A Clue
in the
Crumbs

Also available by Lucy Burdette

Key West Food Critic Mysteries

Other Novels

A Clue
in the
Crumbs

A KEY WEST FOOD
CRITIC MYSTERY

Lucy Burdette

CROOKED
LANE

NEW YORK

Published in the United States by Crooked Lane Books, an imprint of The Quick Brown Fox & Company LLC.

Crooked Lane Books and its logo are trademarks of The Quick Brown Fox & Company LLC.

Library of Congress Catalog-in-Publication data available upon request.

ISBN (hardcover): 978-1-63910-430-7
ISBN (ebook): 978-1-63910-431-4

Cover illustration by Griesbach/Martucci

Printed in the United States.

www.crookedlanebooks.com

Crooked Lane Books
34 West 27th St., 10th Floor
New York, NY 10001

First Edition: August 2023

10 9 8 7 6 5 4 3 2 1

For Yvonne, Jane, Carol, Comer, and Phyllis—because old friends are the best friends

Chapter One

It wasn't a real restaurant so much as an erratic takeout joint, supported by loyal customers willing to overlook the way the place had run down over the years.
                    —KJ Dell'Antonia, *The Chicken Sisters*

*S*ince when has a bad restaurant review been a motive for murder?

That's precisely what my boss at the style magazine *Key Zest* texted me when I expressed my rather dramatic reservations about the possible consequences of trashing local eateries.

Go deeper, she replied. *Ruffle some feathers, Hayley! Man up and do your job!*

Man up? Really?? As for ruffling feathers, that was easy for her to suggest—she's baby-green-bean skinny because she hardly eats, especially not anything greasy, sugary, carb-ish, or otherwise delicious. She doesn't care about alienating local restauranteurs because *she doesn't dine out.*

So now, on the deck of my Key West houseboat, I was deeply absorbed in the article I was attempting to hammer out about whether the Key West food scene was trying too hard to imitate New York. That definitely meant raising questions about prices and menus. Were Key West diners willing to absorb the cost of a forty-two-dollar shrimp cocktail? Or a required tasting menu to the tune of a hundred dollars a pop? Not the Key West locals, I suspected. Maybe the folks visiting the island would be accustomed to this kind of expense and clamor for reservations. Maybe they'd be in the mood to splurge, even if those prices stuck in my own craw.

As I was figuring out how to pose these questions without infuriating anyone, either visitor or resident, a cacophony of sirens went off. One of the disadvantages of living on Key West's Houseboat Row is the proximity to the noise of the fire and police departments. This afternoon the sirens blew loud and long, and I heard another set echo in response, from farther down island. That probably meant both fire stations were calling out their men and women. And that could mean a big fire.

When you mention the word *fire* in Key West, the reaction is fierce. Our island was traumatized by a fire in 1886 that burned most of Old Town to the ground. That fire started in a coffee shop next to the San Carlos Institute, located smack-dab in the middle of Duval Street. The downtown consisted mostly of wooden structures, historically correct and colorful conch homes, set close together, the pride of the city. As the residents learned, our city lay there like a loose pile of tinder during a dry season, waiting for a spark. The fire burned for twelve hours, killed seven people, and destroyed many notable buildings. In the department of horrifying coincidence, the only fire engine on the island had been sent away for repairs.

Naturally, our Key West Fire Department today is better trained and supplied than it was in those days. Even so, our historical district (aka Old Town) is still composed mostly of wood buildings. When notice of a fire goes out over the airwaves, my husband, Nathan, gets alerted and involved if it looks like arson or other suspicious business. I knew Nathan was a police detective when I dated and eventually married him, so I don't complain when he gets pulled away. Even when very important guests are due to arrive that very day. Guests who would have been thrilled to be picked up at the airport in a police SUV.

I saved my file, ran our little dog, Ziggy, out to the parking lot for a quick pit stop, and then went to the houseboat next door. As I expected, my former roommate, Miss Gloria, was pinned to the police scanner. She'd become more interested in crime and police procedure since getting attacked several times over the past few years. Her elderly mah-jongg buddies had chipped in together for this gift for her last birthday, and she'd become addicted almost instantly. She barely glanced up when I stepped onto her deck.

"Sounds like a big one near the bottom of Eaton Street. What do you say we take a run up on your scooter?" she suggested, her eyes sparkling with excitement.

"Haven't you forgotten something?" I asked, wondering for a second whether she really had forgotten, which scared me a bit. Because she was, after all, over eighty years old. More likely, her attention was focused on the police scanner, not our guests. The way I could lose track of time with social media. "Violet and Bettina are due to land in fifteen minutes. We have just enough time to get to the airport and park in the short-term lot so we can be there to greet them."

She thunked the heel of her hand on her forehead. "Ready in a flash." She tucked the scanner into an enormous pocketbook and went into her houseboat, her cats following close behind. She returned with a big grin on her face and her special greeting paraphernalia.

Greeting visitors personally was a tradition on our island. The airport authority had plans for a fancy new arrivals building, but in the meanwhile, visitors tumbled off their planes on steep stairs, trooped across the tarmac under the sun, sweating in their boots and overcoats, and entered through a gauntlet of islanders in shorts and flip-flops. Just inside, twenty yards from the place where they disembarked, a bar served tropical drinks and piped out Jimmy Buffett tunes. Those visitors who'd had to wait an hour or more on the plane after landing because of congestion on the runway or who'd had flight delays for unknown reasons made beelines for that bar. Let the tropical vacation begin! Each exodus from the tarmac into the arrivals area of the terminal reminded me of the opening of a college basketball game when a team was introduced at their home arena: cheering, hand slapping, chest bumping, hand-lettered signs, special little happy dances. That kind of chaotic welcome. Visitors loved to come to Key West, and most hosts loved having them.

For today's pickup, Miss Gloria had hand painted a sign on cardboard: *Key West welcomes the Scone Sisters!* The letters were done in pink and green glitter, and cartoon-style palm trees and tropical drinks with umbrellas danced around the edges. For weeks, Miss Gloria had vacillated over what she should wear, eventually choosing a plaid T-shirt from the sisters' Scottish clan with these words spelled out in sparkling cursive: *Keep calm and eat scones.* She'd special ordered one for each of us. Including Nathan, who'd so far refused to model it.

A Clue in the Crumbs

"Nathan's been called out to the fire," I told her. "So I don't think the police will need us." That was tongue in cheek, of course. Why would they need one old lady and one younger civilian with no police training nosing around? "You can tell me all about what you've heard on the ride over. Is your car in running order?" Her repair of choice for a vehicular issue with her old Buick was slapping on more duct tape. Since I had a scooter and no car and Nathan wasn't available, our transportation options would be either taking an Uber or rumbling over in her beast.

She looked a little insulted. "Of course she is. I took her to the shop last week to make sure she'd be ready to go for Violet and Bettina."

We'd met these two Scottish ladies last year on a so-called honeymoon tour around Scotland. (So-called because Miss Gloria and several members of Nathan's immediate family were included on the trip. Long story, but if you knew Miss Gloria, you'd know there wasn't even a question about inviting her.) There had been an unfortunate death, a fall from the Falkirk Wheel in central Scotland. The victim had turned out to be their son (Violet's) and nephew (Bettina's). The sisters were so grateful about our help in solving the crime that they'd shared with me their prizewinning scone recipe. To die for. Think triple cinnamon and loads of butter.

The sisters had grown famous across the UK after winning the television show contest *The UK Bakes! Scone Edition*. Not only were their scones incredible, but these two slightly dumpy Scottish ladies turned out to "love the camera," as they say in the TV business. They were funny and adorable, and they knew baking inside and out. Now they'd been invited on a tour of our country doing guest demonstrations and judging contests, but most importantly, hunting for the next participants in the American edition of the show. Miss Gloria had invited them to come to Key West early, and desperately wanted them to stay in her houseboat. They were honored and grateful, but other housing arrangements had been made by their agent. Our friend and local chef Martha Hubbard had been drafted to assist with setting up a mini baking contest in town. This would be filmed for television, and if someone really shone, they'd move on to the national contest. If not, it would still be a useful run-through. I'd cleared my schedule to make a special welcome dinner and get ready for at least some of the week's fun.

The scanner in Miss Gloria's pocketbook crackled to life. The dispatcher, whom I thought I recognized as one of Nathan's coworkers, Brigid, said, "There is a report of a large structure fire on Dey near the corner of Greene and Simonton Streets, with smoke and flames visible. Callers report that the building is occupied. Two people were reported fleeing the scene."

This was going to be a doozy. We might not see my hubby tonight at all.

Chapter Two

You'll probably need to call a professional to clean the place. Smoke settles in furniture like gravy on biscuits. Seeps into every nook and cranny.
——Sherry Harris, *From Beer to Eternity*

Violet and Bettina were the last passengers to disembark the plane. Swathed in plaid wool, they entered the crowded arrivals area blinking like badgers emerging from a den into the light. Miss Gloria shrieked with excitement and flapped her glittery sign.

"Welcome! We are so thrilled to have you here in our country." She hugged them each in turn, and they hugged her back. "Give me your coats," she said. "You're going to roast if you stay all wrapped up as if you're visiting the Highlands." I moved forward to take their carry-on bags and pecked them each on the cheek.

"Welcome to Key West!" I said, grinning until my cheeks ached. "Miss Gloria has been dying to show you around our town."

As I remembered, the two sisters looked very much alike, though Bettina was both taller and stockier than her older sister and had distinctive pale-blue eyes, in contrast with Violet's brown. They had similar haircuts—short gray bobs—and wore skirts that fell to their knees and sensible lace-up shoes.

We waited in the teeming baggage area to collect their suitcases, chatting about the trip.

"That's mine," said Bettina, pointing to a huge plaid case with purple ribbons tied onto the handle. "Be a wee bit careful, ma dear; I have a few breakables in there."

I hauled it off the belt; the weight surprised me and nearly pulled me over. Violet's bag came next—the same plaid, but yellow ribbons this time.

"Can we hire a porter?" she asked, watching me grimace as I lifted the second suitcase off the conveyor, just as heavy as the first.

Miss Gloria laughed. "Hayley's our porter. We don't go in for that fancy stuff in Key West."

The ladies took custody of their carry-ons, and I trundled the two enormous bags out of the building. As I dragged the heavy cases on their wobbly wheels to the short-term parking lot, I wondered if the sisters had brought baking equipment with them to take on their tour. Serious chefs carried their knives with them, but for bakers? A special rolling pin? Pastry cutter? A block of marble for rolling dough? It kind of felt like that. Or maybe an implement I hadn't even thought of? I hoisted the bags into the trunk of my friend's car, glad I'd been working out lately.

Between the four of us, we loaded up the Buick with the rest of their stuff and headed home. The two sisters oohed and aahed all the way across town, even though the jaunt from the airport to Houseboat Row was not the most scenic that the island had to offer.

"Wait till we show you the town," said Miss Gloria. "You are going to love visiting our bakeries too. Have you ever had key lime pie?"

"We're looking forward to eating everything you recommend, ma dear," Bettina said, patting her belly.

We piled out of the car, and Miss Gloria herded the sisters up the wooden finger of the dock that led to our boats.

"Thank you, my friend," Miss Gloria said to me. "I know you have work to do, so I can take it from here." She turned to the ladies. "Hayley offered to cook tonight so you don't have to go out and face the restaurant scene when you're jet-lagged."

"Dinner's in about an hour," I said. "I can either run you over to the bed-and-breakfast, or you could relax here on Gloria's deck."

"We could take a catnap if you stay!" Miss Gloria said. "I have a spare room."

The sisters perked up. "That'll be perfect," Violet said, as they followed my friend into her cabin.

"I hope you'll be comfortable in what used to be Hayley and Nathan's bed," I heard Miss Gloria say. "Though if she could cram a six-footer into that space along with a territorial cat, two little ladies should do just fine."

"Cocktails in forty-five minutes or whenever you get here," I said, and headed back to my own houseboat to peel the shrimp and make a salad. I'd considered a million recipes preparing for their visit. Key West pink shrimp was a no-brainer, but in what form? Miss Gloria had nixed a few ideas as too spicy and possibly foreign sounding, particularly the shrimp-in-purgatory recipe that I favored.

"I don't remember eating anything spicy in Scotland," she'd said. "Certainly not something that's traveled that close to hell." We both giggled.

In the end, we'd agreed on garlicky, buttery, Worcestershire-laced baked shrimp with lots of good bread from Old Town Bakery to sop up the sauce. I'd made it for friends and served it with the shells on for a more rustic, hands-on experience, but for our special and jet-lagged guests, I'd decided to peel.

With my prep work completed, I went out to the deck to look for signs of my dinner guests. I was expecting Miss Gloria and the ladies about an hour after I dropped them off. Maybe they'd passed out hard and weren't in the mood for dinner at all. But her deck was empty except for the kitties, T-Bone and Sparky, so I popped over and tapped on the screen door.

Inside, the three women were clustered around Miss Gloria's police scanner. My friend looked up, a guilty expression on her face.

"Sorry, ma dear," said Bettina, looking from my friend to me. "Are we running late?"

Miss Gloria turned off the scanner and ushered the ladies out onto the deck and over to my houseboat. I texted Nathan to let him know they'd arrived and we'd love to see him whenever he could get away. He sent a thumbs-up back, followed by a terse note. *Could be late.*

"We'll have drinks and dinner out here, but I know you two would appreciate my little kitchen. I'll give you the tour first, if that's okay?"

The Scottish ladies twittered their delight.

"Nathan surprised me with this place when he proposed, and it was a total wreck, a gut-and-redo. Obviously, we were constrained by the size of the boat, but I had such fun figuring out what was absolutely necessary—storage, a good oven, counter space for chopping veggies and rolling pastry."

"And don't forget the litter box," called Miss Gloria from the deck.

Evinrude, my gray tiger, took that moment to stretch his long cat body out and sharpen his claws on the little rug in front of the sink. "This guy came south with me when I moved down," I said, grabbing him up and rubbing my chin on the dark M on his head. "All the other animals have been accumulated along the way. And my husband as well."

The ladies laughed and spun around to take in the living area again. "This is absolutely adorable," said Bettina. "Can you imagine, Violet, starting from scratch rather than an old house designed hundreds of years ago?"

"But the history in your Scottish home is wonderful," I said.

Violet nodded. "It looks as though you've thought of everything."

"If it didn't fit, I tried not to be tempted," I said. "Sure, I sometimes yearn for a big kitchen space like the one my first boyfriend had in Key West. But he was such a loser, I'd take Nathan and Miss Gloria and a crowded houseboat anytime."

After a quick peek at our bedroom and the bathroom, I led the ladies back outside and served them little glasses of bubbly pink rosé along with crackers and a small bowl of dip. "This is smoked-fish dip. I thought you being Scottish might enjoy it. It's kind of famous here in Key West—lots of restaurants feature it as a starter. We serve a lot of seafood on our island, because obviously we're surrounded by water. Miss Gloria said you didn't have allergies to worry about?"

"We eat everything, ma dear," Violet said.

"We have constitutions like heilan' coos," added Bettina, referring to the iconic shaggy red cows we'd seen on our western "honeymoon" swing of Scotland. "The only thing that bothers us is a dearth of scones and bread."

"Oh, don't worry, we're very big on carbs in this neighborhood," said Miss Gloria.

After another glass of bubbly and my dinner of pink shrimp and bread and a hearty salad, we took a little break to let our stomachs settle before tackling dessert. I noticed the two Scottish ladies sniffing the air like rabbits.

"Everything okay?" I asked. "You are probably drooping. That flight across the ocean is not for sissies."

"Don't mind us," said Bettina. "Daddy was a fireman, and he taught us early to pay attention to the smell of smoke."

"In fact, he often came home smelling of fires. Mum's scones in the oven and smoke on Daddy's clothes and in his beard—those scents always make us feel nostalgic." Violet added this, her face looking sad. I could imagine she was also thinking of her own son, killed way before his time. Because no one ever expects a child to go before them.

"We were wondering," Miss Gloria said, "whether you'd whisk us on a little tour of Old Town before dessert? Maybe we could even drive by the scene of the fire?"

All three faces looked so wistful and hopeful, I couldn't say no. Besides, I was curious too.

Chapter Three

Whenever someone asks me how I can bake and eat so much and not gain a lot of weight, I say that I practice "bake and release."

—Dorie Greenspan

Along with their pocketbooks, the three ladies loaded into Miss Gloria's Buick, with me at the helm. My friend had taken to driving less over the past year, especially no nighttime excursions. I was happy to pick up the slack, pleased and relieved that she understood and accepted her limitations. She wasn't related to me by blood, but she felt like a beloved grandmother in only the best way.

I drove over the Palm Avenue bridge and took a left on White Street so we could drive south on Southard Street. To me, this street had the quintessential look of old Key West, lined with many small conch homes and big Victorians as well.

"The Christmas decorations are always magnificent along here," Miss Gloria said. "They go all out for Valentine's Day too. Since we've got Saint Patrick's Day this week, you may get lucky and catch a few shamrocks and leprechauns."

"My mother's house is straight ahead toward the Truman Waterfront," I explained to our back-seat guests; "and I'm certain she'll want to have you over. Hopefully, you'll have time to take a tour of Harry Truman's Little White House, where President Truman worked when he wasn't in Washington. It's one of my favorite historical sights on our island."

"We'd love to do that," Bettina said. "Daddy loved Mr. Truman and always thought history gave him a wee bit of a raw deal."

Miss Gloria piped up. "We helped cater a big Cuban-American event there a couple years ago, and our own Hayley solved the murder that ensued."

"Oh mercy, Hayley," said Violet, leaning forward to pat my shoulder, "we had no idea you were a professional detective."

"No offense," Bettina added, "but we'd assumed you stumbled into solving our Scottish murder. Here it turns out you're a crime-solving star!"

I laughed. "Don't tell that to my detective husband—he would hate it. I had a lot of help with the Little White House murder and even more backup. Believe me, I have no professional training. From time to time, I notice unusual details or come up with offbeat ideas that the trained professionals don't think of, that's all. I was especially glad to help bring your son's killer to justice." I glanced over my shoulder to offer a comforting nod. It had been a devastating shock for them to lose the only family member of their younger generation, and I was certain that loss still hurt.

Once we reached the Key West main drag, Duval Street, I took a right heading toward the Seaport. The streets were crowded with cheerful and oblivious tourists, and the sound of music floated, pounded, banged out from the bars along the way. We heard several snippets of "Danny Boy" and saw more green tulle than Key West visitors normally wore.

"Sloppy Joe's was said to be Ernest Hemingway's favorite haunt," I said. "He would write in the mornings, fish in the afternoons, and drink at night. Or so the story goes. He never really set foot in this location of Sloppy Joe's, but that doesn't stop the establishment from capitalizing on his name. If you have time, you might enjoy a tour of Hemingway's home, as well as the walking tour sponsored by the Key West Literary Seminar. But of course, Miss Gloria's cemetery tour should be at the top of your list." I smiled into the rearview mirror. Miss Gloria beamed in response.

"We're doing that later this week," said Bettina. "After the baking contest business is wrapped up, that must be first on our calendars."

The smell of smoke was getting stronger and stronger as we approached the water. Emergency vehicles blocked off the access to Greene Street that led to the harbor, so I parked the car and we got out. Despite the flashing blue lights that came from two cop cars parked catty-corner to discourage onlookers, a small knot of curious people was attempting to dodge the police and get closer to the smoldering building. Before I could stop them, Miss Gloria and our visitors took advantage of the chaos to duck by the officers. I could only follow.

Several fire trucks were lined up on the street, and two firefighters conferred in front of the blackened ruins of the side porch attached to a large Victorian home. Others were manhandling big hoses that had been unspooled from the trucks and aimed at the porch. Streaks of black extended up the side of the house to the second floor. For a moment, I imagined I could still feel the heat of the flames, the beams hissing under the assault of the water. A sharp, acrid smell seemed to coat my nostrils.

"I could swear I smell an accelerant," said Violet. She looked at her sister, who nodded slowly.

"Petrol, most likely." Bettina studied the smoking remains. "Looks like it burned hotter than you might expect with a grease fire in the kitchen or some other accidental cause. Besides, it seems it's mostly contained to this side porch and above."

Violet added, "Probably not faulty electrical wiring for a space heater, either. That's a common culprit in Scotland, but it's quite warm here already." She fanned her face with one hand.

"How do you suppose it started, then?" Miss Gloria asked.

"If you look alongside the wall just past the porch, see the darker patch there?" Violet pointed to a charred heap that I couldn't identify. "To me it looks like something extremely flammable was piled against the side of the house."

"Dry wood, like tinder," said Bettina, "or else paper. And then douse it with a can of petrol and *whoosh*, the whole thing goes up like a bonfire. You can see the bits of black running all the way up the side of the house. With all that wood, they were lucky the whole thing didn't blow."

As we watched, a stocky man in jean shorts and a green T-shirt tight enough to show impressive muscles charged down the street toward the fire scene. He was stopped before he could get to the big home, only yards away from us.

"I'm Vincent Humboldt and I own this place," he shouted, his face red and perspiring. "You can't keep me from going into my own property."

"We can and we will," said a tall police officer, grasping the man's bulging bicep as he tried to push past. "Right now it's not safe for anyone to enter the premises. If you'll come with me, we'd like to ask a few questions." He led the angry man off to the nearest cruiser.

"Did you recognize him?" Miss Gloria asked.

I shook my head as another Key West police officer appeared in front of us. "Ladies, you need to move away from here immediately. It's not safe for onlookers." He scowled, focusing on me as if I looked familiar, like a recurring troublesome problem that he couldn't quite place.

"Sorry, Officer," I muttered, herding my friends back the way we'd come. "You ladies must be exhausted."

"Big day tomorrow," said Bettina, her voice excited even though both sisters looked like they were fading fast. We returned to Miss Gloria's car, and I headed back toward Eaton Street and north to Houseboat Row.

"We'll pop home for dessert, and then I'll take you to your hotel."

Before they could respond, the quick ding of two incoming text messages came from the sisters' bags. Violet rustled through the detritus in her pocketbook and pulled out a brand-new iPhone. "Oh dear," she said, looking shocked. "Our bed-and-breakfast is the very place that was burning. They regret to inform us they cannot provide rooms tonight." She glanced up at her sister, her brows furrowed with worry.

"Oh deary me," Bettina echoed. "Where in the world will we lay our weary heads?"

"Wait," Miss Gloria said. "That was your bed-and-breakfast, and we didn't realize it?"

"We don't know the town and can't keep details like addresses in our heads after all that travel." Violet sounded distressed, as if we thought they'd somehow failed.

"Every traveler has that same problem, really," said Miss Gloria, nodding with reassurance. "When we flew to Scotland for our honeymoon, I could barely remember my name. Besides, every day I forget more than I knew the day before." All three of them laughed.

I chuckled too, especially tickled at the way she described Nathan's and my honeymoon as "ours."

But I sobered up quickly. This *was* a real problem, because in the Key West high season, rooms were scarce to nonexistent. I could call my mother to ask about their guest room, but I knew she had a series of catering events scheduled, so she and her husband Sam would be busy. Besides, I hated to dump every guest who came to the island onto her without planning way ahead.

"My houseboat!" Miss Gloria clapped her hands together. "It was meant to be."

"If you're sure you don't mind . . ." Violet pressed a hand to her forehead, looking weary and worried.

"A weeklong slumber party—what could be better? I happen to know that Hayley baked a cake."

"We humbly and gratefully accept your invitation, at least for tonight," Bettina said. They all three had huge smiles on their faces. "Tomorrow we can sort out something else."

I couldn't help grinning back. "We'll have a bite of cake at my houseboat for dessert, and then Miss Gloria can tuck you in."

We retraced our route and within fifteen minutes landed back at Houseboat Row. Nathan was sitting out on our deck enjoying the evening, and hopefully our leftovers.

A Clue in the Crumbs

"There is your handsome polis," said Bettina, hurrying down the dock and onto the boat to wrap her arms around him.

He greeted the sisters warmly while I went into the kitchen to retrieve the chocolate cake I'd made for our welcome dinner. Though some folks think a chocolate cake is a chocolate cake, my mother had always gotten raves when she made this two-layer recipe with fudgy icing, based on one she'd found in her ancient copy of a Better Homes and Gardens cookbook. Even though the ingredients were nothing fancy, to me it lifted chocolate cake to another level altogether, saying to dinner guests *Welcome!* and *We love you!* I'd never found a recipe to top it.

By the time I returned outside, the ladies had moved on from describing their trip and the wonders of business class seats to quizzing Nathan about the fire.

Looking appalled, he turned to squint at me. "Don't tell me you took our guests to a crime scene already?" he asked, sort of joking but not really.

"Everyone in for cake?" I asked, hoping to divert his attention and keep them from spilling something he would worry about—such as how we'd burst through the police barrier to get close to the fire. Hearing a chorus of yeses, I cut big slices and passed them around.

"Violet and Bettina's father was a firefighter, and so investigating fires runs in their Scottish blood," Miss Gloria explained to Nathan. She had a dab of creamy chocolate icing on her nose, a few crumbs around her lips, and a serious expression on her face. "The wind must be blowing this way, because we all noticed the odor. Plus I heard about it on my scanner," she admitted. "In addition to that, the scene of the fire turned out to be their bed-and-breakfast. That explains why they'll be staying at my place."

Then her eyes sparkled with mischief. "If you're describing it as a crime scene, does that mean arson?"

Nathan scowled; he was not a fan of civilians listening in on and getting drawn into official police business. "Nothing has been determined yet." He crossed his muscular forearms over his stomach and tried to smile, which didn't quite work. "The police have it well in hand. I appreciate all of your interest and concern, but I implore you to leave it to the professionals."

"We promise," said all three of them in solemn voices, holding hands up like courtroom witnesses for emphasis.

I wouldn't have bet any money on them leaving this alone if the opportunity to snoop presented itself.

Chapter Four

Maybe the cat has fallen into the stew, or the lettuce has frozen, or the cake has collapsed. *Eh bien, tant pis.* Usually one's cooking is better than one thinks it is. And if the food is truly vile, then the cook must simply grit her teeth and bear it with a smile, and learn from her mistakes.

—Julia Child, *My Life in France*

Miss Gloria called me bright and early the next morning. "We're going to need a hand getting their equipment to Williams Hall," she said. "Will you please bring over your little rolling grocery cart?"

Because Key West is a mini city, portable grocery carts similar to those found in big cities like New York are common. Everyone had one on Houseboat Row, where a lot of schlepping was involved. It wasn't as simple as pulling into the garage and unloading grocery bags from the car to the kitchen. Residents had to load supplies from the trunk to a cart, then bump the heavy cart up the finger of the dock, and then drag the goods onto their boats. Not for the faint of heart, though Miss Gloria counted shopping expeditions as her exercise for the day, and possibly the week. And she asked for help liberally.

Half an hour before we were due downtown, I rolled my cart to Miss Gloria's boat. The two Scottish ladies were sitting on the deck, each with a cat in her lap and a cup of tea in her hand.

"Good morning," I called out. "Hope everyone slept well."

"Slept well indeed, until our Scottish time zone came calling." That was Bettina.

"Which happened about the time your roosters started calling," added Violet.

"Sorry about that," I said. "Chickens are protected within our city limits, even if they are supremely annoying. Occasionally we can get the bird rescue organization to trap them and move them somewhere else. If we had a humane trap ourselves, we might catch one and ferry it over to the Key West Wildlife Center. But mostly, we learn to live with them."

Miss Gloria emerged from her boat's cabin. "Remember that time we saw a guy trying to scrape a rooster out of his trap into the wildlife center's cage? That rooster had his claws fastened around the wire and was hanging on for dear life." We both chortled. Then I turned my attention to all the stuff on the deck.

Across the remainder of the furniture and on the deck itself, the ladies had spread their baking equipment. I admired a porcelain pie dish, a baking slab, a rectangular baking dish and an oval baking dish and two heavy sheet pans, and as I had suspected, two enormous wooden rolling pins. I tried to restrain myself from coveting everything—imagining the treats I could concoct if only I owned their equipment. I reminded myself there would be no room for all of this in my compact kitchen and that I managed fine with what I had.

After checking out everything, I turned back to them, laughing. "No wonder your suitcases felt a little heavier than the airline limit. Actually, a lot heavier. Even Nathan commented on them." Nathan had volunteered to haul the bags from the parking lot to their room in Miss Gloria's houseboat last night. He'd broken out in a sweat by the time he got them there.

Violet looked a tad chagrined. "We didn't dare appear to be experts without bringing our own equipment. A difference in a pan's thickness or materials can mean the failure of a batch of scones or a burnt Bundt. All on national American TV and streaming live to Scotland, the whole UK, and beyond!"

"Besides," Bettina said, "we're testing equipment for our line of bakeware." She showed me the label on the bottom of one of the pie pans—*Bakeware by the Scone Sisters* was written in script. Above the writing, two intertwined S's steamed out of the slits cut into the top of a pie. She handed the dish to me so I could feel the weight of it.

"These are gorgeous," I said, noticing the perfect heft of the porcelain and the smooth interior surface to which no pastry would dare cling. The outside of the pan was sprinkled with pale-blue polka dots.

"We were asked to suggest ideas for the design on a set of bakeware. The graphic artists tried to translate the essence of us, but nothing really worked," said Violet. "We asked for scones and ended up with indeterminate triangles."

Bettina leaned forward to speak in a stage whisper. "I don't think they listened to a word we said. Finally, our agent located a student who had the idea of the steam coming out of a pie. She's also the one who suggested the polka dots."

"It's priceless," I said. "It's absolutely you!"

The ladies smiled widely. "This will be the first time the pieces are seen in public," said Violet. "Everything turned out so cute, we could eat the pans themselves." All three of the women broke into appreciative chuckles.

"I especially love this one," I said, fingering a square baking pan I'd overlooked at first glance. "I would use this every day."

"Take a look at their knife," exclaimed Miss Gloria, pointing to the small paring knife nestled in a blue velvet cloth. "Not even clumsy me could chop a finger off using that sharp baby."

"That's only a parer. The bigger knives are coming. We didn't bring everything in our suitcases, only the basics to get by in case our shipment didn't arrive. Good thing we did, because our agent, Arvid Smith, said the tracking feature failed. Between that and the fire last night, lord only knows when we might expect it."

"Trust me, there's no such thing as overnight shipping to or from Key West," Miss Gloria said.

I carefully loaded the equipment into my cart, using a stack of beach towels to protect the porcelain. Then I trundled it to the parking lot and transferred everything into Miss Gloria's trunk. The ladies piled into the car, and we set off downtown.

Williams Hall, an enormous white concrete church building at the corner of William and Fleming streets, was constructed in the early 1900s after the hurricane of 1909 wiped out the Uptown Methodist Church. Renovations on the building and the interior had recently been completed with astonishingly beautiful results. The interior of the church portion of the building soared up three stories, with a restored wooden parquet floor, gorgeous wooden pews, and stunning stained-glass windows. The renovation had also added dance, yoga, sewing, and drama studios, plus the magnificent kitchen where Martha Hubbard and other island chefs worked their magic. Our Scottish Scone Sisters would be baking there too, as well as judging the competition for a new contestant to join the American version of their television show, *The UK Bakes!*. I couldn't wait to see them in action.

Chef Martha was waiting for us at the William Street door. "Welcome," she said. "I've heard so much about you!"

"And likewise, for sure," said Bettina, squeezing her wiry frame into a hug. Neither of the visiting ladies blinked at the tattoos covering Martha's arms from elbow to wrist.

"We are thrilled to have you in Key West. Let me give you a quick tour, then on to the main event—the kitchen! Elevator or stairs?"

"Definitely stairs, ma dear," said Violet. "If we keep eating the meals Hayley's preparing, we'll have to buy an extra seat on our next flight." She glanced over at the cart full of equipment. "On the other hand, elevator this time."

Martha laughed and swept us through the church sanctuary, pointing out the original, restored stained glass and beautifully finished wood pews and herringbone floor. On the way to the elevator, she showed us the exercise studio off the main hallway, and then we swooped upstairs. "We have our sewing room here," she said as we emerged from the elevator cab, "with eight machines available for classes. Just in case anyone splits her seams this week, we can patch you right up."

The ladies chuckled.

"And this," said Martha, swinging open a big wooden door, "is our kitchen."

Violet and Bettina spun slowly to take everything in—the parquet floor, pale-blue walls, whitewashed Dade pine ceiling, and finally, the kitchen itself. Bettina ran her hands over the white-patterned counter top, set up both for prep work and as a counter with seating for ten or twelve students who could watch the chef at work. Behind the counter, Violet had made a beeline for the four professional stainless-steel wall ovens.

"I bet she doesn't have to guess temperatures while using these girls," she said to her sister as she patted the top oven. She turned to Martha. "At home, our oven is an antique, with a mind of its own."

"Nothing wrong with old things," Martha said, grinning. "As long as you know how to jolly them along."

"Here, here," said Miss Gloria, pretending to hold up a glass. "Here's a toast from one old thing to a couple of others." We all laughed.

"I've made tea," Martha said, pointing us to the long dining table. "And little cookies. In case anyone feels peckish, we'll have something to nibble on while we plan the week."

We sat around the large rectangular dining table at the end of the kitchen, settling into white upholstered chairs, and Martha poured cups of tea into delicate china bordered with pink roses. On the plate in the middle of the table was a selection of small cookies. Martha saw me eyeing them.

"Almond cloud cookies, pecan pie bars—because why should we only get pecan pie at Thanksgiving?—and these are peanut butter and jelly." She pointed to a grouping of golden cookies with what looked like raspberry jam in the centers. "I wanted to throw a few things together that felt very American in honor of your arrival here in the States." She smiled warmly, and the ladies beamed back.

"Throw a few things together?" I couldn't help muttering. This was the trouble with professional chefs: they made things look so easy that the rest of us felt the urge to try them. Only when we were up to our elbows in flour and realizing we'd forgotten key ingredients and added salt instead of sugar and had neglected to thaw the butter did we realize we'd tackled far more than we could chew without choking.

"The cookies and biscuits are lovely," said Violet, moving one of each kind to her plate. "Now, you mentioned we would go over the schedule for the taping of the show—is there a set time to practice, when do the contestants arrive, and so on. Probably best to tell us things more than once."

Bettina broke in. "Our brains are getting a little less agile as we get older. We have been known to make lists." Each sister brought an iPhone out of her bag and placed it on the table next to the little notepads with Williams Hall logos and fancy ink pens that Martha had provided.

"It's not just getting older," Miss Gloria said, "it's that busy brains get very full, and some things must be pushed out to make room for the new ideas. Isn't that true, Hayley?"

I snickered. "It's very true."

Martha said, "The production team will be arriving shortly to set up cameras and lights. We'll have a short run-through with you two at work so they can begin sound checks and video checks and the like. Then we will break for lunch. I thought we might order sandwiches from Cole's Peace." She glanced at me for confirmation, and I nodded. "The contestants will arrive around one thirty so we can meet them and explain the schedule for the week. Then they will each bake their first recipe. We've done all the shopping ahead, so it should go seamlessly."

"Ha!" said Violet. "They'll need to hear those instructions more than once too. These poor souls are under enough stress without misunderstanding basic expectations."

"Somewhere in there you've scheduled a short nap break, I hope," said Miss Gloria, sounding wistful.

"I hadn't," said Martha.

I lifted my eyebrows. "I could run you home any time you're tired."

Miss Gloria shook her head. "No way I'm missing one minute of this."

"How many contestants have you signed up?" asked Bettina.

"We started with five," said Martha. "Several of them have backed out as the process continued, so I'm afraid we're down to three. Possibly only two. I suppose it all sounds exciting to our home bakers to appear on television with the Scone Sisters, but the reality of competing over a week is a little harder. One woman couldn't get the time off from her job. Another turned up with a recipe that was clearly lifted *word for word* from Cooks Illustrated—with no attribution, and the third was not sure that her husband would allow her to appear on camera."

"Really?" Bettina had her hands parked on her hips. "I hope you urged her to leave that arse!" She clapped a hand over her mouth. "I shouldn't say that in good company, should I?"

Martha grimaced. "I tried to persuade her. She was really gifted, and I told her she deserved a wide audience for her confections. When I phoned her to say she'd made the cut, she said she'd decided cooking and baking for her husband was reward enough. She waffled a bit, so who knows—she might show at the last minute."

While we were busy unpacking the equipment and placing it on the counters where Martha suggested, the lights and camera crew arrived and began to set up. I felt a little bit nervous even watching because of how professional it all looked. But the Scottish ladies were taking it in stride.

"Don't you get rattled in front of a crowd and these cameras?" Miss Gloria asked, leaning her elbows on the end of the counter as several bright lights were switched on.

"I was going to ask the same thing," I said, and winked at Miss Gloria. "Comes from several years of living together, I suppose. Great minds and all that."

"We were slightly bothered at the beginning," said Violet. She patted a wisp of gray hair into place, her brown eyes twinkling. I wondered if her mother might have wished she'd saved the name Violet for Bettina, whose eyes were literally that color. "But everyone kept telling us we were naturals, so after a bit we started to believe it."

"All that needs done really is pay attention to what's in front of you, with measuring and such—and we do know these recipes like old friends. Plus, ham it up a bit. We love giving our opinions about baking, and we love meeting the amateurs and showing them the ropes." Bettina grinned. "Our motto is to be truthful but kind. They are the ones who are nervous as cats, and we're so busy calming them down and trying to set the poor souls at ease that we forget about ourselves."

"Besides, we are old ladies now," Violet added. "What's the worst can happen? Our lipstick smears or our hair is mussed? We don't worry one bit about how we look on the camera." She puffed up her gray hair and pooched her lips, now layered with glossy pink. "If we make a mistake, we own right up to it. That was Julia Child's advice too—never apologize if you make a bad dish. That only makes it worse. Just grin and bear it. She never took herself too seriously, and we don't either. We've added one Scone Sisters tip to those pearls of wisdom—laugh yourself silly."

Even the sternest cameraman chuckled along with her. "Can we get a run-through, please, with the sisters?" he asked Martha.

The ladies moved behind the expanse of white counter and began to lay out their ingredients. All the contestants and the sisters had sent Martha a list ahead of time so everything could be ready to go for today. As they launched into describing their preparations for a basic cinnamon scone, I saw my mother and Sam come in from the back entrance. I waved them over.

"They're completely adorable," my mother whispered when they drew close.

"They are too cute in real time," I whispered back, "but don't they light up the room when they're in front of a camera?"

I watched as they smiled cheerfully into the camera, bantering with each other as they took turns measuring the flour, baking soda, salt, and sugar, and then grated frozen sticks of butter into the dry ingredients.

"The cold butter is absolutely the secret." Violet held a finger up to her lips. "We are sharing it here with you, but please don't pass it on."

Bettina laughed, though she'd surely heard her sister say that line many times. "In truth, we'd love it if you share it, because we want everyone's scones to succeed wildly. My sister thinks it's the temperature of the butter, while I believe it's also the quality of the cinnamon. We did bring ours from Scotland"—she held up a

small glass bottle filled with a warm, cocoa-colored substance—
"but you can find good cinnamon lots of places in your country.
Don't settle for something that has been at the back of your cup-
board for years. Don't take a chance on a store brand either. You
want your flavor to pop!" She clapped her hands together and
mimicked the sound of a pop by smacking her lips.

The two of them stirred the grated butter into the dry ingredients, added a bit of milk, and kneaded the dough lickety-split
into a nice circle. I marveled at how well they worked together,
taking turns, with no fumbling over who'd do the next step.
Their obvious affection made me yearn for a sister. Plus it
reminded me that I hadn't had a good chat with my dear friend
Connie in ages. Even though she lived only two houseboats up
our dock, we'd both been too busy to plan a date.

"Another secret," Violet said, facing her sister again, "is not
to overwork the dough. Nobody will mind one bit if it looks a
little lopsided as long as the scones or biscuits rise high and taste
flaky and delicious. Which they will if you keep that light hand.
Remember, your butter must be good quality too. We, of course,
prefer Scottish or Irish butter, but do use whatever best quality
you have here. Organic, unsalted, if you can."

"She's right, for once," Bettina added, winking at her older
sister. She clapped the flour off her hands. "If you overwork the
dough, you will produce curling stones instead of fluffy scones."

They began to laugh hysterically at their own joke.

Two of the contestants appeared right on schedule, a man
called Harry Sweeting and a young woman named Martina
Bevis, who I thought might win simply on the basis of adorable-
ness. I knew her from seeing her in passing many times while
working out at the gym, but today she was all dolled up. Harry

and Martina each spent a few minutes having makeup applied by one of the TV experts, and then they were both steered behind the counter with Violet and Bettina.

"Welcome, lovelies," Bettina said, "you are winners already by virtue of being here with the Scone Sisters." On cue, Violet laughed. "But naturally, even in good company, it's all about your scones. So let's do have a wee run-through of some tips that will bring out your best. A recipe speaks a different language that sounds foreign to many people, and therefore, it is best to keep it simple. You don't have to cover every step, but talk to us as though you are explaining your ingredients and methods to your granddaughter"—this she directed at Harry before she turned to Martina—"or your grandmother, who is a bit thick and quite possibly hard of hearing." Violet howled with laughter again.

Harry, a dark-haired man with a ruddy face, took the first turn. The camera and light people tried various angles, cutting off his awkward patter and having him start over several times. His face now glistened with sweat, and he had begun to stammer, visibly nervous. I had the distinct impression this wasn't a case of the camera loving its subject.

"Are we ready to try a full run-through?" the lead cameraman asked in a snippy voice. "We don't have an entire millennium to get this show taped."

"I don't believe we'd live that long anyway, ma dear," said Violet, winking and then pointing to her sister. "Carry on, my darling."

Bettina turned to the camera and smiled like an angel. "We are the Scone Sisters, direct from Peebles, Scotland, and we are so pleased to be visiting the southernmost island of Key West."

She patted her hips and grinned. "You can tell by the shape of us that we've tried a scone or two."

"Or three or four," Violet snickered, tapping her gently rounded stomach.

"Here in this kitchen, we are hoping to discover the next champion of *The UK Bakes! Key West Edition*. Key West is our very first stop, and perhaps we will also discover the winner from the entire country right on this gorgeous, tropical island! Our first adventure will be our contestants demonstrating their own scone recipes. They've been asked to bring something that showcases their very best talent. Points, of course, for original-ity, the lightness of the pastry, and please don't tell them"—she pretended to cup her hands around her mouth to whisper—"but appearance in front of the camera counts too."

"You mustn't be discouraged by that. No one," said Violet, stepping forward to loop her arm around her sister's waist, "would have believed that two dowdy, overly middle-aged, chubby Scot-tish women would have made it to where we are today." She turned to face the contestants who were standing off camera. "I tell you that story simply to say that anything can happen, ma dears. If you make an error, do not get dismayed! Play with it, go with it, have fun! But also remember that we are required by contract to be honest in our decisions. Who is first up, Bettina?"

"Harry from Big Pine," said Bettina triumphantly. "If you could first explain what Big Pine is for the viewers who are not familiar with the Florida Keys."

Harry approached the counter and began to describe the island he lived on half an hour north of Key West. Then he told us about his grandmother's recipe for triple-ginger cherry scones. "I added two kinds of ginger that she never would have been able to access back in the day," he said. "Freshly grated ginger and minced candied ginger. That's two kinds of ginger, plus a teaspoon of powdered ginger. Then I added the dried cherries my uncle sends each Christmas from Michigan. So that's three kinds of ginger and my uncle's dried cherries." He held up a small spice jar and another of what looked like molasses. "Plus a generous dollop of molasses as a nod to my southern heritage. That was on my mother's side. That's now three kinds of ginger plus cherries and molasses."

I could only think of a Facebook video I'd seen of an English man cooking a special breakfast egg dish. He'd plopped seven egg yolks in the center of a frying pan and covered them with a small glass bowl. Around the edges, he whipped egg whites right in the pan. By the end of his twenty-minute explanation, during which he'd warned multiple times that he was about to lift the bowl, he'd garnered thousands of comments. Most of the viewers were disgusted by the repetition, which amounted to teasing his audience beyond their tolerance.

"Sounds delightful," said Violet, a whole lot more politely than I could have.

"If not perhaps heavy on strong ingredients?" added Bettina, cocking one of her dark eyebrows. "We shall certainly see whether they fight with each other when you put them in the same bowl. Or whether perhaps they meld seamlessly into something amazing."

Harry was dismissed after he patted his dough out, shaped it into triangles, and popped it into one of the ovens. Next, Martina was invited to the spotlight. The bright lights were kinder to her than they'd been to Harry, bringing out the sparkle in her blue eyes and the bouncy sheen of her short blonde hair.

A Clue in the Crumbs

Martina ran through her recipe for blueberry scones without a hitch, adding that she preferred a mixture of regular and cake flour to keep the scones light. "It's the protein in the flour that can cause the end product to be heavy and dense," she said.

"Fascinating," said Bettina. "You also had a tip about timing?"

"Yes!" said Martina, beaming confidently like a woman who believed she'd won the contest. "Only bake them precisely before you plan to serve."

Her words trailed off when she noticed a commotion at the back door.

Chapter Five

The goal of a recipe is to bridge the experience of a person who has already mastered a dish with that of a person who would like to make it for dinner.

—J. J. Goode, "The Recipe Convention That Dooms Home Cooks," *The New Yorker*, September 3, 2022

All the onlookers and workers turned to look in the direction Martina faced. Another woman had just entered, with glossy golden hair tied in a twist at the back of her head, white pearl earrings, and a pair of oversized black sunglasses. She wasn't beautiful in a classical sense, but she was striking. Her voice, when she called out hello to Martha, was gravelly and distinctive. Perfect for television, I suspected.

"I hope I'm not too late. My apologies for blowing in at the last minute. I was up most of the night last night thinking of this contest, and I finally decided I was foolish to skip it. My sister talked me into it, really." She smiled at Violet and Bettina as if they surely would understand this.

"Come in, come in. Let's get some makeup on and get you started. If you can hop in right away, we will accommodate you." This came from the head cameraman, who had not given in to any other special requests as far as I could tell. The woman moved across the room, took off her glasses, and submitted to the dabbing and buffing of one of the assistants. In the background, Martha and the sisters scrambled to gather her ingredients.

"Can we begin, please?" the crabby cameraman asked.

"I'm ready! I'm Rayna Humboldt, and I have my recipe right here." She tapped the side of her head and smiled as she moved into place behind the counter. She looked directly into the main camera, eyes wide. "Ordinarily, I would never attempt peach scones until the fruit is in season, fresh off the tree from a farm in Georgia. I was going to prepare either pear scones with almond flavoring or cheese and crispy bacon scones, as those are the favorites at our bed-and-breakfast." Her face fell at the mention of either her B and B or the bacon, I couldn't be sure which. "But then I saw these lovely peaches in Fausto's and thought, they really are my favorite." She held up a plastic bag of pink fruit.

Within minutes, she had the fuzzy skins peeled off the peaches and had chopped them into smallish pieces. She stirred her dry ingredients together, grated in her frozen butter, and finally added the whipped mixture of sour cream, milk, and egg. "Last but not least, fold in your peaches, but ever so gently. Place the batter on a piece of parchment paper and shape it into a circle. The batter may appear wet and uncooperative, but do carry on! You're almost home."

She cut her circle of dough into six pieces and pushed them apart a little. "Paint the tops with a bit of egg white, sprinkle with coarse sugar, and voilà—scones. Or today, since this is a special occasion, substitute a bit of almond icing for the sugar once the scones have cooled." She transferred her perfect triangles, bumpy with peaches, onto a cookie sheet and slid it into the oven. While they were baking, she stirred milk and almond flavoring into confectioner's sugar, chattering about the extra zip of sweetness as she worked.

About twenty minutes later, all three kinds of scones had been extracted from the ovens and moved to serving dishes decorated with pink roses around the rims. Rayna painted her frosting on half of her scones and stepped away. Violet and Bettina moved down the counter, describing each contestant's work and sampling it, first plain and then with extra butter. We heard first that Martina's blueberry scone was a tad dry. She looked shocked and disappointed.

"Not to worry, ma dear," said Violet, reaching across the counter to pat her hand. "You are not warmly acquainted with this oven, and it's always trial and error, isn't it? I suspect the temperature may have been set a wee bit high."

The sisters moved to Harry's ginger cherry pastries. Each took a bite and seemed to chew and chew and chew.

"Ummm," said Bettina, swallowing hard and sipping on a glass of water that had magically appeared on the counter in front of her. "A bit heavy, no?" She smiled at Harry. "Next time, maybe cut back the flavoring a smidgen? All those ingredients seem as though they might be fighting each other and thus have weighed down your pastry."

"Sorry, lad," said Violet, nodding vigorously in agreement. "Perhaps spread those ingredients across three scone recipes and one will be a winner." He did not appear to be grinning and bearing this news as Julia Child would have advised.

Finally, the sisters moved to take their places in front of the peach scones. As they exclaimed over Rayna's confections, a stocky man burst through the back door and made a beeline for Rayna. Leaning toward her with both hands on the marble counter, he said in a fierce voice, "I told you I did not want you entering this contest."

Rayna's lips quivered and her eyes shone with tears. "I know you said that, but I thought—"

"You thought wrong," he said, banging his fist on the counter.

Her face crumpled. Now I realized where I'd seen that angry face before—at the scene of the bed-and-breakfast fire. This was Rayna's husband.

The sisters bustled forward to stand on either side of her. "Your wife—I assume you are Mr. Humboldt—is a very talented baker," said Bettina. "You are making a big mistake to hold her back from her dream."

"Whoever you are, you have no business commenting on our marriage or my wife," he told her.

"She should certainly have the right to speak for herself," said Violet, squeezing an arm around Rayna's waist.

"I want to stay," she said in a quivery voice, glancing at each of the sisters for support.

"You will not," he said, moving around the counter toward her place by the oven. But Harry had stepped forward to block him, which astonished me.

"You heard the lady. She wants to stay."

"You need to leave the premises," said Martha, moving up to stand next to Harry. "Or I will call the police." She flashed the cell phone that she held in her hand.

I watched the man's face change as he grappled with the options. "I will see you at home," he growled at his wife. Then he bolted back out the door and slammed down the stairs, leaving a shocked audience behind.

I felt the phone buzz in my pocket. I took a quick look: a text had come in from Nathan. Last night's fire was now officially considered arson. He wouldn't ordinarily feel he had to tell me this during the workday, he messaged, but a person of interest appeared to be connected with the Williams Hall contest.

My heart sank. I hated for one more thing to go wrong with this special event.

Call me when you get a minute, okay? I'd like to hear everything you and the other ladies noticed last night. This morning as well. Be careful and stay out of trouble, please.

I texted him back. *I'm so sorry to hear that. How awful! Don't worry about us, we're plenty busy here. No time for trouble.* I paused, then added, *Can you tell me the name?*

The three dots on my screen indicated he was typing.

Rayna Humboldt.

The woman we'd been waiting for all morning, never sure she'd come. Who'd floated in at the last moment and was in the process of blowing the other two contestants away with her pillowy peach scones with almond icing. The woman who'd been reduced to tears by her furious husband.

I moved to the stairwell, where I wouldn't disturb anyone else, and called him right back. "Why in the world would she set fire to her own business?" This was a rhetorical question more than anything, because Nathan probably didn't know the answer yet and wouldn't be spilling it to me if he did. "This is heartbreaking," I said, knowing he would understand how much Miss Gloria and Martha and I had been looking forward to the contest.

"It is," he answered. "We would have brought her in to the station this morning, but there isn't enough evidence to question her formally. Is the filming of today's episode over?"

Was this why she'd shown up so late? I had a million questions. I told him about the incident with Mr. Humboldt crashing into the kitchen and threatening his wife. "They've got all three of the contestants in front of the camera now to talk about tomorrow's taping. Rayna's kind of a mess, so I don't think it will go on much longer. Plus Miss Gloria and the sisters look knackered, so I'll be bringing them home shortly."

"Is Rayna in danger?" he asked.

"I honestly have no idea."

"I'm going to have another detective meet her downstairs and escort her home and check that out. Meanwhile, is your mother there?" he asked. "Or Sam? Can one of them possibly take the women back to Houseboat Row? I'd like to come over and interview Martha Hubbard, and it would be good if you could stay and give me your opinions and observations. You know what's important with this cooking stuff, more than I ever will. Martha might have some background on the Humboldts, and maybe she will be more forthcoming if you're there too."

Martha had had an unpleasant run-in with the police several years ago and would be feeling anxious and stiff with his questions.

"I'm sure they'd be happy to take the women," I said, feeling a little burst of pride that he thought I might help. "Do I say anything to them about why I'm staying to meet you? Why you're coming?"

I could hear his deep sigh. "It will all come out soon enough, but if you can finesse avoiding giving the reason, that's probably better for now."

Chapter Six

As for a suspect, she said, "We don't have a particular demographic, except it's someone who wants to make a really delicious pastry."

—Carol Pogash, "During Bakery Break-In, Only Recipes Are Taken," *The New York Times*, March 6, 2015

I sat at the dining room table with Martha and Nathan, where only hours ago I'd nibbled tea and cookies and giggled with the Scottish sisters. Now Martha looked serious and a bit nervous. Actually, quite a bit.

"Can I make you a coffee?" she asked, glancing at Nathan. A chef would always be the caretaker.

"Thank you, no. If we could get right to it, I have some questions."

I reached across the table to put my hand on top of his. "Is Rayna considered a suspect in the arson?"

Martha might not have noticed it, but I saw the slight lines tug on my husband's forehead and the way the corners of his lips tipped down. Nathan was a bit annoyed that I was getting ahead of him.

"This is a good question, to which we do not yet have an answer." He turned back to focus on Martha. "However, the building where the fire occurred belongs to her husband. Let's start with the incident today."

We took turns filling in the details—how Rayna had turned up at the last minute, baked spectacular scones, and then been verbally abused by her demanding husband, who'd appeared out of nowhere.

"I think he would have dragged her away like a caveman if Harry and Martha hadn't blocked his path."

"I had my finger on my phone," said Martha, "ready to dial 911."

"Always a good idea," Nathan said, nodding his approval. "Never hesitate. We'd rather you call over something that turns out to be nothing than not call and someone gets hurt. If you could, tell us everything you remember about Rayna's first appearance when she was trying out for the contest."

Martha sat back in her chair and pushed away an inch or two from the table, as if she still found Nathan intimidating. Which, to be honest, happened with most people who didn't know him well.

"We thought she was a perfect candidate for the show. She seemed relaxed, and she had a full command of both her recipe and the kitchen, even though she'd never set foot in the building before. Not everyone can do this." She narrowed her eyes at him as if he might contradict her.

He held both hands up and smiled. "From a man who has absolutely no expertise in the culinary arts and relies helplessly on his wife to feed him, I bow to your opinions. Besides, my boss insists that I come across as a piece of wood when on camera."

I laughed out loud, getting a little more enjoyment out of his description than he might have liked—even though he was the one who'd made the joke. Martha snickered too but fell quiet when she saw the serious look on his face.

Too late, I realized I shouldn't laugh about the one major flaw that could keep him from a big police department promotion—even if he brought it up. Unless he was *clearly* laughing at himself and inviting me to join him. The Key West chief of police, which I knew he'd like to be one day, spent a good chunk of time interacting with the public—giving holiday speeches and commemorations, posing for photo opportunities, calming distressed citizens during crises, and the like. These public appearances were not his strength. His smarts and doggedness and deep sense of justice were.

"Did you get the impression that Rayna was upset or anxious about anything?" he continued.

Martha took a moment to think this over, running her fingers across the intricate tattoo ringing her arm above her left elbow. "She was worried about her husband getting mad that she wanted to be a part of the contest."

"Can you say more about that?"

Martha nodded. "We tried to encourage her, because she was such a natural." She glanced my way. "You know the way the Scone Sisters take to the camera and come alive as soon as the lights flash on? They never appear the least bit nervous, and you feel like they're talking straight to you. You, meaning you in particular, but that translates to all the viewers everywhere."

"Yes," I said, "they're incredible. I agree. Just the little bit I saw today, Rayna seems to have some of that same talent."

"Can you say more about the issue with the husband?" Nathan asked. "Can you remember any details about what she thought he might do if he found out?"

Martha wrinkled her nose and squinted. "Well, she didn't say anything specific, other than that she realized belatedly that he'd never approve. She didn't mention that until we told her she'd made the cut, and then it was like she suddenly recognized she'd gotten ahead of herself with the decision to try out for the role. She didn't say this, but I did get the sense he's jealous and controlling. Actually, we did see exactly that in action."

"Anything else?" Nathan asked. "Did she act as though he'd threatened her? Or that he would?"

"Not exactly. More like he makes the decisions for the family and she follows along. Here's an example. You obviously know they own the bed-and-breakfast on Dey Street. They're a couple of blocks from that French bakery, Au Citron Vert, on Greene Street. When the B and B first opened, Rayna told me the new bakery owner came over to ask whether they would like deliveries of their pastries for morning breakfasts. Apparently, she'd already had a conversation with him and agreed that this might be a good idea. His pastries are divine, and it would save her some time. But when the baker showed up to discuss the nuts and bolts with Rayna's husband, he laughed in the guy's face. He said that no frenchified wannabe could hold a candle to his wife's cooking."

"She sure didn't strike me as someone who would be that subservient to her husband. Didn't it seem like she had a ton of confidence?" I asked Martha.

"She did. But it waxed and waned. On the one hand, she was waiting to break out from his domination. But then she scared herself when she did something she knew he wouldn't like."

By now, I was intensely curious. Surely Rayna wouldn't have gone home and argued with her husband about the baking contest, then set their place on fire. To what end would she have done it? To punish him because he was bossy? And then she'd had the guts to show up for a TV show taping the next morning?

Martha's eyes widened suddenly, as she must have been thinking along the same lines. "Don't tell me she set her own bed-and-breakfast on fire."

Nathan shook his head. "I'm sorry, but I can't release any information about an ongoing investigation just now."

Which I interpreted to mean that the police very much might be thinking that.

"That's why any little details you can remember could help us solve this," he said grimly.

"I suppose you've already gotten a guest list and interviewed anyone staying there?" I asked. "It's possible they'd have overheard an argument—or maybe one of them was angry at the husband for something?"

"We have done," he said, and turned back to Martha. "What do you know about the special equipment that the Scone Sisters brought with them?"

She crossed her arms over her stomach, holding an elbow in each hand. "Hmm. Not a lot. They brought a few pieces with them, right, Hayley? Isn't that what we lugged up here this morning?"

"It's gorgeous, top-of-the-line stuff with the cutest designs on it," I said wistfully. "It's very expensive, and when they succeed with their tour, I suspect the prices will shoot up." Then I shifted to wondering what this could possibly have to do with a fire.

"Oh my gosh," I said suddenly. "That's where Violet and Bettina were to be staying. Because of the fire, they got bumped out of their room. Don't tell me this is related to them?"

"We simply don't know enough yet to say." Nathan turned back to Martha. "Could you tell me what you know about the other contestants? Were they acquainted before the contest? Did they seem to have any special connections, either with each other or someone else in the room?"

Martha thought about that for a moment. "I can't remember Harry talking with anyone—he's a little different. It's like he misses a lot of nuances in conversations with the people around him. Or possibly, to be generous, he was very nervous and that made him stiffen up. In some ways, it was hard to envision why he'd enter the contest." She frowned a bit, remembering. "It was like watching someone who loves to sing but can't carry a tune in a bucket deciding to perform in public."

I nodded. "He didn't seem that dexterous in front of the cameras either—he kept repeating himself in an annoying way. I didn't taste his scone, but it barely rose. With all those winter ingredients, his recipe was very heavy. Curling-stone heavy."

Martha snickered. Nathan didn't. Now wasn't the time to joke—something serious was happening.

"I didn't notice any friendly interactions among any of the candidates," I added, "not while I was there."

"Martina was chatting with everyone ahead of time," Martha said. "She works as a personal trainer at the WeBeFit gym, so chatty conversation comes easily. But I wouldn't have said she knew the others."

"No one was commiserating with Rayna for having a rotten husband, for example?" I asked. That would be too obvious and easy. The longer I knew my Nathan, the more I appreciated how tedious police work could sometimes be, and the amount of persistent digging it took to solve a case. He'd taught me that you should never take anything offered at face value. Many people lied to the police, for many reasons—not all of them related to the crime at hand. Solving a case often required help from the community too—like during New Year's week this year when two men had pushed a dry-as-tinder Christmas tree against the famous Southernmost Point Buoy and set it afire. Surveillance cameras recorded some of the action, and a local bartender identified the perpetrators after their photos were shared by the police on social media.

A text from my mother lit up my phone, which I'd set on the table. "Oops, I forgot to ask. Okay to accept an invite for us and the ladies to Mom and Sam's house tonight for dinner?" I asked Nathan.

"Sure," he said. "I'll pick you all up. That will give me a chance to get their impressions about the day." He turned back to Martha. "Let me know if you think of anything else, or if you notice unusual interactions between the contestants this week."

"Will do," she said, as we stood up and headed to the door leading out of the kitchen. "Hopefully, it doesn't get any worse than this. We've got too many balls in the air to keep this contest afloat as is." She grinned at me. "Please make sure you get the ladies tucked into bed early—we need them spunky for tomorrow's filming."

Chapter Seven

Are they ghastly or gorgeous? A terror or temptation? For me that's the wonder of mushrooms, the riddle. They could be poisonous. Then again, they could be soup.

—Frank Bruni

As usual, my mother had put on a glorious spread for dinner.

"I didn't try to make Scottish food," she said with a laugh, after she and Sam had welcomed the guests. "Who could compete with you ladies? I ended up deciding on a Crock-Pot chicken cacciatore, even though I'm not Italian and neither are you. The recipe probably isn't Italian either! Anyway, I could let it simmer all day long and not worry about it while we watched you amazingly talented women in front of the camera."

"Besides, the Crock-Pot dinner allowed my wife to focus on a glorious dessert," Sam added. That made my mouth water— what had she made that he'd describe this way?

"We are simply gobsmacked by your hospitality and will happily eat whatever you serve us," said Violet, and her sister nodded vigorously beside her.

"Let's have a wee cocktail out on the porch," Sam said, herding them out to the deck. "We loved your show today, ladies. You are going to be stars all across America. I've made a pitcher of mojitos, but we also have the usual wine, beer, gin and tonic, seltzer, soft drinks. You name it."

The sisters and Miss Gloria settled into their deck chairs with deep sighs and accepted tall glasses beaded with moisture, ribboned with mint, and topped with slices of lime. The Key West weather was cooperating too—the humidity had broken a bit and the sun was behind enough clouds to moderate the temperature and pinken the sky.

"Can you imagine sitting outside for cocktails at this time of year back home?" asked Violet.

Bettina shook her head and laughed. "I checked this morning. Forty-two degrees the high at noon, with sleet expected after dark. This is surely heaven."

Sam served up Scottish cheese shortbreads laced with a bit of heat from cayenne pepper, along with pink shrimp cocktails and mushrooms stuffed with Parmesan and cream cheese.

"This way we have a mushroom theme going," said Sam. "Though lord only knows what nationality that suggests."

After twenty minutes of chatter, I could see all three ladies were getting a little loopy as they sipped down their cocktails. My mother noticed it as well.

"You all have had such a long day. What if we go ahead and eat and let Nathan get you home to bed?"

"They do have another long day tomorrow," I said. "The next competition should be very exciting to watch."

"We've taken the day off the catering business just for that reason," said Sam as he helped usher the guests into the dining room.

Once the plates were loaded with chicken, mushrooms, and peppers in a flavorful tomato sauce over fresh egg noodles and a lovely tossed salad made by Sam, Bettina asked Nathan, "Can you tell us anything about the fire?"

He settled his knife and fork on the edge of his plate. "It certainly looks like arson, which is probably not news to you. In fact, the fire was hot enough that it could have burned the place down. It was only dumb luck that a passerby noticed, and then that the fire department got there so quickly. I wonder if you wouldn't mind describing what you saw last night when Hayley drove you to Greene Street?" That was Nathan, probing gently.

"As I said right away, I smelled an accelerant." Violet was talking but looking at her sister for confirmation.

Bettina nodded her head in agreement. "It looked as though something highly flammable had been piled against the side of the house. With both an accelerant and the extra kindling, either it seemed like an amateur at work or someone who wanted to make sure the job was done." She explained to Nathan again how their father had been a firefighter and then rose to chief before his knees gave out and he had to retire. "For our bedtime stories when he came home at night, we always wanted to hear who'd set a fire that day and how Daddy put it out. I can't imagine there was a fire every single day, so maybe he embellished his work."

"Mother hated that," Violet said, smiling softly. "She hated everything to do with his job. We overheard her telling our aunt that he came home smelling of ashes and death."

"He made us practice over and over how to escape from a fire," Bettina said. "Drop to the ground and follow your sniffer to the fresh air. Touch a door before you open it—if it's hot, go out another way. We had a big hammer to break our bedroom window and coils of rope to drop out and shimmy down." She grinned at her sister. "We got pretty good at that and blew away the other girls in PE once we started school."

When supper was finished, I helped Sam remove the plates and carry them to the kitchen. My mother carried a gorgeous caramel cake to the dining room. "It's turned out the best ever, in your honor," she said, placing it between the sisters. "This is from a *Southern Cakes* cookbook that I love. Coffee or an after-dinner drink for anyone?"

"Just the cake." Bettina grinned. "It will be a slice of heaven and the perfect nightcap."

Mom cut generous slices of the cake, the inside a pale yellow surrounded by a crunchy layer of golden caramel. After scraping up every crumb on our plates, we loaded into the car, the three sleepy ladies in the back of Nathan's SUV and me in front. As he turned on the engine, his radio crackled to life.

"There's a report of a dog walker finding a body in the alley off Greene Street near the site of last night's fire. Please check in with location."

Nathan spoke into his mouthpiece. "I'm nearby and will ride over now."

In his current job as lieutenant, he would not be called upon to work this case. But as close as we were to the action, I understood that he'd feel the need to drive over and make sure no important step in dealing with the scene was overlooked. Plus the dispatcher had reported it as near last night's fire. That was already very much on his radar.

He parked on Simonton Street, a block away from the bed-and-breakfast, put his flashers on, then turned to look at our guests and Miss Gloria in the back seat. "This shouldn't take long. I'll wait until the detective on duty and the coroner arrive to make sure the proper procedures are being followed." He paused, looking at the concerned faces. "No one here will be getting out of the car to poke around the crime scene, is that understood?" He crooked a smile to soften his words a bit. But he meant it.

Miss Gloria saluted and the others nodded, all three of them looking subdued.

"I suppose that means me as well."

Glancing at me, Nathan barely cracked a second smile. "If you don't mind, it does."

Out the car window, now fogged a bit with our breathing in spite of the AC Nathan had left running, I could see the dog walker. He was sitting on the curb, his feet in the street and his animal pressing into his side. In the light of a nearby streetlamp and the neon palm tree flashing in the window of the 7 Artists and Friends Gallery, his face looked shocked. The dog was short but long and muscular, speckled with black and white like a blue merle Aussie. One of those designer dogs, I thought. Maybe with a lot less energy than our Ziggy, but probably better behaved. He reached up to lick his owner's face.

Ziggy himself had found a body last fall, and he hadn't sat around panting or leaning against me or comforting me while I figured out who to call. He'd dug around the dead man in such an excited way that I worried the crime scene would be destroyed. The memory of that day came rushing in—the horror of finding the corpse and the emotional turmoil that followed as the murderer was hunted down over the next couple of days. I felt sorry for the good citizen crouched there beside the road. A body is the last thing a dog walker thinks of finding on an evening outing.

Two Key West Police Department patrol cars pulled up, and Nathan strode over to meet them. After a few minutes of conversation, one of the officers, a heavyset balding man, jogged down the alley, his gait lighter than I would have predicted for a man of his size. The other stationed himself at the entrance and directed the gathering crowd to disperse.

Then the coroner's car arrived, which I recognized from previous crime scenes, although it wasn't marked as such. Nathan chatted with the man briefly, and they walked over to the alley and disappeared for a few minutes. I could feel the anxiety mounting among the ladies in the back seat.

"It could be anything," I said to my friends. "Somebody could've had a heart attack, or it could've been a homeless person who died of exposure."

Miss Gloria burst in. "Since when did anyone die of exposure in March in Key West?"

"Point well taken," I said, smiling gently. "It's just that we've had such a nice evening and sometimes our fears and our imagination are worse than the truth, so I don't want to assume it's something awful."

"Hard not to," she grumbled, "when the corpse was found right near the scene of the arson. Plus the bed-and-breakfast belonged to the husband of one of our contestants. Plus our dear friends were supposed to be staying there." I silently agreed that it added up to trouble.

Bettina patted her on the shoulder. "We'll all learn soon enough, ma dear."

A Clue in the Crumbs

Nathan emerged from the alley, returned to the dog walker, and squatted down to his level. The man appeared distressed, and his dog pressed up against him and licked his face again.

"Isn't that Paul, the new owner of Au Citron Vert?" Miss Gloria asked.

That was the same pastry shop owner who had approached Rayna's husband about providing baked goods for their breakfasts. Now I was super curious about his impressions of that incident as well as what he'd found tonight. After his last experience as a suspect, he wasn't going to react well to questioning by stern police officers. I was sure of that.

Nathan arrived back at the car half an hour later, a grim expression on his face. We all knew better than to ask, but he said it anyway.

"Ongoing investigation." Followed by a heavy sigh.

Chapter Eight

A kitchen, by the way, is the perfect setting for a murderous plot—it's hot, fast, heavy work, involving people who are probably more accustomed to acting on their feelings than talking them out.

—Lucy Burdette, "Food and Mystery:
A Perfect Pairing," CrimeReads

Lots of people never make it past the main drag in Key West— that is, Duval Street. But there are many adorable alleys off the beaten path hiding both spectacular private homes and bed-and-breakfasts. Sometimes the only thing giving a place away is the sound of a waterfall hidden by a clump of tropical shrubbery, or the clinking of breakfast dishes on an outside porch behind a wooden fence. Rayna's husband's bed-and-breakfast was one of those.

After I dropped the three ladies off at Williams Hall the next morning to do a run-through of the new day's work, I decided to wander in the direction of the B and B to glance over the crime scene on the way to having a chat with Paul at the little French bakery. He might tell me something in person that he wouldn't tell a cop. He'd been burned by his last experience of interrogation as a suspect and so was likely to clam up if uniforms showed up at his store.

I thought for a minute about seeking Nathan's approval, but over the last two years of our marriage, we'd come to a tentative and unspoken agreement. Truth: sometimes people talked to me who wouldn't talk to him. He understood that and even appreciated it, especially following his father's visit last fall. He would always worry about my safety, but I was getting better about not acting like a silly woman who'd go into a dark basement alone after hearing a suspicious noise. If the cops were done questioning Paul, I couldn't see how it would hurt to ask for a few impressions myself.

I found a spot to park Miss Gloria's Buick at the north end of Greene Street and trotted toward Humboldt's Happy Home, the bed-and-breakfast belonging to Rayna's husband. The building was located on Dey Street, a one-way lane connecting Simonton and Elizabeth Streets. The alley was open to traffic this morning, with no sign of last night's tragedy aside from a piece of yellow crime scene tape hugging the old home's porch and a handful of orange cones that blocked off the small backyard. The charred timbers and siding on the west side of the home still gave off an acrid smell, but I saw no evidence this morning pointing to the place where the body had lain. There was no sign of life in the old building either—no lights, no lazy movement of ceiling fans, no noise or lovely scents of baking from the kitchen. The cottage at the back of the property, which had probably started life as a shed, was also quiet and dark.

I returned to Greene Street, passed a tattoo shop and Sloppy Joe's, and arrived at Au Citron Vert. The place had been decorated to resemble a Parisian pâtisserie, no fake palm trees or Jimmy Buffett slogans in evidence. Though the original owner had been killed several years ago, her right-hand man, Paul Redford, had bought the establishment and now ran it successfully. Inside, there were round café tables, dark-maroon leather chairs, and a glass case brimming with the kind of pastry you might find in France. He'd gotten more and more confident as his experience grew, serving napoleons, éclairs, pralines, fruit tarts, and the flakiest croissants on the island. He also made what I considered to be the best key lime pie in Key West—and there was a lot of competition. I tried not to go in too often, because it was impossible not to buy his confections and equally impossible not to gobble them on the spot. This morning, the tables brimmed with visitors sipping tea from china cups and devouring the pastry. Paul was alone behind the register, so I approached. He looked a bit peaked, the skin below his eyes showing dark demilunes of exhaustion. He wore a pale-green shirt decorated with a basket of darker-green limes along with the words *Au Citron Vert* and *Key Lime Pie et plus*, or *key lime pie and more*.

"I'm really sorry to hear what happened last night," I said, after greeting him. "It had to be brutal, being so close to that."

"I suppose you'd know," he said, busying himself straightening the pastries in the glistening case so he didn't have to look me in the eye, almost as if the two of us were now in a club that no one wanted to join. "I've been thoroughly grilled by the police and assured them I know nothing other than what I saw on the street."

I'd come hoping to learn what happened, so I leaned on the counter, lowered my voice to a whisper, and asked the hard question. "What did you find?"

"At first I thought it was a random bag of trash. Or even a homeless person sleeping."

"Either one of those would be quite possible," I agreed. "But if you're like me, you went closer to check, in case someone needed your help."

He nodded, his face looking grim. "Glacier pulled me in, so I had no choice."

"The dog," I said. "He's a cutie. I love the colors of his fur and the whole shape of him. Dogs are like men that way; sometimes you just fall for the look of them."

He snorted with laughter.

"How did you come up with the name?"

Paul chuckled again, the muscles in his face beginning to look less tense. "If you saw us last night, you probably weren't close enough to notice the one pale-blue eye—that's our glacier connection. He's part Bernese mountain dog, part poodle, aka Bernedoodle. He was a pandemic puppy who failed to adapt when his owners had to go back to work, because he wants to be with his people all the time. My sister grabbed him from a shelter in Miami and insisted I take him."

I heard a sharp woof from the back room. "He can't understand why he's not allowed in the shop." Paul grinned.

I smiled back. "Did you recognize the man you found?"

His grin fell away. "He was facedown," Paul said with a big shudder.

We were distracted by a text that came in on my phone, followed by a second. I glanced at it quickly to be sure there wasn't a family emergency. Both were from Miss Gloria's older son, Frank. "Give me a sec?" I asked Paul.

Mom's not returning my calls and she didn't call at our usual time Sunday. I want to make sure she's okay, read the first.

Assuming so, can you remind her to call her family? read the second.

I texted him right back. *She's fine, she's great. The Scottish baking sisters are staying with her and she's all a-twitter. I will nudge her to call you ASAP.*

The phone calls kept her sons from worrying too much about leaving an old woman alone in a houseboat in the Keys. I'd remind her of that, though she'd object to being classified as an old woman. I knew better than to mention anything about a murder or a fire to her son. With her family, I tried to keep things light without bending the truth. If I truly felt she was incapable of living alone, I certainly wouldn't ignore it. But I'd tackle the issue with her first. She was capable of facing facts if and when that time came, and she deserved the chance to make her own decisions, unless she became mentally incapacitated and thus incapable of making them. She'd made me promise to step in and help out should that happen.

As soon as I finished typing and sending the message to Frank, I decided I should buy a selection of pastries while I was here. This would demonstrate goodwill to Paul and provide the ladies something to snack on later when they arrived back home, at which point they might be drooping and in need of some sugar. Our Houseboat Row neighbor, Connie, had been hoping to meet Violet and Bettina. She'd suggested a spot of tea later today, which might work out depending how long the taping session lasted. But I certainly wouldn't have time to bake.

Connie herself, with an active toddler and another on the way, plus a full-time flourishing cleaning business, would not be getting anywhere near an oven.

As Paul was packing up my pastries in a white box and taking my credit card, a third text came in, this time from Miss Gloria. It was rife with typos and had an air of desperation.

Did you get my text? Can you come right away? Dead man was Rayna's husband. She never showed up today and everybody's at sixes and sevens. Especially Martha. They've called off the work for today. We're all so upset and addled and I can't remember how to work the Uber. I would rather not try to walk home with our Scottish ladies.

I texted back immediately and told her I would be there within minutes.

"I've got to go," I told Paul, stashing the card back in my wallet. I jotted my phone number on one of his cards and pushed it over to him. "Will you call me if you hear anything new?"

"I will." He looked quite curious. "Did you get some bad news?"

I considered this quickly. He was going to hear sooner rather than later if everybody at Williams Hall had heard. Maybe he'd have a useful reaction.

"The body that you found last night? That was Rayna's husband."

He gulped, his Adam's apple traveling down his neck and back up. The color in his face drained, almost matching the greenish hue of his shirt. "I didn't recognize him, I swear. As I said, he was facedown with his head half buried in the bushes and a big knife in his back. All the blood everywhere." Those were details he had not told me before.

His face had gone ghostly pale now, and he began to look woozy, as if he might pass out. I had the sense that his brain had only now begun to process what he'd seen.

"Why don't you sit down for a minute?" I suggested. "Can I get you a drink of water? Or a cold cloth?"

He shook me off and pulled in a shuddering breath. "I'll be fine. It's just the idea that I saw someone murdered whom I knew—that freaks me out. Even if I didn't know him well and honestly didn't like what I knew."

He looked instantly worried, as if he shouldn't have mentioned that.

"I know," I said. "That's brutal, seeing someone killed. Sometimes your mind can't really absorb what's in front of you. Did you by any chance see Rayna last night?"

He shook his head no. "If she was there, she didn't come out. I hope they headed her off before she got home. How horrible it would have been for her to see her husband like that." He looked as though he might cry.

A group of chattering women had come into the shop and waited to take over my place at the register. "We'll talk another time," I called out to him as I stepped aside. "I'll be in touch, but please call if you think of anything that might be important to this case."

I trotted back to the car, drove to Williams Hall, and found a parking space only a block away. I vaulted up the stairs to the second floor and hurried into the kitchen. The ladies, all three of them looking subdued, were sitting at the wooden table on the white upholstered chairs. Martha was huddled with the camera people and one of Nathan's detective friends.

"Thank goodness you're here!" Miss Gloria got right to her feet and gathered her bag and the sweater she'd brought in case the air conditioning was jacked up too high. "We are all in a bit of shock, and we need carbohydrates and caffeine."

"Luckily, I just stocked up on both. Did the police already question you? Is it okay for you to leave?"

"They told us they'd be contacting us with further questions," said Miss Gloria. She tipped her head at the detective and whispered to me, "Hopefully, that will be Nathan, because this guy has no social skills."

Which I figured meant he wasn't inclined to tell them what the cops already knew. Or maybe not leave out hard questions just because they were older than the usual suspects in an investigation. It was probably more the latter, because she looked rattled, as did her friends. I put a comforting hand on her back, noticing the sharp bony protrusions, and reminded myself that she was more fragile than either she or I liked to think. "Come on, I'm parked only a block away."

On the way to the car, I called my friend Connie. "We're coming home early, unexpectedly, and I'm in possession of a sack of pastries. Do you want to join us for coffee? We could use a distraction."

"Sure, what happened?"

"Unfortunately, the husband of one of the Scone Sisters' contestants has been murdered."

After appropriate murmurings of dismay, she agreed to meet us in half an hour, and I drove home to the houseboat.

"We'll come to you," said Miss Gloria, as she got out of the front seat and steamed up the dock with the sisters in her wake. "Give us a minute to stash our stuff and freshen up."

Chapter Nine

On the other hand, if you're looking for information on real-world problems, you might want to look to someone who doesn't bake cookies for a living.

—*David Lebovitz Newsletter*, May 23, 2022

I put the kettle on and set the pastries out on my favorite green-leaf platter, a wedding gift from one of my mother's dear friends. Fifteen minutes later, I had a pot of freshly brewed coffee ready out on the deck, along with hot water and tea bags, assorted sugars and milks, and the pastries.

The three ladies arrived minutes later, still quieter than usual. Connie bounced down the finger of the dock, happy, I was sure, to be off work and off childcare duty, at least for the moment. We introduced her to the Scone Sisters, and they shared hugs all around.

"You look amazing," I told her, holding her away for inspection. "You are positively glowing."

She grinned. "Thanks. I'm in the pregnancy sweet spot where I'm well past barfing every half hour, and I'm not quite so big I can't tie my own shoes."

The ladies howled with laughter.

"I don't think I ever got past the morning sickness stage," Violet said, a cloud of grief passing over her face. "Not until I held that precious boy in my arms." She shook the sadness off and smiled at Connie.

"Now, everyone get comfortable and let's have something hot and something sweet," I said. "Sounds like it was a rough morning in the kitchen."

Once they were settled with drinks and snacks and had finished quizzing Connie about her toddler, Claire, and the new baby who was coming in a couple of months, I asked the ladies to describe what had happened.

Bettina said, "We knew right away that something was off kilter when Rayna didn't show up. We were quite astonished, because her performance yesterday was so clearly superior to that of the others. She seemed thrilled to be involved and really excited about today's taping."

"Except for the ugly scene when her husband tried to drag her off by the hair," said Miss Gloria.

Violet nodded, adding, "Quite naturally, her not coming makes perfect sense in hindsight, because who would show up to a baking contest when one's husband has been murdered? A person needs to pull in and take care of herself after a tragic loss."

She knew this better than almost anyone, having experienced the violent and shocking death of her own son.

"Did you hear anything new about the murder from the detective? Are there suspects?" she asked.

I hadn't heard a peep from Nathan, but he wasn't in the habit of keeping me apprised of breaking news in active cases. I would quiz him gently once he got home.

"Unfortunately, I imagine she herself has to be one of those under suspicion," Bettina said. "Don't they always look at the closest relatives? Plus we all witnessed that ugliness in the kitchen. Several of us might have been happy to murder him ourselves."

"I've missed a lot of excitement," said Connie. "Who are you all talking about?"

Together we explained about the baking contest and the woman who'd shown up late, apparently appearing against her husband's wishes.

"She was brilliant," said Bettina, shaking her head sadly. "Those peach scones were to die for."

Violet patted her sister on the back. "Perhaps not the best wording to use under these circumstances?"

"Oh dear, I didn't think," Bettina said.

"Last night as we were leaving Sam and Mom's place, Nathan got word that a dog walker had stumbled over a body," I continued. "Turned out the dog walker is the pastry chef from Au Citron Vert. The guy who baked these amazing treats." I pointed to the green plate, now empty of everything except crumbs. "We learned this morning that the dead man owned the bed-and-breakfast that was torched the other day and that he was Rayna's husband. He appeared at yesterday's taping and tried to force his wife to leave." I glanced at my phone to see if there were any updates and noticed Nathan had sent another text right after Miss Gloria's. I'd been too distracted to notice.

"Don't forget to tell her that Bettina and Violet were supposed to be staying there," piped up Miss Gloria. "Until the fire incident, after which all reservations were canceled. Which was fine, because I love having them here with me. Did you hear anything about how the poor man was killed?"

I sighed, once again wondering how much to say. "They found him facedown with a big knife in his back."

Both sisters blanched. I felt guilty that I had shocked them by telling too much.

Violet leaned over to pat my hand. "Don't worry, dear, it's not that we're so fragile. It's that our best knife was among the equipment that has gone missing. Lucky for us, we brought some things in our luggage. We finally tracked down our agent yesterday, and he reported that our things have not arrived. He was supposed to bring all our shipped luggage to the Williams Hall kitchen, where he's not shown his face. He was so eager to take us on as clients that he was calling us daily. But once we got here, not a jot."

"Diddly squat," Bettina agreed. "Not so much as a *Welcome to America*. He's supposed to be representing us and smoothing our way, but so far, nothing. In fact"—she glanced at her sister—"I'm not convinced that he has the slightest idea where our shipped equipment is." She paused, looking worried. "Can you describe the knife?"

It seemed like a major coincidence that their knife would have ended up in this man's back. Hopefully, we could rule that out right away. I glanced at my phone to read my husband's text again. "Nathan says it was a butcher or carving knife, and it looked old. It had a wooden handle with rivets, and the blade itself had an unusual curve."

Violet pressed a palm to her throat. "Oh dear, I don't like that at all. It sounds too much like ours."

"I'm so confused," Connie said. "The pastry chef was murdered?"

"No, no," said Miss Gloria with a strained laugh. "That would be a true tragedy. We're all talking at once, so no wonder you don't have it straight. The dead man was Rayna Humboldt's husband."

A connection seemed to snap into place in Connie's memory. "Remember I told you that one of my workers had to leave the island for a family emergency and I've had trouble replacing her?"

I nodded. One of the chronic problems for businesses on our little island was getting enough help to do the work, especially during the tourist high season. The cost of housing had shot up so high that people with one ordinary job had a hard time affording it.

"I've been pitching in and taking some of her shifts. One of her regular jobs is cleaning for Mr. Humboldt's bed-and-breakfast. She often worked the ten AM–to–two PM shift, getting ready for new visitors and tidying up the rooms of the people staying on."

"Were you acquainted with Rayna's husband? What was he like?" Violet asked.

"I can't say that I liked working with that man, not one bit. He was always critical, picking on the smallest things that we hadn't gotten right—supposing the pillowcases weren't folded just so, or he'd found an imaginary dust bunny under a bed." Connie squinted her eyes, thinking. "I overheard them arguing a time or two. He was plain nasty."

Bettina touched her hand to her face, covering her eye with her palm. "I didn't think much of it at the time, but didn't it seem like Rayna was wearing a pile of makeup when she turned up for yesterday's practice taping? At the time, I assumed she came camera ready and had applied her own foundation and eye makeup in advance because she knew she was running late. But now I'm wondering whether she was trying to cover something up. Maybe my subconscious noticed a bruise?"

"Like she had a shiner," Miss Gloria burst out. "I had one of those one time when I stumbled at night and had an altercation with the nightstand. I wore a thick paste of concealer for two weeks because I was afraid everyone would think Frank had hit me. Plus my face looked butt ugly, as one of my own sons was rude enough to say on FaceTime." She let out a peal of laughter, then settled down as the seriousness of the situation weighed on all of us.

"Didn't you also have a black eye that time you got hit on the head right on this dock?" Connie asked. "Hayley was staying with me at the time, remember? If I'm right, she found you and called the ambulance."

The memory came flooding back to me, how terrifying it had been to assume the heap along the finger was a pile of garbage and then have Miss Gloria's small body take shape among the shadows. I hadn't known her well enough to understand what a terrible loss it would have been if she hadn't recovered. "Awful night," I said, reaching over to squeeze my friend's hand.

She winked at me. "It was, but I bounced back, and since then I've lived through worse. Back to Rayna's problem," she said. "Let's think about that black eye and what led up to it."

"Do you suppose her husband clocked her and she fought back and stabbed him?" Violet asked.

"It's possible," I said. "But he was stabbed last night, and Bettina thinks she noticed the bruising earlier. I can guarantee that a body wouldn't lie in that alley for long without someone finding it. The streets on either side of it are very busy, especially at night. Maybe Rayna was on a slow burn about the blow and finally erupted?" I glanced around the little circle of women.

"If you had to say," Miss Gloria asked, "what color was the bruise under the makeup?" She held up her hand before Bettina could answer. "Let me explain why that might be important. A shiner is darker at first when the eye is swollen from the pooling blood. In fact, after Hayley found me, I remember waking up in the hospital early the next morning in a complete panic, thinking I'd gone blind. I pressed the nurse call button about a thousand times, and she came rushing in. Once I told her the problem, she explained how all the blood and other fluids had drained down into my eyelid and the poor thing was drooping over my eye like a full diaper." She patted her cheek. "We got a good chuckle out of that description. A bruise morphs to yellow and purple as the days go by and the blood disperses." She paused to think, or was it for a dramatic reveal?

"In other words, if we knew the color of her skin underneath the makeup, we might be able to figure out approximately when he hit her. Whether she felt threatened and so on."

I could only sit back and listen to my friend with astonishment. She'd missed her calling as a detective.

"*If* he did hit her," said Violet. "Unfortunately, stabbing someone in the back a few days or even a day after one had been struck would not exactly be considered self-defense. Not in Scotland, anyway. If a person has a way out of a dangerous situation, she is bound by law to use it."

"What did you think of Harry stepping up to protect Rayna from her husband yesterday?" I asked.

"Gobsmacked," said Bettina. "Never would have predicted that. He seemed like an every-man-for-himself kind of guy up to that point."

"Is it possible they're having a fling?" Miss Gloria asked.

"Absolutely never crossed my mind," I said. "They don't go together, even in my wildest imagination."

"Agreed. We have the day off from the contest," said Miss Gloria, brushing the crumbs off her lap and folding up her napkin. "We should use the time wisely. Interviewing suspects and so on. There are a lot of avenues to explore with this case."

"I was thinking more along the lines of taking our guests to lunch," I said with a laugh. "I'm doing a roundup for *Key Zest* called 'Paradise Lunched.' Opinions about food are always welcome."

Opinions were *not* always welcome at the Key West Police Department, so if I could keep the ladies distracted, Nathan would be grateful.

Chapter Ten

Annie looked up, then realized she was still holding the bread knife, as if it were some sort of weapon, and set it down on the counter.

—Ann Cleeves, *The Rising Tide*

The Seaside Café, on the grounds of the Southernmost House, was best known for its fantastic location on a beach overlooking the Atlantic Ocean. It had gotten a boost in reputation after former *New York Times* food critic Sam Sifton visited earlier in the winter and raved about the lobster pizza. I figured if we arrived when it opened at eleven thirty, we'd have an easier time scoring a table overlooking the water. The Duval Street party crowd tended to move slowly in the morning and take their lunches late. I didn't know how the café's pizza would stand up in comparison to my beloved Clemente's, but certainly the atmosphere and ocean-side scenery gave it a leg up.

"I wish I could join you but must get back to work," Connie said. She promised to talk with her other employees about the possibility that Rayna had been abused by her husband. "I'll text you later," she told me. "Keep me posted about any new information."

The café at the Southernmost House did not take reservations, but as I'd hoped, we were seated easily at a table on the sand bordering the beach. The ladies exclaimed over the beautiful Victorian yellow-pink-and-turquoise home with its turrets and fancy dentil crown moldings. Miss Gloria explained that it had been built in 1897 and gone through many different iterations over the years.

"You can walk to the Southernmost Point easily from here, although that's not really a repeat attraction," she said. "Once and done."

"But folks do stand in line for hours and hours to get their photo taken in front of that buoy," I said. "We can do the same if it's important to you."

Bettina and Violet looked at each other, then shrugged in unison. "Not so much."

"They call this the quiet end of Duval Street, although there's plenty of action," Miss Gloria added. "It's not as crazy as the far end, with the Bull and Whistle and Sloppy Joe's and so on. Not to mention the clothing-optional bar, called Garden of Eden. They have a rooftop garden where you can tan your privates," she said, grinning.

"I hardly know how to respond to that," Violet said, sputtering a bit. "Just to say that our weather in Scotland wouldn't lend itself to such an establishment."

For a few minutes, we studied the menu.

"What do you think about having a cocktail?" Miss Gloria asked. She was looking at the Scottish ladies rather than me. Maybe she assumed I would object.

"What are your plans this afternoon?" I asked.

"A good long nap," said Violet with a snicker. "But to be serious for a minute, having one's knife discovered in the back of a dead man will take the starch out of you. A cocktail sounds lovely."

After we'd ordered—the grilled caprese sandwich for me, a hot-honey-and-salami pizza and a mixed green salad with strawberries for the Scottish ladies, a lobster biscuit for Miss Gloria, and the lobster pizza for the table, I asked, "Could you tell me about the knife, and your bakeware? And your agent. It puzzles me that we haven't seen anything of him since you arrived in town. I would have thought he'd attend the events at Williams Hall."

"Believe you me, it puzzles us as well," said Bettina. "He was all over us by phone and text when we were getting ready to come. We all agreed that we'd stay at that particular bed-and-breakfast. He insisted he would take care of having the bakeware and equipment shipped, all of it."

"We knew better than that, from experience traveling around Great Britain and Scotland," said Violet. "One should not assume that one's luggage will make it to the next destination whole."

"You seemed quite convinced that the knife found in Rayna's husband was yours."

The waitress appeared to deliver our drinks—tropical crushes for the sisters, a painkiller for Miss Gloria, and iced tea for me.

The sisters exchanged a knowing look. "It sounds exactly like a knife that belonged to our grandmother, and she got it from her mother. It was made in Germany, and it looked a bit long in the tooth, but it could be sharpened like no other knife I've known. The blade had a little curve in it from generations of women honing and carving. Plus it had those rivets on the handle. Exactly as your husband described."

A Clue in the Crumbs

I could imagine how distressed they must feel, thinking that a family heirloom had been used in a murder. Maybe it wasn't so. On the other hand, the knife sounded utterly distinctive, and that made me grateful that the ladies had been eating supper with my family when the man was killed. There was no way they could be suspected in the death.

"In other words, if your knife was used in the attack, your luggage must have arrived at the bed-and-breakfast by yesterday. Someone dug through it to find it, or else happened upon it when they needed a weapon." I pushed my glass of tea aside to make room for the food arriving at our table—we'd ordered enough for a small army. "Was it packed by itself? Would anyone have known it was there?"

"Good question," said Miss Gloria, draining her painkiller and nodding at the waiter to bring another before I could protest.

"It was in a wooden box along with our serrated bread knife and a duo of parers. One can never assume that any kitchen outside our own home in Peebles would come with sharp blades. We brought the third paring knife with us in the checked bag, just in case," said Violet, a wistful expression on her face. "All that aside, the velvet padding that held the knives still carries the scent of our mother's kitchen. So we never feel homesick when we travel for a gig, silly as it might sound."

"Not silly at all," said Miss Gloria firmly. "But you can't be certain that the murder weapon is your knife." She strove to find the positive in every situation, no matter how grim it looked at first blush.

"Unfortunately, it sounds like it, though," said Bettina.

"Assuming the knife was yours, as I said before, either someone knew where to look for it or they were rooting through your stuff and came across the box. Imagine you're the murderer. Seems like you'd look in the kitchen before searching someone's random luggage, no?" I asked. "Unless this person knew where to look and for what."

"Nobody other than our agent knew about the goods we'd shipped," said Violet.

"Not exactly so," said Bettina. "Remember I phoned a few days ago and informed Mr. Humboldt to be on the lookout for a shipment of our kitchenware? So he was aware. We don't know who else was staying there, or whether they'd have overheard us talking to him on the telephone, or whether they'd have reason to paw through our luggage. Perhaps Connie or one of her workers might have noticed when our shipment arrived?"

"Unfortunately, it seems likely that Rayna would have known about the arrival of your belongings as well," I said. I took a bite of my sandwich, chewing slowly and noting in my mind the toasted baguette, the ripe tomatoes and fresh basil, and the creamy mozzarella. "You should eat before everything gets cold," I said, sliding a slice of each of the pizzas onto my plate. "Oops," I added, looking at the sisters. "Is it okay that I try your pizza?"

"Absolutely!" said Violet.

"Question of the day," said Miss Gloria, clinking the ice in her glass as she slurped the new drink. "Supposing the murder weapon was your knife. Did someone plan that purposely to throw suspicion on you? Or was it a case of a lucky find for a seat-of-the-pants murderer?"

She shoveled a piece of hot lobster pizza into her mouth. "And one more question: supposing again that it was your knife in that man's back. After that, can you imagine using it in your kitchen?"

Chapter Eleven

But there are a few absolute, ironclad rules that I think protect us from losing our tenuous hold on civilization and sliding into the chaotic abyss, and one of them is this: Sandwiches must be cut in half on the diagonal.

—Emily Heil, "Sandwiches Must be Cut Diagonally and I'm Not Taking Questions," *The Washington Post*, October 4, 2023

While the ladies went back to Miss Gloria's boat to snooze off their cocktails and lunch and the shock of the murder, I wrote up the first segment of "Paradise Lunched." Seaside tables, the background playlist of birds and waves, lobster pizza, and pretty cocktails—what was not to like? Then I made myself a cup of coffee and sat on the deck with my animals to think about who might have murdered Rayna's husband. I didn't like the so-called coincidence of Violet and Bettina getting booked into the bed-and-breakfast where a man was killed and a fire was set. Why might their knife have been used in the murder? No one had mentioned it yet, but I began to wonder if it was possible that one or both of them had been targeted—that they were meant to be painted as villains.

But why? It was hard to imagine them doing anything that would create enemies. Although envy over another person's success came in many forms, even when not solicited. Maybe especially when not solicited.

Where was this so-called agent who had been so eager to sign the sisters before they arrived in the United States? Was there a lot of money involved in selling their bakeware? From the pieces they'd managed to pack in their suitcases, I'd seen that it was pricy and elegantly beautiful. I wondered now if the person who landed the license would stand to rake in a boatload of money. The answer might well depend on how well our friends were received on American TV. Despite the way they described themselves as post middle age and slightly dumpy, they had astonishing charisma. I believed they were going to be a major hit. After all, who would've predicted that *The UK Bakes!* would become a television sensation? Americans loved all things from the United Kingdom, but especially if they were Scottish.

My thoughts wandered back to their agent. Where was he staying now? Had the authorities allowed the bed-and-breakfast to open up to registered guests? This being the high, high season in Key West, the owners would stand to lose a lot of money if they were closed indefinitely. On the other hand, one of those owners was now dead. Perhaps Rayna didn't care about money right now. Maybe she wasn't the next in line to inherit anyway. Even married couples sometimes kept their assets separate.

I texted my friend Connie. *When you're talking to your cleaning employee, can you find out whether Rayna's bed-and-breakfast is open for business again? Also, has anyone seen the sisters' agent who is supposed to be staying there? Is there any word on the street about the murder?*

That was a lot of sensitive information to expect the cleaning crew to know. But Connie was both curious and resourceful. Her crew trusted her and would probably tell her tidbits that they'd hold back from the cops for their own reasons. Next, I texted Miss Gloria.

Don't forget to call your sons. I have a dinner date with Nathan tonight, at Little Pearl. Not his cup of tea at all but he promised weeks and weeks ago since he was working on Valentine's Day. Will you and the ladies be okay without us?

She texted right back. *No prob. Mrs. Dubisson has invited us to dinner at her place, so we'll be well fed and nearby.* She ended the message with hearts and a thumbs-up. I felt relieved about the ladies staying close to home and glad to have a night off from entertaining. Most of all, I was glad to have a night alone with my husband.

My Nathan was not a tasting-menu kind of guy. But he was a guy who wanted to keep his wife happy, so he'd agreed to a date night at Little Pearl this evening. The tiny restaurant, located in an unlikely Old Town neighborhood, had been the location of Seven Fish when I arrived on the island, consisting of a small white one-story stucco building with a five-seat bar and terrible acoustics. Even so, Seven Fish had turned out some delightful fish dishes, served one of my all-time favorite meat loaves, and cooked a banana walnut chicken to die for. That was the gist of my first-ever restaurant review, written when I was trying out for the food critic position at *Key Zest*. I could have recited my piece by memory.

Seven Fish's successor, Little Pearl, hadn't started out with a tasting menu, but the upheaval of the pandemic and its resulting staffing issues had pushed them in that direction. They produced fancy food at big prices, but even so, the restaurant was fully booked most nights for all three seatings. On that basis alone, it seemed to be a hit, and my boss Palamina had been lobbying for me to try it. Nathan knew all this, so he was putting a good face on our date. For my part, I would be sure to let him choose first. For one thing, I wanted him to eat what appealed to him. For another, I'd be happy to remain incognito—or as much so as possible in our small town.

Early on in my food-writing career, hardly anyone had sniffed around my reviews as though I were a dog in heat. Folks didn't know me, and my words carried no weight. That wasn't the case right now. *Key Zest* was becoming the best-read e-zine on the island, and my restaurant reviews were a big part of the equation. If intrepid food critic Hayley Snow didn't rave about a meal, or especially if she did, people paid attention.

That had become a bit of a problem. I couldn't fairly represent ordinary citizens spending their hard-earned money on a rare night out when the owner of the place was fluttering around the table plying me with a little extra taste of this or special that. No way a regular diner would get that much attention, including an exposition on the genesis of this dish or that. Besides, this was supposed to be a Valentine's Day special dinner with Nathan, even though we were a good month past Valentine's Day. To avoid as much fuss as possible, I'd made the reservation in the name of Bransford, bought a pair of clear tortoiseshell glasses, and dressed very casually, like a tourist might.

I waited outside the small restaurant, having agreed to meet Nathan here, since he was coming from the other side of town. Seeing his familiar shape striding from the direction of the cemetery, I felt both safe and shivery at the same time. We exchanged kisses and a big hug, and I followed him inside to our table. I ordered a glass of wine, he ordered a beer, and we studied the menu.

"Did you have a good day?" I asked him.

"It's all relative in this business, isn't it?" he said. But then he smiled. "We're close to putting a few bad guys away where they belong, so that's a plus. This morning I had coffee at Five Brothers with some interested local citizens."

Chief Brandenburg had had a brainstorm about trying to make his officers more accessible to the community, with the hope that the community would in turn come forward with tips and information when they needed it. Authentic Cuban coffee at an authentic Cuban takeout place frequented by locals would be the lubricant.

"After that, I gave a talk to sixth graders about becoming our community partners." He made a face. "My impression is that kids that age aren't interested much in partnering with anyone but each other."

"I remember those days," I said, grinning. "I thought my mother was a dork and my father a hopeless loser. Don't even get me started on the new stepmother. I certainly wouldn't have chatted with a cop." I laughed, thinking about how much my life had changed for the better. My mother was now a dear friend and trusted confidant, and I adored her husband, Sam. I knew that my father, despite his flaws, loved both me and his stepson. I could see now that my stepmother had only contributed positive things to the family equation. Most of all, I loved my police officer husband.

"How's it going with Miss Gloria and her entourage?" Nathan asked.

"Tough day," I said. I described the ladies' distress after they'd gotten word that it was Rayna's husband who'd died. "Of course, Martha and the people running the contest are distraught about the delay. It took her a lot of persuading to convince the producer that an event in Key West at her venue would be successful. At this point, it's a mess."

The waiter returned with our drinks and asked if we were ready to order. I motioned for my husband to give his choices first.

"Are you sure? I can be flexible and eat whatever you need me to eat."

That made me laugh. *Flexibility* and *food* and *Nathan* were not words that were often used in the same sentence. He chose the everything-bagel Tater Tots, chicken-fried Wagyu, and braised short ribs. I worked around him, filling in with lots of fish, a beet salad, and Asian-inspired vegetables.

While we waited for our first course, I told Nathan more about what was going on at Williams Hall, followed by a summary of my conversation with Paul Redford at the pastry shop. "I don't suppose you need us to try to track down this Mysterious Agent."

Nathan grinned. "It's a lovely offer, but I think we can handle it."

"I don't suppose there's anything you can tell me about suspects? Rayna, maybe? Or . . ."

Nathan narrowed his eyes a bit. "You know I'll tell you the minute I can."

We had eaten our way through the first three courses when a text came in on my phone. I couldn't help glancing at it. This was not only a Pavlovian response to a phone addiction; I was worried about my pal Miss Gloria and whether she and her Scottish friends would stay out of trouble without me to herd them. This time the worry was warranted.

Can you

The text was cut off, but then a call came in from Miss Gloria. I glanced at Nathan. "There's no reason she would be calling unless there's a problem."

"Take it," he said, his brow furrowing with concern.

"Can you and Nathan possibly come home? I'm so sorry to interrupt, but Violet and Bettina's agent is here on the boat."

Her voice sounded shaky.

"Are you in danger? Has he threatened you? Should we call 911?"

"No," she said, "I have a funny feeling about him, that's all. Just get here quick as you can."

Nathan was already motioning for the check. "We can't fit in dessert," he said to the waiter. "In fact, our babysitter called; there's a problem. Could we get the bill?"

"Oh goodness," said the waiter, "let me get that for you right away."

Chapter Twelve

So with Martha whacking away at the chopping block, anchor Jane Clayson laid out the worsening crisis and attempted to get the domestic diva to explain herself. "This will all be resolved in the very near future and I will be exonerated of any ridiculousness," Martha said, rolling her eyes and resuming her cabbage shredding. But Clayson, usually Martha's kitchen helper, continued to grill her. Exasperated, Martha huffed: "I want to focus on my salad."
—Keith Naughton, *Newsweek*, July 7, 2002

As I sped back to Houseboat Row, I expected the worst. I parked my scooter and trotted up the finger toward my friend's boat. Nathan was fast on my heels. The two Scottish ladies were splayed in lounge chairs on her deck, each with a cat draped over her stomach. Evinrude, my gray tiger, blinked and cocked one ear from his place on Violet's lap when he saw me. Bettina's cat accoutrement, T-Bone, didn't even look up. A youngish man with dark hair shorn fashionably short on the sides, whom I assumed to be the agent, was sitting in one of Miss Gloria's low beach chairs, sipping a mug of what I figured was tea. Although she had been known to serve after-dinner drinks in mugs. He did not look at all threatening. Miss Gloria emerged from her cabin with her own mug and gave a quick nod of thanks to the two of us. Then her eyes bulged a bit and she shook her head, as though we shouldn't ask what the heck was going on—confusing me, and I assumed Nathan as well.

"How was your dinner, ma dears?" Bettina asked. "We didn't expect you home so soon."

Which meant either she wasn't nervous like my friend or she didn't know Miss Gloria had phoned. Or she was an amazing actress.

Nathan came up behind me and took a step onto the deck. The boat rocked a bit with his weight. He stared directly at the man in the low chair, thinking, I was sure, about how worried Miss Gloria had sounded on the phone. And how that worry didn't seem to fit the scene.

"I'm Lieutenant Nathan Bransford, KWPD and next-door neighbor to this lovely lady. This is my wife, Hayley. You are?"

"Arvid Smith," he said, saluting Nathan and waving at me. "I am lucky enough to be representing these sisters as they travel the country. I'm in charge of letting the American people know about their talent and their beautiful bakeware." He flashed a big smile. "Unfortunately, as you know, some of these goods were damaged in the fire off of Greene Street."

"We don't know about damages, but I would like to," said Nathan sternly.

"What can you tell us about our knife?" Violet asked, her eyes flashing fiercely. "How did it possibly end up in that poor man's back?"

He grimaced. "Unfortunately, nothing. I know everyone has been wondering where I disappeared to, and that's what

I came to explain." Arvid's phone rang, and he glanced at the screen.

"So sorry," he said, scrambling out of the low chair. "I need to take this pronto. Speak to me," he said into the phone. He hopped off Miss Gloria's houseboat and headed toward the parking lot, listening.

"What is this about their knife?" Nathan asked in a low voice. I realized that I'd left out that very important bit of information when I'd told him about our day.

As Bettina explained that they suspected their knife had been used to murder Mr. Humboldt, I tried to puzzle out exactly what was going on here. The two Scottish women didn't seem worried or frightened, but I remembered that Miss Gloria's voice had been hushed when she called, as though she'd not wanted to be overheard. Something was not right with this picture.

Nathan asked, "Are you absolutely certain it was your knife in the man's back? I haven't seen a forensics report in the station yet."

"You described it perfectly, with the worn, curved blade, and those rivets." That was Violet, who'd sat up straight, looking solemn now, as if wanting to get everything right for Nathan. "It was hard to think it could be anything but our knife. That's where the knife was, right in the box that was supposed to be shipped to the bed-and-breakfast where we were supposed to be staying." She looked at her sister, bereft. "We should never have brought it with us. It makes me a wee bit sick to think of it gone forever."

"Had you experienced anything threatening in the weeks leading up to this trip? Unusual calls or warnings, fan mail that left you unsettled, anything like that?" Nathan asked.

"Oh no," said Violet. "We were so excited about coming, and we've gotten a lot of positive feedback from the States. We

even got email from people who had seen our show in the UK—
however they manage to view it across the pond. Our fans were
thrilled that we were bringing everything to America. Honestly,
we are thrilled as well."

"What about this Mr. Arvid Smith?" Nathan continued,
tilting his head in the direction that the man had disappeared.
"What do you know about his background? How did you get
lined up with him? Did you have other people who lobbied to
represent you? If so, why did you choose him?"

The sisters looked at each other, faces worried. "That is an
extremely good question," said Violet, nodding slowly. "Lots of
good questions."

"Astute," added Bettina. "We should have thought to ask
these questions ourselves, but we liked him so much, and he was
very persistent."

"Very," added Violet, pressing her lips together. "Perhaps
that should have been a warning signal?"

"Let's go back to the beginning," Nathan said, leaning
against Miss Gloria's deck railing. He was probably trying not
to frighten them, but he was tall and fierce and very serious. I
perched on the end of Miss Gloria's lounge chair, ready to inter-
vene with reassurance if needed. "How did the U.S. tour come
about?"

"You know we launched a new show and it began to do well
shortly after you visited Scotland? We'd won the scone edition
of that other baking contest with our cinnamon scone recipe,
remember?" She looked at Nathan until he nodded. Whether he
remembered this or not, he would want her to continue.

"After you left, our popularity continued to blow up, with
our viewing numbers off the chart. We had no idea why, but we

were determined to enjoy every moment and not let this little gleam of fame go to our heads. Then our producers started talking about a spin-off show in the U.S., and how we would travel about your country, headlining contests to find the very best American bakers," Bettina said, then paused, a small frown on her face. "Honestly, we thought it was ridiculous."

"But one day we were talking with Miss Gloria and telling her about all the silliness, and she begged us to come here for a visit. Next thing you know, we were getting all excited about seeing your island. Not that it took much begging," added Violet. "We simply couldn't wait to see you all again."

"We happened to mention to our UK producer that we were planning to visit friends in Florida. Then he got excited about how we could launch the tour from Miami. With a bit of sly maneuvering," said Bettina, with a wink, "we were able to suggest starting the baking-star search in Key West. The rest is history."

As I listened, I wondered whether one of the sisters was slyer than the other, or whether they always worked as a team. My money was on Bettina.

"Somewhere during that time, the notion of designing Scone Sisters bakeware came up. We thought that was even more ridiculous, of course," said Bettina. "We ignored it at first. It was enough that the producer of the show agreed to finance the Key West stop, as suggested by Gloria. We were happy with that; we didn't want more. But all these people started to lobby us about representing our interests in our line of so-called products. We didn't have any such items."

Violet frowned. "We never would have conceived of designing products named after us. We couldn't have imagined such a thing ourselves. I can't keep straight who started it; do you remember, Bettina?"

Bettina shook her head, and Violet continued to talk. "At first it seemed a wee bit greedy. Or maybe more than a wee bit."

"We were doing the baking show because it brought us such joy," Bettina said. "We needed joy in our lives. With the bakeware idea, we worried that we'd get so focused on the money that we'd do something ridiculous and end up in jail. People allow that to happen when a lot of money is at stake. Even Martha Stewart, who's food royalty in your country, got carried away with dollars and ended up serving prison time."

Miss Gloria looked huffy, her eyes bulging a bit like a disgruntled iguana. "There is no way you two would do anything illegal. You have the highest standards about everything." She scooped up her black cat, Sparky, and he meowed in agreement—or protest—then squirmed until she put him back down.

"Thank you for your confidence, dear," said Bettina. She turned to her sister. "But we still worried. Remember that nice girl Alison Roman who wrote wonderful cookbooks and made it sound as though entertaining a crowd was a dream come true? But she wasn't a fan of people turning themselves into a brand to sell merchandise."

"She got into a heap of trouble for calling out women who she thought leveraged their popularity to make money on commercial products. Branding themselves. Exactly like cookware with our name on it," said Violet. She looked like she was going to dissolve into tears.

"Who specifically talked you into the idea of the Scone Sisters baking equipment?" I asked. "Can you remember?"

"As we mentioned, agents came out of the woodwork after our show ratings climbed," Bettina explained. "We couldn't see why we would need an agent, and so we repelled their advances. We were very reluctant to get mixed up with something like this. If the bakeware was cheap enough that ordinary people without a lot of extra wealth could buy it, were we not taking their much-needed money better spent on their kids or their table? Wouldn't ordinary pans without our logo cost less and do them just as well? If the bakeware was too expensive, such that ordinary people couldn't afford it, that didn't seem right either. We really didn't want to get involved."

"Next thing you know, the producer talked us into taking meetings with people who wanted to represent us and find just the right designers." Violet rubbed the cat on her lap, and I really thought she would cry. "One of them suggested that a line of Scone Sisters baked goods would be more in line with our brand. We could just imagine a collection of dry pound cakes with our names on the plastic wrapping. How totally embarrassing."

"It made us shudder, all this talk about being true to our brand. We didn't have a brand. We were a couple of small-town Scottish sisters who knew how to whip up a cake or a dozen scones or what have you," said Bettina.

Violet picked up the thread again. "But then Arvid came along—he actually flew to Scotland and then hired a car to drive to Peebles to meet with us. He sat at our kitchen table overlooking the backyard. Remember that table, Hayley?"

I did remember. It was etched into my brain as one of the sadder days of my life. I'd sat at their table, which was covered by baked goods from distressed neighbors and friends, sipping tea with the sisters and listening to Violet grieve the fresh loss of her son.

"Arvid explained that it wasn't the cakes or the pans or even the fancy flours and special European butter that people loved, it was that we represented family. He said that our love for each other came through so clearly as we baked. That's what people adored about us and what they yearned for in their own lives." Violet really did have tears shining in her eyes now, and a hand pressed over her heart. She took a shuddering breath. "Our connection is similar to what you and Gloria have."

I reached behind me to take Miss Gloria's hand and give it a squeeze.

"Arvid told us that his mother had just lost her sister, her very best friend in her whole world, a friend she'd had her entire long life. He said she was distraught but that watching us work together on our show helped her remember the sweetness and not just the sad."

"You could imagine," said Bettina, glancing at her sister, "that we were all a puddle of tears by that point. After we'd mopped each other up, he said that he'd taken the liberty of having an artist that he adored draw up a logo. By then we'd been shown hundreds of designs that felt wrong. He'd had a small Highland company make up a few sample pans."

Bettina got up and went into Miss Gloria's cabin and came back with the baking pan I'd seen when they unpacked their suitcases. She showed it to Nathan, who spent several minutes studying the steaming pie.

"Isn't it the most darling thing you've ever seen? This is what sealed the deal."

Nathan gave a shrug and smiled. "I'm not the best judge of baking pans, but it's attractive."

I was of two minds about their agent as I listened to them talk. On the one hand, he might really be a warm, sweet man who'd seen something special in the sisters and wanted to show that goodness to the world. On the other hand, he might have focused on their soft, sad underbelly because they could be exploited so easily. Did his mother really have a sister who had just died?

Nathan said, "So he showed you the attractive design, and then what?"

"We still had some concerns, but the design was simply adorable. We felt like it captured our essence, if any logo could. Arvid convinced us to try the pans and see what we thought. We baked some of our recipes using his equipment and had to agree that the materials transmitted the heat perfectly," Bettina said. "We ourselves would have bought a whole set of those baking dishes if we hadn't already been given them gratis." She sighed. "So we said yes. Now look at the mess we're in. A man murdered with our family heirloom knife. The TV show in ruins. Serious stress on our dear hostess."

The sisters reached for Miss Gloria's hands. My friend flashed a determined smile and stood up.

"Don't be ridiculous. There is not a soul in the police department or anywhere in Key West who thinks you have anything to do with any of these situations. Let's just tell Lieutenant Bransford everything we know and let him sort out the details."

"Your friend Gloria is very wise," said Nathan with a small smile in return. "At least this time."

Miss Gloria batted at his arm.

We talked a while longer but seemed to get nowhere, and the ladies were drooping.

"Where did that young man get to, anyway?" asked Violet, with a puzzled look on her face. "What was he rushing off to and why hasn't he come back?"

A Clue in the Crumbs

"I'll run up to the parking lot," Nathan said. He came back several minutes later. "No sign of him. You haven't gotten a phone call or text explaining where he went?"

The sisters checked their phones. "Nothing," said Violet.

Now I was getting worried. Obviously, something strange enough had happened with Arvid that Miss Gloria had interrupted the first private dinner Nathan and I had had in weeks.

"Do you mind saying why you decided to call me at the restaurant?" I asked.

Miss Gloria waved me off. "Pfft, I can't really remember, but obviously, I overreacted. Though we're glad you're home just the same."

I glanced at Nathan, wondering if he too was beginning to worry about her mental acuity.

"You think of anything else or hear from Arvid, you know I'm right next door," said Nathan as we headed off to our house, Evinrude and Ziggy trotting behind us.

Nathan took the dog for a quick walk as I got ready for bed. So many questions had been raised but not answered. What did we really know about this agent? Why were the sisters so important to him? What would he get out of it? Was it worth murdering someone over? Or did he have enemies determined to ruin him and the sisters all at once? Did he live in Key West? Why had the sisters agreed to stay in that particular bed-and-breakfast? Was he involved in that? Why had Miss Gloria called us home abruptly? Why didn't she want to talk about it? There were so many places to start, so many dangling ends.

Right before getting into bed, Nathan shared another text with more details from the crime scene, including several that chilled me. The crime scene technicians had found shards of a white ceramic baking pan under the porch near the dead man. Possibly he'd been both hit on the head and stabbed in the back. Possibly both pieces of equipment used in the murder belonged to the Scone Sisters.

"That's why I was so interested in their logo," he said. "One of the broken pieces looked exactly the same as what you described the other night."

"Was their stuff used to implicate them?" I asked. "I absolutely cannot believe they were involved in this murder themselves. Not possible. That aside, as far as they know, their boxes were never delivered."

"We'll figure it out," he said, leaning in for a good-night kiss.

He drifted off right away—a gift. My mind was spinning with the loose threads of the murder case, mostly circling the question of how the Scone Sisters had gotten mixed up with it. What phone call had their agent received that caused him to leave Houseboat Row and not return? Or was it the presence of Nathan that scared him off? This wasn't out of the question, as those with a guilty conscience found Nathan particularly intimidating.

I pushed myself to think more broadly about unanswered questions. Had none of the neighbors seen or heard anything the night the man was murdered? What did we really know about the relationship between Rayna and her husband? Had one or both grown up in Key West? Had there been something going on with Rayna and Harry, or did he simply step up to do the right thing when he thought Vincent was threatening Rayna?

As Nathan slept and I did not, I decided to get up and do something useful. Evinrude hopped off the bed and followed me out to the kitchen. I gave him a few treats and made myself a cup of herbal tea, then went out onto the deck with my laptop. A blanket of darkness had settled in around us, broken up by the streetlights on Palm Avenue and the spotlight attached to our laundry building in the parking lot. There was a hum of cars from North Roosevelt and a low-pitched clatter and wheeze from the Renharts' air conditioner the next boat over.

I remembered when I first arrived in Key West that I'd insisted to Connie that I was never again going to join Face-book. It felt childish and passé, filled with people I hardly knew bragging about the contents of their trumped-up best lives. She had laughed, saying, "You'll have no idea what's happening in this town unless you're on Facebook. There are at least a dozen local pages, and they'll help you if there's a power outage, or a hurricane, or any other more serious issues. Or if you just want to complain about something in Key West, you'll find plenty of people to join you."

Remembering this, I woke up my computer and navigated to the Key West locals' page.

There were the usual snarky comments about tourists and the price of housing and food, for which I couldn't blame the complainers. As I scrolled farther down to see older posts, I came across a conversation about the murder.

A friend of a friend who lives in that neighborhood said that man got exactly what he deserved.

What did that mean? What had he done? Did anyone deserve to be murdered?

Chapter Thirteen

The smell of that buttered toast simply talked to Toad, and with no uncertain voice; talked of warm kitchens, of breakfasts on bright frosty mornings, of cosy parlour firesides on winter evenings, when one's ramble was over and slippered feet were propped on the fender, of the purring of contented cats, and the twitter of sleepy canaries.

—Kenneth Grahame, *The Wind in the Willows*

The next morning, Nathan left for work early. Having slept poorly, I dozed for a luxurious extra half hour. I woke for good when Connie texted.

My coworker who cleans for the bed-and-breakfast has agreed to talk with us. Pretty sure she knows more than what she's told me so far. Can you meet us at Harpoon Harry's at 9 o'clock? She needs to leave for work at 9:30. As do I! She finished her message with a quartet of emojis, a bagel, a fried egg, a broom, and a sweating face.

I came out of our cabin, blinking in the bright light of a sunny day, and went over to knock on Miss Gloria's door. The ladies were having coffee at the kitchen table. Their hands were folded around their mugs. A plate of buttered toast, another of mango and pineapple slices, and two jars of homemade jam rested on the table.

"Good morning, Hayley," said Violet. "Look, Gloria cooked for us this morning. Won't you come and join us?" She patted the bench beside her.

My friend was absolutely beaming at the idea that she'd cooked for her guests. Toast, coffee, and sliced fruit was the perfect menu for her kitchen skills. Seeing the three of them clustered around that familiar banquette brought on a wave of nostalgia for the many mornings I'd spent there with Miss Gloria. Just because a new turn of life was a good one didn't mean you wouldn't miss something treasured from the past.

"Good morning! I can't stay; I'm running out to meet Connie for breakfast. What time does Martha want you at Williams Hall? Assuming the show must go on?"

Miss Gloria nodded and patted a smear of raspberry jam off her lips. "She's hopeful but not necessarily optimistic, if that makes sense. In fact, she's worried sick that the competition might be canceled. Anyhoo, we're supposed to be there at eleven. I don't know if she actually has someone to replace Rayna or if she's hoping she'll show up or what. But we can take an Uber if that time's inconvenient."

"Not at all," I said. I didn't want to miss the chance to hear what Martha might have learned about the murder. Not to mention see who might show up and who wouldn't. Plus keep tabs on the ladies, especially considering how nervous Miss Gloria had been last night. "I'm going to run out for a bit, but I'll be back by ten-thirty-ish to pick you up. Have you heard from your agent?" I asked the two sisters.

"Crickets," said Violet. "And you can trust us that we've texted him about a hundred times."

"That's so weird. Could I speak to you privately for a minute?" I asked Miss Gloria. I couldn't think of a more subtle way to ask why she'd called us home from dinner so abruptly.

She popped up from her seat and followed me out to the deck. "Is something wrong?" she asked.

"I've been worrying about last night," I said. "I couldn't figure out why you needed us home, and yet you didn't seem to want to talk about it. Violet and Bettina didn't seem concerned, but I'm thinking something about their agent must really have spooked you."

She nodded slowly. "Exactly. Two things. He told us that he's visited Key West several times, after coming with his fraternity brothers for spring break. So it's possible he knows people in our town, including the man who was murdered."

"Okay," I said. "Good observation." But certainly not a reason to panic.

"Second," she said, "he asked the sisters a lot of questions about their father, the fireman, and what they noticed about the fire at the B and B the other night. He's fascinated by fire. I could see that in his face."

"You think he's a firebug?" This possibility made me feel queasy, as he seemed quite involved with the two women and I hated thinking about them getting hurt in any way.

"Not necessarily," she said. "I got worried, that's all. It was just a crazy feeling, and I called." She looked a little sick now, as if she'd done something wrong, ruined the night for Nathan and me.

"I'm glad you did, and so is Nathan. Your safety is way more important than one restaurant meal. Let me know the minute you hear from him, okay? I'll be back in about an hour to scoop you up."

I hugged her quickly and trotted up the finger to the parking lot to grab my scooter and buzz across the island to the harbor. As I drove, I mulled over Miss Gloria's information. At least I had a little bit more of a sense of why she'd called us home. Had Arvid Smith set that fire? He'd certainly had access, plus access to the Scone Sisters. Why in the world would he want to implicate them in a gruesome murder by using a weapon that belonged to them? I forced myself to set this aside for the moment and concentrate on where I was going and what I was doing.

At the busy corner of Caroline and Margaret Streets, Harpoon Harry's was easily recognizable because of the orangy-pink stucco walls and cerulean-blue doors, usually thrown wide open to encourage visitors. The walls inside were chockablock with bright paintings, old-fashioned signs, and a collection of license plates. At the register, shelves bore an enticing choice of layer cakes, and beyond that was a gorgeous collection of alcohol bottles. The decor suggested that visitors would find fun but nothing fancy, just good food and fine drinks at a reasonable price. A guest would never have to negotiate such foodie trills as truffle oil or fennel pollen or beef marrow while dining here.

I found Connie and her coworker at a table for four at the window. Usually, the staff refused to seat a party until everyone was present, but Connie was a longtime local and probably knew the hostess. I took a seat, and Connie introduced me to Ines. She was small but sturdy looking with a long dark braid down her back. Connie had told me she'd be unlikely to say much to the police, as several members of her family had immigration statuses that might be judged a bit murky.

Connie rested a hand on her back. "Ines is one of my best workers. She must have joined me right after you left."

"That's been a while," I said.

Connie grinned. "Yes, and I wouldn't have said that you were one of my best workers. You were too busy solving mysteries."

I laughed. "Including the mysteries of my poor judgment in getting involved with bad boyfriends."

The waitress came to take our orders. I took a quick glance at the menu, tempted by the marble Jack patty melt, the hot pastrami on rye with potato salad, and the three-egg omelet with bacon and cheese. Instead I went for one egg over easy and a toasted poppy-seed bagel, hold the butter and cream cheese. I'd been eating out frequently over the past two weeks, with more restaurant food to come—in fact, I was due at Goldman's Deli for a one o'clock lunch. The only way to keep my fighting weight was to eat reasonably most of the time and drag myself to the dreaded appointments at the gym.

I handed the menu back and turned to Ines. "I really appreciate your willingness to talk to me."

She glanced at Connie's face and then back over to mine. "I don't know that I know anything, if you know what I mean. I certainly don't know who killed that man. Or why."

I was a little surprised that she didn't have an accent, considering Connie's comment about her undocumented relatives. "But you know the people who own the place and what they're like, and maybe what their relationship was like? Maybe who's been on the outs lately with Mr. Humboldt? Did he have any beefs with either customers or vendors?"

I remembered from my short stint in the cleaning business how much a worker might overhear if she blended quietly into the background. Still, I worried that I'd dumped too many questions on Ines all at once. I switched tactics.

"Maybe we could just start with what it was like working for them. Did it seem like this was his business or both of theirs?" That was a softball question to get her thinking, as I guessed a husband and wife would own the business together. "Who did the training, things like that."

The waitress came to deliver our food and fill our coffee cups. I watched Ines stir sugar and creamer into her mug, then carve off a small bite of toast.

"He was definitely in the driver's seat," she said, placing her knife and fork back down. "He was fussy in every way, and he knew that the competition in this town was tough. He wanted to get five-star reviews in spite of his outrageous room prices. Or maybe to justify them. A month or so ago, a guest posted on one of the travel review sites that their room smelled a bit musty. He was so angry! He had us clean every inch of that place practically down to the studs. Even Rayna—Mrs. Humboldt, that is—was put to work that day."

"I was there too," said Connie, pausing midbite over her cheese omelet. "He did not want to hear anything about how we live in the tropics and the place was old and it couldn't possibly smell like it was new construction no matter how hard we cleaned. I thought he might fire my company." She grinned. "In his heart of hearts, he knows we are the best on the island."

"I wonder if either of you met another guest who was supposed to be staying at the inn. His name is Arvid Smith, and he's the agent representing the Scone Sisters. I'm almost certain he would have arrived before the fire. But now he seems to have evaporated."

"Yes," said Ines. "I believe he checked in the afternoon before the fire. But I don't know anything more. We were asked to deliver any packages to the hall outside his room, but nothing arrived while we were there."

"Mrs. Humboldt was very excited to have the Scottish ladies staying there," Connie said. "She said her husband was happy about it too. I don't know if he expected them to mention his bed-and-breakfast on TV or what."

"But yet he didn't want his wife to compete?" I asked, glancing at Ines.

"He knew she was an amazing baker," said Ines. "Because all the guests raved about her pastries." She blushed and glanced down at her plate. "She even gave us the leftovers to take home. They were honestly the best croissants and muffins on the island. I don't think he wanted to lose that. I don't think he wanted to lose *her*. Had she won, she would have been traveling, right?"

"Right," I said. "Did they ever fight about that? Did you ever see him push her or hit her?" I was thinking of the bruising that Bettina noticed during the first day of taping. But Ines pressed her lips together, making it obvious she didn't want to respond. Did that mean she knew something but couldn't say, or did it mean she objected to the question?

"So sorry to cut this short, but I need to get to work," Ines said, adding a wink as an afterthought. "My boss is very strict."

"Mine too," said Connie. She followed Ines to the door, turning to shrug at me as if she didn't know exactly what Ines had reacted to. "I'll call you later, okay?"

Chapter Fourteen

How can a country be called great if its bread tastes like Kleenex?

—Julia Child

We arrived at Williams Hall before eleven, and Martha motioned urgently for me to come over. She looked as though she hadn't slept for even a minute.

"I've tried everyone I can think of to find another contestant—calling, texting, emailing all across town. The real chefs have jobs and can't take time off. Nobody is available, not anyone we'd want. If our lineup is dull, the producer will kill the entire Key West stop. I've promised my bosses here that this sideshow would put Williams Hall on the map."

I took a big breath, hoping she'd breathe along with me. "Have you heard anything from Rayna? Maybe she needed a few days off to deal with the shock of her husband's murder. I could totally understand that."

"Not a peep," said Martha. "I ran by the B and B this morning, but it appears to be closed, and the neighbor I talked with hasn't seen her. Worst of all, the showrunner posted some clips from yesterday's taping on the show's website and Facebook page. I've been checking the comments left by viewers. They are brutal," she finished glumly.

"Are the comments signed or anonymous?" I asked. "Could they have been made by the other chefs competing here? Martina or Harry?"

"What difference would it make?" she asked. "If people read those reviews, not a soul would watch the show."

Across the room, Martha noticed the producer waving in our direction.

"Chin up," I said, because I couldn't think of a darn thing that would be useful. *Buck up? Everything will turn out for the best? If it's meant to be, it will happen?* All nonsense, and she'd know it instantly.

A few minutes later, Martha called for attention from the folks milling around the big kitchen. "We've decided to go ahead with the day's taping even without Rayna. We can edit her segment in when she shows up, and fingers crossed, she will. She's suffered a terrible loss, and she probably needs some time to absorb it."

Violet looked disappointed, if not surprised. "The showrunner posted video from yesterday on their Facebook page, looking for feedback," she told me in a low voice. I shouldn't have been startled that she was savvy about these things. "Rayna got the only raves. She was clearly going to be our star. Unfortunately, the other two candidates have yet to display any special magic."

Based on what I'd heard from Martha, that was a kind way of putting it. Looking at the faces around me, I suspected that everyone had the same sinking feeling. Martina was adorable and chatty with the workers, and while on camera—all good. I knew she was a talented musician, but from what I'd seen yesterday, she couldn't bake her way out of a paper bag. Harry, on the other hand, had neither asset. No charm, no skills. Why in the world had he been chosen for the competition? Why had he even applied?

"So true," said Miss Gloria. "Plus Harry's scones resembled dog turds. Hate to say it," she added, "but sometimes you just gotta speak the truth to power."

That didn't exactly fit the situation here, and she'd said it a little louder than possibly she'd intended, but she got pretty much the whole kitchen laughing. Harry, who'd been standing at the far end of the long counter, heard it too. His face reddened with embarrassment and anger. I had a sudden shiver of understanding that he might be the kind of guy who would stab someone in the back if he was angry enough. Though I hadn't gotten any sense of a motive, no obvious reason why he'd kill Rayna's husband. Maybe protecting a friend or lover? I should try to have a chat with him during a down moment.

Martha looked around the big space, probably desperately hoping that Rayna would make a last-minute appearance, and barring that, that some other baker would rise to the occasion. She put both hands on the counter, leaned forward, and spoke to the crowd.

"Today is quick-bread day. We are certainly looking forward to the creations of Martina and Harry. But is there anyone else who might pitch in to fill up this space for us? Just for today. You wouldn't have to be an expert baker by any means. As I mentioned, we can splice Rayna in when she's recovered a bit from the shock of recent terrible events."

From what I'd seen in the past couple of years, Martha was a very calm person, with a lot of experience running stressful events. She catered fancy parties involving more than sixty people passing hors d'oeuvres that she'd cooked right in front of the crowd, and I'd never seen her break a sweat. But this felt different; she was deeply invested in having the week's events go well. She wanted to show off Williams Hall as well as her own cooking skills and, more generally, the foodie scene in Key West. Those goals meant the world to her. At this moment, we could see them glugging down the drain.

"Hayley," she called. "Can you think of anyone who would be a reasonable stand-in?"

"Not me," I said, taking a step back. "I have so many conflicts of interest it's beginning to look like a spider's web."

We could all see that Martha was growing distraught as the minutes ticked by. The contest was in trouble. Bettina's gaze roved over the audience and lighted on my mother and Sam.

"We haven't talked about a baking duo," she said to Violet and Martha, "but why not? My sister and I do it all the time in the UK, and our people love it." She pointed at my mother and Sam. "We know they can cook, and they're sweet as treacle."

Coming from behind me, I recognized Sam's voice whispering to my mother.

"You know that Irish soda bread we're baking to take to Hayley's house in a few days for her Saint Paddy's Day dinner? We could try that out here. This kitchen is heaven."

I turned around to watch this conversation unfold.

"We are not television material," my mother hissed back to him.

"We would be place fillers," he said, adding a chuckle. "The last time you made that bread, it was out of this world. Remember you said you were planning to add caraway seeds and serve it to a crowd because it was delicious? Here's your chance. This is definitely a crowd." Grinning widely, he gestured to the camera people, producer, Martha, the Scottish ladies, the audience.

I clapped my hands together and then squeezed her wrist. "Mom, I think it's a great solution. You help Martha out plus get the bread recipe nailed. You could even use your appearance in this contest when you advertise the catering business. Win-win-win!"

My mother bit her lip, looking unconvinced. "Okay, let's try it," she said to Martha, who raised her arms as if her team had scored a big goal. She whisked my mother off to the makeup station.

I glanced at my cell phone. It was almost one and I absolutely couldn't bail on this lunch. I didn't want to bail anyway— I hadn't seen Lorenzo in forever. He was my tarot card–reading friend and one of the wisest people I knew. I could describe the events of the week, and he'd be able to zero in on puzzle pieces I was missing. He could also tell me straight out if he was sensing danger in our vicinity. Aside from Rayna's poor husband, of course, who'd already encountered danger.

I trotted over to the table where my mother was getting buffed up. She had a mixture of delight and terror on her carefully drawn face.

"I'm heading to Goldman's Bagels to meet Lorenzo for a quick lunch. Can I pick up something for you?"

The makeup artist took a step back to let her talk. My mother put a hand on her stomach. "I'm way too nervous to eat," she said. "I hope this doesn't become a disaster. How can it not be?"

"You'll be brilliant," I said. "Even if you're not, you'll try to enjoy the experience, right? And when you finish, you'll have a great story to tell. Isn't that what you always told me growing up?"

She groaned. "What goes around comes around." Then she grabbed my hand. "Hurry back. I'll feel better if I can see your face in the crowd."

"No boozing it up on lunch break," said Sam from his perch at the bar.

Chapter Fifteen

Do you know what would happen to us if anyone knew
we had a rat in our kitchen? They'd close us down.
                    —Skinner, in Jan Pinkava's *Ratatouille*

Goldman's Deli was another old-fashioned restaurant in Key
West, with a vibe similar to Harpoon Harry's. Because of
the expected high-season traffic on North Roosevelt, I decided
to take my scooter rather than Miss Gloria's big car. It was
definitely easier to maneuver than the Buick, and even easier
to park. Almost all the big grocery chains were located out on
this northern border of the island, along with shops like Home
Depot and T.J.Maxx and Gordon's Food Service, so the traffic
was no surprise. The deli was tucked into a large shopping center
anchored by Winn-Dixie. It was an unassuming storefront, but
as it served good diner-style food at reasonable prices and had
the best bagels on the island, it was often crowded.

Lorenzo was already seated at a table inside, with a parking
lot view. I'd met him almost as soon as I moved to Key West,
and he'd been a trusted confidant and friend ever since. He
spent almost every evening at a table set up on Mallory Square,

reading tarot cards for worried tourists. Over this period of time, his dark curls had become tinged with gray, and to me he seemed to grow ever wiser, if a little sadder about the state of the world. He stood up to kiss my cheek and gestured at the table.

"Is this okay? Too loud? Too warm?"

I laughed. "It's perfect."

The waitress bustled by with menus and plastic glasses of ice water. "Do you need a few minutes?"

"I know what I want, if you do?" I looked at Lorenzo, and he nodded. "Tuna melt with potato chips," I said, handing the menu back to the waitress. I rarely ordered potato chips, but they were the perfect side for a buttery, cheesy tuna melt—pure comfort food in a tough time. "Plus a cup of coffee with milk." I wasn't drooping yet, but I could imagine I would be after the influx of carbs and fat, and I had a long afternoon ahead at Williams Hall.

"And for me, raisin bagel, double toasted, with chicken salad, lettuce, tomato, onion." Lorenzo smiled up at the waitress and then back at me. "I always order the same thing. I know what I like and I know I can digest it." As the waitress bustled off, he asked, "Lots going on in your life?"

"Always. Especially now. But how could you tell?"

He laughed. "It's not always in the cards. This time you were a little late and seem harried and"—he winked—"you only have one earring on."

I pressed a hand to my naked earlobe. "Busted."

While we waited for our lunches to be delivered, I filled Lorenzo in on the events of the week. "Honestly, I was expecting a quiet week and tons of fun watching the Scone Sisters do their thing. Instead, we're investigating a murder case and arson."

Lorenzo choked on a sip of water, then a big grin spread over his face. "Does Nathan know he has assistance on this case?"

I grimaced in return at his teasing. "I'm using the word *we* very loosely. But think about this: Violet and Bettina's heirloom knife was used to murder the man. And possibly one of their specially marked baking pans was used to knock him out. Pure coincidence? I think not. But it couldn't have been one of them, because we were at dinner together at my mother's place when the man was killed. Before we went to dinner, they were on Houseboat Row—they weren't ever out of my sight. I can't imagine one of them did it anyway, because they're not young women, they're super sweet, and they're more prone to noshing on baked goods then executing a murder. Wouldn't stabbing a large man in the back take someone tall and strong? Finally, what would be the point of killing this guy? They didn't know him. They'd barely laid eyes on him."

Lorenzo leaned forward and pressed his palm to the back of my hand. I only now noticed I was clutching the side of the table. The warmth of his hand felt reassuring in a way I hadn't consciously realized I craved. "As far as you know, they don't know him. But okay, you've convinced me that in spite of the knife, the ladies weren't the perpetrators. What else are you thinking?"

I took in a deep breath, pushing the air all the way down to my belly and then letting it out slowly. "I'm worried about what in the world is going on with their agent. He's the one who talked them into using their logo on these special pans once it became known that they were coming to the U.S. Last night he visited Miss Gloria's boat. She called us home early, sounding panicked. Once we showed up, he looked nervous. He said hello, then took a phone call and disappeared. Poof, gone. Is that because he's the murderer? Or was it because the sight of Nathan frightened him to death?"

"Possible," said Lorenzo, keeping a straight face. "We're all a bit scared of your husband."

I grimaced. This was more true than Nathan would want to admit. He was working hard on appearing approachable to the public, but his natural tendency was to look fierce. "If he was the killer, maybe as soon as he saw Nathan, he realized the police would be hot on his trail. Or was he for some perverse reason trying to implicate the sisters? Why would he talk them into using this equipment and then employ it to murder someone? It doesn't make sense. But I'm worried. I'm worried about their safety and their reputation and all of it."

Lorenzo had picked up the deck of cards lying on the table, well used and well loved, as I knew from other readings. I could imagine all the people who had looked to him for direction in their lives. Thousands of them, confused, in pain, sad, hopeful, scared. I'd come to him with each of those feelings at various times. He always provided wisdom appropriate to the problem. Sometimes what people heard didn't match exactly what he'd said, but he was confident they would absorb what they needed. So even if his words weren't what I thought I wanted them to be, they would prove to be exactly right in the end.

"Three cards okay?"

I nodded.

Lorenzo paused with his eyes closed for a brief meditation, then dealt out the Page of Wands, the King of Swords, and the Tower. He put his finger on the Page of Wands card, featuring a young man dressed in red, carrying a staff. "This card can mean there is a lot of excitement and many possibilities ahead, but maybe there is a sense of discouragement. This card can be a trigger of courage—you should act on this opportunity."

He glanced up to see if I understood. I nodded, though honestly I never felt at the time of a reading that I understood everything he and the cards were telling me. Did this have to do with my new responsibilities at *Key Zest*, which weren't going that well? (Maybe that was because my focus was elsewhere?) Or with my role in solving the murder case? Or was there a message for me in this card about the Scone Sisters' agent? In time, that understanding would come. I hoped.

Lorenzo touched the second card. "You will remember that Queens rule with the heart, and Kings rule with the mind. The King of Swords represents a mature man who, while very supportive, does not like to show his emotions—he can be clinical and stern. But he will help."

That would have to be Nathan. Lorenzo grinned, and I thought he was picturing Nathan too.

"Finally, the Tower. This card signals upheavals and destruction."

I hated pulling this card because it scared me—a tall building with flames licking out of the top, a bolt of lightning, bodies falling.

Lorenzo smiled gently. "Always remember that the destruction is often of something that no longer serves you. What feels frightening will probably be freeing. Questions?" he asked, after he'd finished.

It always took time before I could absorb and understand his message. I shook my head.

"I know you must be worried about the murder case and the effect it might have on your Scottish guests. I imagine there are suspects other than their agent?"

I nodded. "Actually, now that you think of it, I've been imagining that everyone connected with the contest could have killed the man."

"Why is that?"

"For one, he didn't want his wife to enter the competition. At that point, she withdrew. A few days later she changed her mind and showed up in the kitchen with what Bettina thought might be the remnants of a black eye. She was the clear front runner in this contest. But then Mr. Humboldt appeared and tried to drag her out of the kitchen. Abused wives sometimes snap, right? Although that seems overly obvious."

"Anyone else?" my friend asked.

"Martina and Harry really didn't stand a chance of winning with Rayna in the running. But now she's mourning or grieving, or even possibly guilty of murder, or maybe she knows who the murderer is and she's afraid. Anyway, she's missing in action. I suppose the other two are hoping for a breakout now that she's disappeared."

"Do you think Harry or Martina might have killed Rayna's husband to get her out of the way?"

"It's possible. The winner of this contest goes on to perform nationally." I paused to let my mouth catch up with my mind. "It hadn't occurred to me to wonder what the prizes are. Probably a big cash purse. But it could be something even more important, like the chance to open their own restaurant or work with a renowned pastry chef." I was thinking aloud now, puzzling out important questions that hadn't materialized until Lorenzo mentioned them. "On the other hand, maybe the most logical solution is that the Scone Sisters' agent killed Humboldt because of some previous connection we know nothing about. The agent may have argued against Violet and Bettina staying at the dead man's bed-and-breakfast but ended up booking there too. All three of them were driven out by a fire on their first night in town. Could all of this be coincidence?"

His eyes got even wider.

"There's more," I said, leaning forward to whisper. "Miss Gloria called us home from date night last night because she was worried this agent—his name is Arvid, by the way—has a history of being a firebug. Or at least a deep interest in fire. Coincidentally or not, Violet and Bettina's father was a fireman." I stopped speaking and slumped into my chair. "Are you receiving any messages from the universe about this mess?"

I didn't really expect him to be able to deliver anything like that; that's not how his gift worked. But he sometimes had sparks, bits of light that illuminated the path later on. I leaned forward to absorb whatever he said.

My friend cocked his head like a curious bird. "From what you've told me, I would want to know who had access to their knife. Who had a previous relationship with the man who died? Who stood to gain the most from his death? Or who became enraged by something he did when he was alive? One truth I've come to know is that batterers in a relationship usually lash out more than once."

I sat back in my chair again and crumpled my napkin. The waitress delivered our meals, and we began to eat. "Those are excellent thoughts and questions."

Lorenzo smiled. "Did you ever watch that cooking show called *Rat in the Kitchen*? One of the performing chefs is a saboteur, but nobody knows who it is. The person does things like overseasoning a competitor's sauce or exchanging rotten ingredients for fresh, or even replacing sugar with salt in baked goods. This reminds me of that. Although no one gets murdered on the show." Now he looked a little sad. "It's not only in Key West where money drives the world."

"You always come through." Belatedly, I noticed the dark circles under his blue eyes. "How are you doing, by the way? I didn't ask you anything about your life." I'd been too busy recounting my own problems and gobbling my sandwich.

His eyes blinked closed and then back open. "You know that Uranus is in my house, and that means a rocky stretch, a lot of disruption. But I'm coming out of it. I am fine." He paused. "I will be fine."

Lorenzo believed deeply in the meanings forecasted by astrological charts, and what he saw there reflected his truth. It was often spot-on. This reminded me of what my friend Eric the psychologist always told me: the caretakers in this world could appear to be all together emotionally, but the weight of carrying other peoples' problems could begin to create tiny fissures in their hearts. Emotional stress fractures, to say it another way. It was important for a caretaker to reach out so that someone could support them too. Otherwise, the heart might shatter along the lines of those hairline cracks. Lorenzo, like Eric, was a kind person with a big heart whose first impulse was to carry other people forward when they couldn't move themselves.

My phone beeped a warning. "Sorry to eat and run, but Mom and Sam have been drafted into the contest, at least for today. I promised my mother that my smiling face would be in the audience."

His eyes got wide.

I explained about the two of them agreeing to stand in as placeholders during the day's filming. "My mother's as nervous as I've ever seen her."

Lorenzo reached for the check.

"This lunch is definitely on me," I told my friend. "It's not even worth arguing about. I know you have to get back home and get dressed for sunset. I'll see you soon, I hope? I do want to bring our Scottish visitors over to meet you. They've heard so much about you. Or maybe, even better, you can come to dinner on the pier."

He bowed, his hands folded to say *namaste* and thanks. Then he hurried off to his bicycle, and I went to the counter to pay the check. While I waited for my change, I perused the listings on the posters tacked to the bulletin board beyond the cash register. As always, in the Key West high season, there were more events available than a reasonable human being could attend. Art shows, theater productions, musical acts, historical tours, lectures at the library—the choices were astonishing. I noticed that Martina would be giving a concert tonight on the rooftop at the Studios of Key West. This was a lovely venue, outdoors with a great view, a bar, and an excellent sound system. Our visitors would love this, but I suspected that after the busy day they were having, the women would be too tired to attend.

Chapter Sixteen

Recipes do not make food taste good; people do.
—Judy Rodgers, *Zuni Café Cookbook*

By the time I returned to Williams Hall, the quick-bread contest was about to begin. Violet and Bettina called the bakers to join them behind the long counter in front of the ovens. I studied Martina and Harry more carefully this time, in light of the murder. Could I sense extreme desperation from either of them? Because that's what it would take to kill a man with a butcher knife and a baking pan, I thought.

Martha took the space at the far end to assist as needed. She did her best to smile in a lighthearted and welcoming way, but she looked tense to me. The camera swung around to focus on Bettina's face, and the cameraman pointed at her. The sisters bustled forward to take their places between Martha and the baking contestants.

"Welcome to the southernmost edition of *The UK Bakes!*, American-style. We are so lucky to have landed in Key West, Florida, for this segment of the show! We are your visiting Scottish hosts, Bettina and Violet Booth, and it's our grand pleasure to be here today. As you know, our contestants will all have a chance this afternoon to prepare the quick bread they've selected as a favorite, in front of the studio audience." She winked at the small crowd encircling the counter.

"In Scotland," Violet said, "which as you know is a very old country—"

"Almost as old as we are," Bettina said, and the audience laughed.

Violet squeezed one eye shut and shook her head. "My sister . . . Before we watch you prepare your recipes, we'd love to hear what you've chosen to bake and why. Do you have a special emotional connection to this bread?" She glanced down the row at Martina, Harry, and my mother. "Let's see, shall we start with Harry?" She patted the counter beside her, gesturing for him to approach that space.

Harry moved stiffly to join her and smiled broadly, showing all his teeth. I could imagine his mother instructing him that that kind of smile would help him look friendly in photos. It did not.

"Mine is a lemony lemon bread. It's based on something that Alison Roman cooks and calls her house dessert," Harry said. "She makes it with turmeric, which I find counterintuitive and peculiar. I left that ingredient out, replaced it with ground ginger, plus increased the lemon, both rind and juice, and decreased the sugar."

"Lemon bread. With ginger. So unusual," said Bettina. Her eyes widened enough to let the audience suspect she was dubious.

"Sounds lovely. Cannot wait to try it," said Violet, the skin around her eyes crinkling with humor. "Aside from your connection to Alison Roman, does the bread have any significance in your family history?"

He took a moment, looking a bit perplexed. "Not really. In the cake family, my family preferred chocolate to lemon. All of our baked goods came courtesy of Pepperidge Farm. My mother told me that baking from scratch was overrated."

He got a loud laugh, though from the look on his face, I didn't think he'd meant to be funny.

"Thank you," said Violet. "Next, let's have Martina Bevis come forward."

Martina bounced over, reminding me of Tigger in *Winnie the Pooh*. She was grinning from ear to ear, as though she could hardly wait to share the details of her quick bread.

She didn't wait for a question from the sisters. "My recipe comes directly from my Czech grandmother," she said proudly. "It's actually a yeast bread, so not technically quick. The hallmarks are rum-soaked raisins and slivered almonds. Babicka—that means grandmother—often made this at Christmastime, though it could be eaten any time of year. My Czech ancestors would say, *When homemade vánočka comes out of the oven, Christmas is on the doorstep!*"

"Thank you; it sounds lovely. We adore family history sifting into our baked goods," said Violet. "We've allowed Martina to start her yeast bread ahead of time so it can bake along with the others."

I thought she looked a bit annoyed, as this monkey wrench would surely mess up their timing. Bettina took a turn with the patter.

"Last but never least, we invite Janet and her handsome husband, Sam, to come forward. Please tell us about your bread."

"We will be preparing Irish soda bread," my mother said in a voice so quiet I had to strain to hear her. She had grown very confident in her everyday Key West life as a caterer, but not so much when the circumstances were new and challenging. Like this.

"You will need to speak up," said the man behind the camera. "We can't hear you."

My mother looked mortified. "Irish soda bread," she repeated, almost shouting this time. Bettina patted her on the back.

"Try a teeny notch down in volume. Any family connections with this recipe?"

"I always thought my family was one hundred percent French," said my mother. "But I've recently learned on an ancestry site that I had a great-grandmother who immigrated from Ireland in the mid-1800s. Her family had no money, and there must have been very few opportunities for a young woman. Annie Ryan from Clonin, Ireland. I never knew her, nor did I have the chance to eat her food. But this recipe is in her honor. Imagine how brave she must have been to leave her beloved country alone and cross a great sea to a new land."

Her eyes sparkled with intensity as she described the hardships that resulted in Annie's migration—the famine and persecution.

"Unlike some other quick breads, there is butter in this recipe. You may choose to use raisins or not. Caraway seeds are also optional, though aficionados of the recipe insist there's no point in making it without them. I tend to agree." She grinned at Sam, who was looking delighted as she blossomed right in front of us.

Violet clapped her hands. "Wonderful; let's have the baking begin. For this episode, we will have each of you working simultaneously at a station along the counter. The folks doing the filming will move from one to the other to zero in on your techniques."

I watched the action for the next half hour, until Martha announced that time was up and the breads needed to go into the oven. "If the contestants could meet us at the end of the counter, we'll film short interviews with each of you during that time."

While the bread was baking and the contestants were talking, I went to join Miss Gloria at the big table on the other side of the room, where we chatted about the events of the past few days. "How is Lorenzo?" she asked.

As I told Miss Gloria about our lunch, I was able to put into words what I had noticed but not completely absorbed.

"Lorenzo looked tired and a little mournful," I said. "I hate that."

"The work he does is draining," she said. "So many troubled people come to him for advice. Plus he sits there on Mallory Square for hours with all that zaniness surrounding him."

Mallory Square was located at the very bottom of Key West, overlooking the water and, in the distance, ritzy Sunset Key and shaggy Wisteria Island. Visitors gathered on this plaza to watch the sunset and enjoy street performers and cocktails. The party scene tended to have a crazy vibe—this was not a place for quiet contemplation.

"I'd have to think those nights take a lot out of him," Miss Gloria added. "What made you think he was mournful?"

"I got the sense that he's been wondering whether what he does really helps people. That made me feel a little sad, because of course it does. People come because they're looking for guidance at one particular moment in their lives, and he provides it."

Miss Gloria patted my hand. "Of course. But it's a question that all of us ask at some moments—probably more than one. Is our life useful? Are we doing the best we can to contribute to the good of the universe? All of our dreams and intentions can be overwhelmed by the bad news and the loud chatter in the world outside." She studied my face. "Anything else?"

"He did say that people don't always hear what he thinks he's told them. That doesn't bother him—he's like a therapist whose patients refract feedback through their own lenses. He says that most people hear in his readings exactly the message they need to receive."

Miss Gloria sat back, nodding in agreement. "What do we do next about this murder case?"

"It's not really our case, is it?" I said with a laugh. "But I wonder if we could figure out who the heck Arvid Smith is and pass what we learn on to Nathan."

I typed Arvid's name into the search bar and scrolled through the results that came up on my phone. Unfortunately, almost all of them led to pages about a musician particularly known for playing the sitar. He did not resemble our handsome dark-haired agent Arvid one bit. I showed her the screen.

"That's not him," she said. "You would think a TV agent would have all kinds of hits from all kinds of publicity. What does it mean that he doesn't show up at all?"

"Good question. Either he's had very limited success, or he's not who he says he is."

"Makes me wonder how carefully Violet and Bettina checked him out before they hired him," said Miss Gloria, sending a worried look across the room to her friends. "Type me in and see what you get."

A funny request, but I did as she'd asked. Instantly, I wished I hadn't. At the top of the screen, there was a link to an article in the *Key West Citizen* from several years ago.

Gloria Peterson, age 77, was attacked and left for dead on the Tarpon Pier dock last night. She was taken to the Lower Keys Medical Center for treatment and remains in guarded condition. Neighbors denied having heard or seen the perpetrators. Police are asking anyone with information about the crime to contact them.

I had been one of those neighbors, and I'd always felt bad about not being there for her. I'd also wondered if my actions had caused her troubles and I'd been too wound up with my own problems to notice.

She took the phone from my fingers, skimmed the piece, and handed it back.

"Pfft," she said. "That's old news. What we really ought to be doing is going door-to-door and interviewing the neighbors around that bed-and-breakfast."

"I'm certain the police are all over that," I said, glancing up from the screen. Nathan would abhor that suggestion. "They won't want a group of untrained civilians stumbling around the vicinity of the crime scene."

"But what if there was a rooftop or some other high perch where someone was watching the night sky and happened into being an observer? Maybe they didn't even realize at the time that it was a murder." Miss Gloria looked very excited.

As little as I wanted any of the ladies to think they were part of the police investigation, she had a point. I remembered that Martina was performing on classical guitar tonight at Hugh's View—the space atop the Studios of Key West, which had been fashioned into a popular sunset happy hour and concert spot, named after a local philanthropist.

124

"Like Hugh's View," I said. "Except from what I recall, the trees would've made it hard to see what's happening at the street level. It's more of a bird's-eye view than anything."

"Used to be you could go to the La Concha, that hotel on Duval Street. They had a wonderful outside bar high up above the chaos," said Miss Gloria. "Unfortunately, it's been turned into a private spa, and they don't encourage us hoi polloi."

Martina approached our end of the table with a shy smile on her face. "So sorry to interrupt, but I hope you might be interested in my concert tonight." She dealt out two postcards from a small stack. The cards showed a photo of her seated, a guitar on her lap. "I'm performing at the Studios, and if you're not doing anything later . . ."

"Thanks for the invitation. It's a very busy week," I said, smiling, wondering if the universe was piling on, telling us to *take a look.*

Despite the urge to look for clues to a murder from on high, we probably wouldn't make it out tonight. The ladies would be exhausted. But I reminded myself to talk with Martina the next time I went to the gym. I'd seen her perform on classical guitar—she was very talented. As so often happened in Key West, people who seemed like one thing—a jock, for example—turned out to have other impressive talents. None of that meant she wasn't capable of murder.

As for Harry of the heavy scones and sour lemon bread—he was a big question mark so far. And where the heck was Arvid Smith? Had he disappeared because he was guilty?

It would all boil down to motive. Who'd known Mr. Humboldt and disliked him well enough to wish him dead?

Chapter Seventeen

The old days were slower. People buttered their bread
without guilt and sat down to dinner en famille.
                    —Laurie Colwin, *Home Cooking:*
                            A Writer in the Kitchen

We returned to the kitchen area, where the sisters were
talking about baking as a way to connect with one's
ancestors. "That's why we always ask the question about the lin-
eage of a bread or cake, because many times the baked good
means so much more to the baker than merely a shot of sugar,"
said Bettina.

"It's almost as if the ancestors were giving a precious gift of love
to those bakers, who then share it with the people around them,"
said Violet. "I love how your American food writer Laurie Colwin
said it: *No one who cooks, cooks alone. Even at her most solitary, a
cook in the kitchen is surrounded by generations of cooks past, the
advice and menus of cooks present, the wisdom of cookbook writers.*"

All three ovens began to chime in unison, announcing that
their baked goods were ready. Martina, Harry, and my mother
rushed back to the counter.

A Clue in the Crumbs

Bettina rubbed her hands together, a big smile on her face. "This is my very favorite moment in the process—a viewing of the fruits of our labor. *Your* labor this time."

Violet was grinning too. "Shall we let them take their breads out of the oven, or shall we do the honors?"

"Remember that contest we hosted in Edinburgh when that contestant dropped her tray of mashed potato scones? Tatties o'er the side!" Bettina shrieked with laughter, then winked at the three bakers. "Best we do it, lads and lassies."

First, they removed Harry's lemon bread from the oven at the far end. The crowd on my side of the counter pressed a little closer. I couldn't see too much, but enough to notice that the bread appeared very brown and sunken on one end. Harry looked devastated.

Bettina patted him on the back. "Not to worry, ma dear. As they say in the old country, failing means yer playin'."

Martina's bread was taken out next. Instead of coming out too flat, this one had risen up over the edges of the pan, then burned down the sides and dripped onto the oven floor. This explained the burning smell I'd noticed the last few minutes.

"Possibly," said Violet kindly, "your grandmother's measurements don't translate well to the U.S.?"

Finally, the sisters went to my mother's oven and pulled out a perfectly round, light-brown loaf of bread. Even though I wasn't hungry, the scent made my mouth water.

"Now," said Violet, "we will let the products rest for ten minutes. This is very important for you bakers at home, because the steam inside helps your breads and cakes to rise." She tapped on the soda bread, which made a lovely hollow noise. "The rest allows for better slicing as well; no ragged edges to appall your guests."

"Who will be our winners for today's segment?" Bettina mused. "Should it be Harry's family lemon bread? Or Martina's grandmother's Christmas bread? Or the Irish soda bread perhaps made by Janet's great-grandmother?"

Minutes later, after a bit more chatter and stories about their ancestors, the sisters returned to Harry's bread and invited him up for the tasting. Using the parchment paper that had been tucked under the batter and protruded from the edges, Bettina removed the bread from its pan. "Now the moment you've all been waiting for," she said as she sliced into the end of the loaf, which was crumbly and appeared dry. She cut off three tiny bites, one each for the two of them and one for Harry. They popped the bread into their mouths, and we watched them chew. I was pretty sure that Violet was struggling to mask the pucker of her face. Bettina didn't even try.

"Perhaps, ma dear," she said, patting him on the back again, "perhaps put a tad bit of that sugar back in next time. The lemon comes through oh so clearly."

Violet nodded vigorously and took a big swallow from the water glass that Martha had set out for each of them. "Perhaps maybe a wee bitty less of the dried ginger too?"

Next, they tasted Martina's Christmas bread, which appeared to have wet dough in the middle when they cut into it. "All ovens are different, deary," said Bettina, "and perhaps the one your grandmother used ran a little hotter than this one." She winked at Martina, whose face had fallen like Harry's loaf. "The bread has promise, though. I did get a lovely taste of rum raisin."

Finally, they moved on to my mother's Irish soda bread. Violet sliced into it, and I could see the steam wafting up. The texture of the bread looked appealing, and the smell was to die for.

Violet's eyes fluttered shut as she chewed on her bite. "This is heavenly," she said. "I would not even put butter on the table. It's rich and moist as is."

"Here we must disagree," said Bettina. "Bread is always better slathered with butter."

The camera people moved the length of the counter, filming each bread and its baker. Bettina clapped her hands together to get everyone's attention. "Tomorrow," she said, "we will be baking easy desserts, otherwise known as loaf cakes. I cannot wait to see what our talented contestants have in store for us! We will see you all promptly at ten thirty AM."

As the work for the day was wrapping up, I checked my phone and realized I had missed a call from Nathan. I moved into the hallway to listen to the message.

"I'm going to need to make a showing at City Hall at five o'clock," his voice mail said. "Chief Brandenburg is being commended for twenty years of service. Plus citizens are demanding to hear from the police department about the murder and why we haven't wrapped things up yet. Let me know dinner plans, and I will try my best to join you."

I couldn't get annoyed, because he took his job very seriously and he seriously wanted the promotion to captain. The other fellow in the running was a competitive contender, so it wouldn't do for Nathan to slack off because he had houseguests.

I approached the counter, where the Scone Sisters were talking with Martha and the producer, with Miss Gloria looking on. The ladies looked sleepy, which was how I felt at this point too.

"I was thinking I could call for a dinner reservation at Salute. It's right on the ocean, people play volleyball on the beach in front of the tables for our entertainment, and the food is good—fish and so on. For dessert, let me just say you shouldn't pass up their homemade ice cream sandwich. But whenever you ladies are ready, I'll ferry you home to the houseboat for a rest."

"Divine," said Violet. "All of it!"

On the way home, Miss Gloria quizzed her guests about their impressions of the baking performances today. "I shouldn't ask you this, because she's practically family, but wasn't Janet amazing? And her Sam is so cute, the perfect sidekick. Is Nathan driving us to the restaurant?"

"Nathan may or may not make it—he has a command performance at City Hall. It will all depend on how the meeting goes. Sometimes these things drag on incessantly with community comments. He can't very well walk out in the middle of someone's rant."

"What meeting?" asked Miss Gloria.

"It's the usual monthly city commission meeting, with a special commendation for the police chief. After that, he has to stay on, as the public has clamored for an opportunity to press the police about the details of the murder and why it hasn't been solved."

Both sisters perked up as I explained.

"Do they let the noncitizen public into these meetings?" Bettina asked. "We would love to see your politics in motion."

"They do," I said, thinking if luck was with me, they'd be too zonked to add in another stop. "It's usually pretty dry stuff."

Chapter Eighteen

A *grudge* is not a *resentment*. Sure, they're made of the same material—poison—but while resentment is concentrated, a grudge is watered down, drinkable and refreshingly effervescent, the low-calorie lager to resentment's bootleg grain alcohol.

—Alex McElroy, "Why Holding a Grudge Is So
Satisfying," *The New York Times Magazine*,
January 2022

After walking Ziggy and feeding both animals, I retired to the bedroom to rest for ten minutes. Fortunately, I'd set my alarm, and it went off just as I'd drifted into a deep sleep and felt like I could have slept all night. I washed my face, put on a swingy purple yoga skirt, a white tee, and pearl earrings, and headed over to Miss Gloria's to collect the ladies. Still a bit groggy myself, I imagined they were seriously wilting.

Instead, all three were tapping toes on the deck.

"We were beginning to worry that you'd forgotten!" said Miss Gloria.

I shook my head in amazement. The sisters didn't look like they'd been working under the glare of lights and cameras all day, not to mention recovering from an international plane flight across the pond only days before.

"Our reservation at Salute is for six o'clock," I told them. "We could walk the length of the White Street Pier before we go to the restaurant, if you're not too tired?"

"Oh," said Violet, her face disappointed. "I thought we were going to City Hall to watch your Nathan battle the civilians. We all took power naps and woke up full of energy."

They didn't understand just how dull one of these evenings could be. "Are you certain you want to go to this meeting? It's super tedious stuff—they drone on in astonishing detail."

"We want to see Nathan in action," insisted Bettina. "It will help us understand how your country works. Not to mention your husband."

"Okay," I said, laughing. "But don't bring any weapons in your purses in case we're searched."

The City Hall in Key West was built on the site of the Glynn Archer Elementary School, famous for its appearance in the 1955 movie *The Rose Tattoo*. Built as a new structure within the old walls, the gorgeous white stucco building had every modern convenience the administration might need, including hurricane-proof windows, without losing its sense of history. A huge auditorium served as the city commission's chambers, and this was where tonight's meeting would take place.

Many of the seats were already filled when we arrived, and the commission members and mayor were filing in to take their places at the dais in the front of the room. The counter in front of their seats was high enough that they all appeared pint sized, a bit like Goldilocks in the big bear's chair. I ushered the ladies in, pointing out folding chairs in the last row on the right, as we would likely want to slip out well before the meeting was concluded.

On the opposite side of the room, a line of uniformed police officers, including Nathan, leaned against the back wall. Nathan and another lieutenant were in the running for promotion to captain, with an eye toward eventually rising to chief. That meant their behavior was being watched carefully at public events like this one, as well as in news reports about the police force—both by Nathan's higher-ups and in the community. I caught his eye and gave him a little wave. He looked surprised to see us. Astonished was more like it.

The meeting began, and we were asked to stand and recite the Pledge of Allegiance. Then a minister offered a prayer for reasonableness in a time of divisive politics. Tall order, I thought. The mayor began the meeting by declaring the day "Peter Arnow Day," named after a photographer who'd been active many years in battling the AIDS epidemic. While listening to the accolades, I noticed that a man several rows in front of Nathan was getting restless.

He turned to my husband. "What kind of progress has been made on the murder case?" he asked in a loud voice.

Nathan smiled through gritted teeth and answered softly, "We'll be talking about that topic very shortly." He gestured toward the front of the room.

"How do you propose to become chief of police when you can't solve one vicious crime?" The man's voice had moved from merely loud to belligerent.

"We are certainly working on that, sir," Nathan said, looking grim.

But the man grew more agitated. He hurled accusations and questions at Nathan and the policeman around him. "Whose side are you on? Criminals or citizens? What have you done for us so far? Are you going to wait until more of your citizens are murdered with their bodies left bleeding on the sidewalk?"

Within an instant, several cops approached him. "If you can't calm down, sir, you will have to leave the room," said a burly, swarthy officer with a crew cut.

This only served to make the man more agitated. He shouted again, repeating, "Whose side are you on?"

"There's only one side, sir," said my husband quietly. "We always stand with the citizens."

"Exactly who are you protecting?" the man yelled at Nathan. "It's certainly not us!"

The tension in the hall crackled. Five uniformed police surrounded the man, grabbed his arms, and escorted him to a back door and quickly outside.

Mayor Teri called for the room's attention, ignoring the altercation. "Next, we would like to laud police chief Sean Brandenburg for twenty years of service."

Nathan and the other officers trooped up to the front of the room and stood behind the chief. The city manager commended him and, after listing his accomplishments, gave him a watch and a commemorative coin. The chief thanked the city, his wife, and the department, and complimented Key West citizens for working with the police. With the exception of Nathan and the chief, the officers trooped back to their original positions. This was not a good sign, as the chief would have allowed Nathan to answer questions without his presence if things were going well.

A Clue in the Crumbs

I squeezed my hands into fists, hoping my husband wouldn't be harassed, and if he was, praying he could keep his temper in check. He was undoubtedly already rattled by the man who'd been evicted.

Mayor Teri leaned into her microphone. "Now Lieutenant Bransford and Chief Brandenburg will take questions from the public about the recent crime. Please come up to one of the podiums, state your name and address, and briefly ask your question."

A man in khaki shorts and flip-flops was the first to speak. "We do not feel safe in this town," he said. "Ordinary citizens are attacked near their businesses and left to die." He pointed at the two men and slapped his palm on the podium.

"Why has no one been arrested? Why has no information been provided to the citizens paying your salaries? Well?" He spread his arms out, glaring at Nathan. "What can you say about that, Mr. Wants-to-Be-Chief-but-Doesn't-Have-What-It-Takes?"

Several people in the audience snickered, and I felt the same urge, but it was from sheer anxiety more than finding the man funny. In fact, I was horrified for my husband. How did this man even know he was angling for a promotion, and why would he blame Nathan for lack of progress on the case? This was exactly the kind of situation that could spiral downward quickly if he didn't react well.

Nathan cleared his throat and smoothed his shirt collar. "I understand your concerns, and the police department shares them. We are entirely committed to solving this vicious crime and bringing the murderer to justice. Our investigation has been wide ranging, and we have several suspects in our sights."

"When might you be sharing some of this expert information with the citizens?" the man asked, his voice dripping with sarcasm.

The skin on Nathan's neck above his collar was beginning to redden. He took a shallow breath. "I'm sure you understand that it is impossible for us to share information about suspects and possible scenarios until that information is confirmed. Preferably after a suspect is arrested."

The man pounded the podium again. "We have no confidence that anything is happening in your department, sir."

The chief took a step closer to Nathan and whispered something to him. Nathan shrugged but then nodded.

"What we know is that Mr. Humboldt exited the back of his bed-and-breakfast to the yard behind on the evening of the murder. The perpetrator was likely to have been waiting for him there behind the garbage dumpster. There may or may not have been a verbal altercation, and it appears that Mr. Humboldt began to walk away when he was attacked. A dog walker found the body and alerted the emergency medical crews, but the victim had passed away by the time they arrived."

Nathan crossed his arms over his chest and glared at the citizen. "This is what we know and are able to say about what happened. We have no information about the motive for the attack, nor are we ready to make arrests or discuss the details of the murder. We encourage citizens who may have some information about the crime to contact us directly."

Oh, this was bad—he'd said earlier, right after getting pressured by this civilian, that the department had suspects. This sounded like a repetition of what most people would already know, perhaps a speech encouraged by the chief, supposedly to calm town residents. I was afraid it would push people in the other direction.

"Your time is up, sir," said Mayor Teri to the man at the podium.

I heard pockets of outraged and fearful chatter in the audience.

The angry man stomped away, making space for a chubby woman with thin blonde hair.

"My name is Ellen McFadden, and I live on Whitehead Street. I may have some information to share. The night that man was killed, my husband and I were taking some visitors on a bar crawl. We'd been to the Waterfront Brewery and Schooner Wharf Bar and were on our way to Sloppy Joe's." She looked embarrassed but determined. "We'd had a few drinks, if you must know, but I did see a man running from the direction of Dey Street. A young man with dark hair. I told my husband he appeared to be bloody—"

Nathan took several steps toward her, holding his hand out and forcing a smile to his lips. "Thank you, ma'am. It would be best if you didn't say anything further in public. Thank you very much for speaking out. Could you wait for me outside and we'll continue our conversation? One of our officers will escort you out and wait with you."

"Certainly, Lieutenant," she said, and hurried up the aisle to the vestibule that opened into the hall, a stocky officer with a crew cut in her wake.

Bettina leaned over to me. "We are going to use the loo and will meet you by the front door in a few?"

I nodded and whispered back, "Be there soon."

Nathan answered a few more questions—more than adequately, I thought. But at this moment, our jumpy island needed much more than adequate responses. We needed definitive answers and arrests. Once he and the chief returned to their seats, Miss Gloria and I left to find the sisters.

They were outside the building, near the large painted tiger statue that had been rescued from the school during the City Hall renovation and then replaced in its original position. The guardian officer of the woman who believed she'd seen a bloody man running from the scene of the murder was on his cell phone with his back to her. Our Scottish women pals appeared to be grilling the witness.

Chapter Nineteen

"I wouldn't thank the Lord," she said, pulling that same 14-inch chef's knife out of her bag. He gasped. Like most cooks, Elizabeth insisted on using her own knives.
—Bonnie Garmus, *Lessons in Chemistry*

"Everyone all set?" I asked brightly as I approached, hoping to head off any further interference in the police case. I'd learned from living with Nathan that the more frequently a witness told a story, especially when questioned by an untrained interviewer, the more the story could change. Not in factual ways, either. People didn't mean to fabricate extra details, but this could happen in the retelling.

"We were just asking this nice young woman about what she saw the night of the murder," said Bettina. I noticed her taking her phone back from the woman's hand.

"That might have been him," the witness said, brushing a wisp of blonde hair off her forehead. "To be honest, we had more drinks than I admitted to the officer. But he definitely had dark hair and a nice build like this man."

"May I see?" I asked, reaching for the phone. As I'd feared, it was a picture of the two sisters with their agent, Arvid Smith. "Do wait here for Lieutenant Bransford," I told Ellen the citizen. "He will be very interested to hear about any details you might remember." Then I herded the ladies to the back parking lot where we'd left the Buick, and we climbed in.

Violet leaned forward from her place in the back seat. "I hope we didn't make a mistake, talking to that witness. I hope we didn't muck up your dear husband's case."

I glanced at her in the rearview mirror; her face was furrowed with doubt. "Not to worry; Nathan and his department are experts at this sort of thing. Let's enjoy the evening, and we can chat more with a drink in front of us."

"A capital idea!" said Miss Gloria.

I drove the few blocks from the town hall to Salute, a restaurant on the edge of the Atlantic. Their kitchen offered reliably fresh seafood and delicious cocktails, but the setting was the biggest draw. It was rustic and open air so diners could watch bicyclists ride by, beach volleyball players batting at balls beyond that, and behind it all, a stretch of white sand leading to the Atlantic Ocean.

"Aw, I think we've literally died and gone to heaven," said Bettina as we were ushered to a table near the open-air window. Miss Gloria and I spent a few minutes reviewing the menu choices for the sisters.

"Grouper and shrimp cakes versus sautéed yellowtail snapper—those are my favorites," said Miss Gloria. "Unless I'm in the mood for spaghetti and meatballs, though Hayley could whip those up for us in an instant."

A willowy waitress wearing her hair twirled up in a knot and a flowy skirt introduced herself as Marlene. "I'll be taking care of you tonight." She listed off the specials.

"Thank you, ma dear. You dress like an artist," said Violet, "and move like a dancer."

The woman beamed. "I *am* an artist, and a yoga teacher too. I paint in a studio on Dey Street. You can see some of my work at the Key West Collective on Caroline Street."

"What kind of painting do you do?" Bettina asked.

"My husband and I make books together. It's a little hard to explain on the fly." She glanced around the restaurant, where every table was now filled. I imagined she had a million places to be, food to deliver, customers to chat up. "I paint on the right hand of a page, and then he writes poetry inspired by the art on the left. We journal like this every day while we travel, but we've been working like mad for the last month to get ready for a show. The project was inspired by a Facebook page called Out My Window. During the pandemic, people from all over the world posted photographs of exactly that—what they could see from inside their home. It was a way of connecting when no one could travel and everyone felt claustrophobic. During the lockdown, we attempted something similar. I painted and collaged and he wrote about what we saw outside our window. But forgive me, I'm babbling."

She grinned. "In fact, I'm headed back to work to finish some details after my shift here. Can I get you some drinks while you look at the menu?"

"I think we can give you everything at once, if that's okay?" I asked.

"Of course!"

We put in orders for mojitos and shrimp and grouper for me and the sisters, mussels with garlic for Miss Gloria. "Will you set aside two of your ice cream sandwiches before they sell out?" This had happened to me once in the past. It was deeply disappointing to have a vision of homemade cookies wrapped around ice cream in your mind and heart, and then have the reality snatched away.

"Of course." She winked and whirled off to take drink orders at the large and rowdy table beside us. I watched her go, noticing that Miss Gloria was watching too.

"That's some project she has going. I hope it's a busy street," said Bettina, with a laugh. "Or it could be a boring book."

"Not really," I said slowly. "It's an alley. The alley where Mr. Humboldt's body was found."

"Holy cattails," said Bettina.

While we sipped on drinks and waited for our meals to be delivered, I asked the sisters to tell us more about their missing agent. I didn't want to make them feel bad about having chosen him, but I had so many questions and worries.

"I know you told us that he connected with you because his mother's sister had recently died. Do I have that right? When you selected him, did you know where he was from? Or what kind of experience he's had in the business of representing celebrities?"

Bettina twittered. "Celebrities! How you do go on."

But Violet wasn't laughing. "This bothers me a lot. Unfortunately, it's become clear that we didn't ask nearly as much as we should have before we hired him. We liked his manner and we snatched him up, a pig in a bloody poke. For all we know, he was the shakin's o' the pocky and we got sucked in."

"Shakin's of the pocky?" Miss Gloria asked.

"The leavings in the bottom of a bag," said Violet. "Or the last bairn in a long line. Smallest pig in the litter."

"The dregs, you mean," exclaimed Miss Gloria.

I wanted to laugh, but Violet looked so concerned. "Maybe he's fine. Maybe there's a good reason that he's disappeared," I said. "What I've learned from hanging around with too many cops is that the biggest part of a murder investigation is asking lots of questions, considering information that you didn't even know you hadn't looked at or noticed was missing."

"Hayley and I used Google on him earlier," said Miss Gloria. "The only Arvid Smith that came up was an older guy who plays the sitar. But wait, you have a picture of your agent that you were showing that woman outside City Hall. Show her that. Maybe she'll notice a clue."

Violet pulled out her phone and scrolled to the photo, then passed it to us. In this photo, the man I'd seen briefly on Miss Gloria's deck had his arms thrown around the two sisters. They were all laughing.

"We had just agreed to sign with him," she said glumly. "We were so exhilarated—we had no idea he'd do a runner, and a man would be murdered, and our Key West contest would be left in tatters."

"It can't be as bad as all that," I said. "Though it will be good to find out if your Arvid is really who he said he is, and why he's disappeared."

Marlene the waitress appeared at the table with our dinner plates balanced on her arms.

"I never understand how a person can carry that many dishes at once without dropping anything or dripping hot liquid on themselves or the customers," said Miss Gloria. "You are a waitress rock star." We all laughed.

"Thank you," said Marlene as she settled the food on the table. "You are now my favorite customers."

"It smells amazing," said Miss Gloria. "Wait until you get the tip." The other ladies chittered.

"Can I get you anything else?" Marlene asked, a big smile on her face.

The expression on Miss Gloria's face shifted, as if she'd just remembered something important. She got a lot of mileage out of looking innocent while asking hard questions. "Whoa, wait. You said your studio is on Dey Street. Isn't that where . . . ?"

Marlene's smile trembled. "Yes, so tragic. Now, unfortunately, murder is our deadly claim to fame. Hope you enjoy your dinners. I'll check back with you shortly."

"But wait." Miss Gloria put a hand on her wrist. "Could we visit your studio sometime to see your process?"

Marlene's face lit up again. "Of course, but text me ahead." She jotted the number on my friend's napkin.

Chapter Twenty

I was startled by a thought: what makes our ritual meals so powerful is not that we gather with our families, but that we gather with our ghosts.
—Ruth Reichl, *La Briffe,* December 8, 2021

After we finished our dinners and enjoyed the ice cream sandwiches—milk chocolate ice cream pressed between two crispy chocolate chip cookies—I assessed my charges and determined that they still looked amazingly energetic. "Should we make a quick stop at the Studios of Key West to have a nightcap and catch a few songs from Martina?"

The ladies exchanged glances.

"Absolutely!" said Bettina. "We did not come to America to go to bed early. We can do that perfectly well in Peebles, Scotland."

I drove them across town and found a place to park on Simonton Street, around the corner from the studios. We could see the lights on the rooftop of the four-story white stucco art deco building and hear the strains of a guitar.

"We haven't missed a thing," I said. I held the door open, and we took the elevator up to Hugh's View, an open-air performance space and bar. Martina was set up under the lights and a wavy metal rooftop, with the guitar in her lap and one foot on a stool.

I settled the ladies on folding chairs with a good view of Martina and the city of Key West spread out behind her.

"She sounds amazing," whispered Violet. "This is where her true talent lies. Someone needs to kindly steer her away from baking." She raised her eyebrows at her sister, as though Bettina were the one responsible for tackling the tricky people issues, and we all laughed.

At intermission, I took drink orders and went to the small bar in the back corner, where my trainer from WeBeFit, Leigh, was moonlighting as the bartender.

"Lots of excitement in your world, I hear," she said.

"Always," I said, "but what do you know?"

"You didn't hear it from me," said Leigh, "but Martina had a brief interaction with Rayna before all of this blew up. She's a good judge of character if you can read between the lines." Which I took to mean she wouldn't gossip but she might know something. Leigh pushed the drinks across the bar to me with a smile and turned to the next customer.

I carried the wine back to our seats, noticing that Martina was standing by herself near the stage. "Let's say hello to the star," I suggested, and headed over, the three women steaming along behind me with drinks in hand.

"You sound beautiful," said Violet. "What a talented musician you are."

Martina smiled shyly and thanked us for coming.

"I particularly like the second song," I said, though that sounded ridiculously uninformed to my ears. She played classical music, not songs. "I haven't had the chance to ask you what made you decide to enter the baking contest, when you have so much else going on in your life."

"I adore their program." She took a quick glance at the sisters, who grinned back. "I've watched every episode of your *UK Bakes!* show. You"—she reached to touch Bettina's hand—"remind me of my grandmother in Prague. She was full of energy and so smart and so kind. She was forever baking things and taking them to neighbors who might be sad or sick. I didn't pay enough attention to her when she was still alive and I had the chance. In a way, being on the set with you two makes me feel closer to her."

"If that isn't the sweetest thing, ma dear," said Bettina, stepping forward to hug her. "You'll find that baking her recipes over your lifetime will serve the same purpose. She'll always be with you in your kitchen."

"Without the stress of performing," Violet added with a laugh. "Did you know the other contestants before signing up for the contest?"

"Harry I've never met, though I've seen your mom before." She glanced at me and grinned. "She's a hoot."

"And Rayna?"

A shadow crossed Martina's face. "I shouldn't say . . ."

Bettina reached for her hand again. "You can trust us, ma dear."

Martina glanced around the milling audience to see if anyone would be eavesdropping. There were a few groups of people near us chatting over glasses of wine, but no one appeared to be listening in.

"She came to the gym for one introductory visit, but her heart wasn't in it. I couldn't tell whether her husband had wanted her to come but she wasn't interested, or whether she wanted to come and he discouraged her. Either way, she struck me as a sweet soul, a little lost. Someone who might have trouble standing up for herself unless she was really pushed hard. That's it. I need to refresh myself before the rest of the show."

We thanked her and returned to our seats. "Well," said Violet. "What did you think of her?"

"She can't be a murderer," said Bettina, "not with her taste in role models." She winked at her sister. "She barely knew Rayna or her husband, if she's to be believed. Everything she said was vague enough that it's hard to take seriously as information related to solving a crime."

The same thought I'd had.

When the music had finished, we moved to the wall overlooking the canopy of trees and, beyond that, the water. Though we were facing in the direction of the bed-and-breakfast where Mr. Humboldt had been killed, the buildings closest to us were obscured by the trees' lush greenery.

"Hard to imagine that anyone could have seen what happened the night of the murder from this vantage point," I said, feeling discouraged.

"Maybe if you had a pair of binoculars and knew exactly where to look," said Miss Gloria with a wistful sigh. Her face suddenly lit up. "You know that crazy place on Dey Street that Lorenzo won't go in? That's exactly the same place where our waitress's studio is."

"Who is Lorenzo, and why won't he go in?" asked Bettina.

"I can't believe we haven't introduced you yet! He's a good friend and a tarot card reader, and he's very sensitive to, well, pretty much everything. But especially anything the slightest bit supernatural," said Miss Gloria.

I explained more. "A few months ago, we went to the Dey Street compound to see an art show. Lorenzo stopped short on our way into the courtyard and refused to go any further. 'I know some very strange things have gone on in this place,' he said when we asked what was wrong."

I gave my wineglass to a passing waiter.

"I told him you don't really have to be a tarot card reader to get that," I said. "After all, it's home to a bunch of artists and musicians known for partying hard. But he wouldn't set one foot further. He said he was getting a very troubling vibe. The energy was all wrong. He's not a timid person either."

The Scottish sisters laughed. "That will not put us off in the slightest," Bettina said. "You know yourselves from your visit to Scotland last year that our country abounds with thin places. We like to sit quietly and absorb those feelings when we notice them. Sometimes old souls are trying to tell us something. Sounds as if this may be one of your thin places in Key West. Maybe Lorenzo misinterpreted the message."

That felt right, even though I hadn't put those words together to describe it. A thin place, we'd learned in Scotland while visiting Nathan's sister, was a place where heaven and earth felt very close together—the veil between them was thin.

"Or maybe this place has a thin veil between hell and earth, rather than heaven," said Miss Gloria. I thought she'd meant that as a joke to lighten the mood, but no one laughed.

"What does this place look like? What stands out as particularly weird or fey?" Violet asked.

"It's an old compound that belonged to the artist Susie DePoo. She used to invite other artists to work and sometimes stay there. The place is kind of a wreck, looks like it could fall down around you at any moment, but it hosts an amazing artistic community. There are some studios, plus musicians live there during the high season when they perform around town. They could never afford regular housing otherwise." As I described the scene, I realized I still didn't exactly understand Lorenzo's reaction. Was it possible that someone had died here? Or was there another connection to the current murder? Had Lorenzo sensed a violent death coming? Maybe he was even sensing Mr. Humboldt's murder. Although that had occurred in the street, not in the artists' compound.

"Marlene said she and her husband have been working late hours to get ready for a show. What if they were there the night of the murder?" I asked, then met Miss Gloria's eyes. "It's possible they might have seen something, even if they didn't realize it at the time. It's only a few blocks away from here. Let's go over, if you're up for it, and we'll see if her studio light is on."

We left the concert area, took the elevator down to the first floor, and headed across town on foot on Simonton Street. The ladies were starting to flag, but we were so close that it seemed a shame to skip the opportunity to talk with Marlene. We turned right on Dey Street. The windows of the Humboldts' bed-and-breakfast on the left were mostly dark, except for a light on the porch and another fainter light inside, high up on the third floor toward the back of the house. The shed at the back of the property was also lit up. I could make out a long black patch on the left side of the building where the fire had burned. I wondered if the fire or police department had released the property back to Rayna. It didn't appear that guests were staying there. That thought reminded me to check back in with Connie to see if she'd found out anything new. Certainly no one had contacted the sisters about reclaiming their original reservation.

Susie DePoo's palace, on the right, was an old, wooden, two-story structure with a gate beside it that led into a courtyard with several smaller wooden shed-like buildings surrounding it. I could imagine this whole place would have gone up like dry kindling if the blaze had jumped the alley before the fire department arrived.

"She's here," Gloria called back to me. "I texted her. She said we could come up for a bit." I followed the ladies into the courtyard and up a steep set of wooden stairs to the second-floor room overlooking the street. Marlene was waiting for us on a screened-in porch, looking tired, still in the clothes she'd worn to wait on our table. She carried the scent of a restaurant kitchen in her hair. I wondered idly why so many people in my life had a name starting with *Mar*: Marlene, Martina, Martha. I'd have to concentrate to use the right name for the right person. I snapped my focus back to Marlene.

"Thank you for seeing us," I said. "We won't take up a lot of your time. We are helping unofficially with the case of the murder that happened across the street."

She studied each of our faces, looking puzzled.

"I can't quite figure out what your interest is in this case," she said. Her face was drawn, exhausted, which made sense after a day devoted to her own work, followed by a busy shift waitressing.

"I know; we don't look much like police, do we, ma dear?" Bettina laughed. "We wondered if you and your husband might have seen something related to the murder that night."

"No," she said. "As I told the officer who talked with us after our neighbor was found, we were very involved with our own work and didn't notice anything until the police department arrived with lights and sirens. That we took notice of."

"No screams? No argument? No sounds of distress?"

She shook her head again and gestured for us to follow her into the slanted ceiling studio, where a series of colorful journals were laid out on tables. "We were having a heavy discussion about our book—which side of the page should be art and which should be poetry. He thought the art should come first, but I was not so sure. We've always done it the other way. But as he points out, isn't the idea of all this work to open our hearts and minds?"

We spent a few minutes looking over the beautiful books—striking colors and bright birds and hennaed hands on the right-hand pages, handwritten words on the left. I bent closer to read one page:

> *Perhaps it would be best for me*
> *To write only on the front,*
> *But I <u>always</u> want to keep in mind,*
> <u>*Every page has two sides.*</u>

"That's why we're such a good team," Marlene said, smiling warmly. "My husband is always asking questions, and that helps me do the same."

Hearing a bit of rustling behind me, I turned to see that the two sisters had wriggled behind Marlene's worktable to look out the small window, the only one in this part of the studio. "It would not have been easy to see what was going on in that alley," said Violet. Miss Gloria squeezed in with them to peer out.

"Exactly," said Marlene.

"Do you have the pages you were working on that night?" I asked.

"Let me see if I can scramble them up. They were sketches, because we were trying out several scenarios. At that stage, it wouldn't have turned into something we would display or sell." She grinned. "Especially since the hub and I were in disagreement, to put a polite face on it."

She leafed through her drawers and returned with a couple of sketched pages. Again, the right sides had been daubed with bright colors—yellow, red, and orange. There was a broken object in the center of one page that looked like a flower vase. "I think these are from that night."

The colors reminded me of flames. Could Marlene and her husband have seen someone setting that fire and not realized what they were seeing and how important the information could be? The arson was something we'd all put on the back burner, so to speak, as it had been overtaken by the murder.

"So these pages were created on the night of the murder?" I asked. "Or was it the fire?"

"Actually, I think it was the fire," she said. "Tell me again why you ladies are involved with this?"

I explained how Violet and Bettina were visiting to film the Key West edition of their show.

"Unfortunately, our agent looks like a murder suspect, because he was staying across the street and now he's vanished entirely, without a word to us to explain himself," added Violet. "His name is Arvid Smith." She extracted her phone from her handbag and found the photo of Arvid with the two sisters.

Marlene studied it and then handed it back. "I am pretty sure that's not Arvid."

"He's our agent, so I think we know his name," said Bettina straightening her shoulders.

"Who do you think is it, then?" I asked, feeling an uncomfortable tingling.

"His name is Tim Trahant, and he practices Chinese medicine. I heard him give a talk a couple of weeks ago arranged by the French acupuncturist in town, Michel."

This sounded completely wacky. "That can't very well be," I said. "Our Scottish visitors hired him out of a whole lineup of potential agents for their American appearances. He did not present himself as a practitioner of Chinese medicine."

The two women were nodding vigorously as I spoke. "Not a mention of herbs nor needles," Violet said.

Marlene shrugged gracefully. "I could be wrong. Your photo is a bit out of focus, and I certainly don't know Tim well—I only met him the one time. I am a longtime yoga devotee, and the topic of traditional Chinese medicine interested me. I can't imagine why he'd show up in Scotland under those circumstances."

Miss Gloria drifted away from the conversation and returned to peer out the small window overlooking Dey Street. She suddenly shrieked. "I swear that's Rayna on the porch of the bed-and-breakfast."

"Are you certain?" asked Bettina, hurrying over to peer over Gloria's shoulder, Violet on her heels. "That's her for sure." The three women dashed out the door and clopped down the stairs, calling out their thanks to Marlene.

"We'll stay in touch?" I told Marlene, waving as I followed the ladies. "I better make sure they don't get into trouble. Thank you for showing us your work and your space," I added. "If it's okay, I'll tell my husband the detective about this. He will probably want to follow up."

"Of course."

Not that I thought running out to tackle a possible murder suspect was a terrific idea, but maybe it wouldn't hurt to say hello to Rayna—if it was really her. There wasn't a lot of light on that porch. Besides, Marlene had dark half-moons of exhaustion under her eyes, and my ladies were starting to drag a bit too. At least this way I could extract them from the Dey Street art studios without a fuss.

I arrived downstairs, jogged through the courtyard, and crossed the street to the bed-and-breakfast. The three ladies were hugging Rayna on her porch. They were talking over themselves, trying to convince her to return to the Williams Hall event the next day. Violet led Rayna to a wicker chair, and they pulled up more chairs and sat around her.

"Even if you don't want to be part of the contest, we'd love to have you come and bake something," said Bettina. "The topic for tomorrow is easy desserts. I know you must have dozens of them up your sleeve. You probably have all the ingredients right there in your kitchen." Bettina gestured at the door to the bed-and-breakfast. "Won't you come back and join us? We miss you terribly."

"It might be good for you, dear," said Violet, when it looked as if Rayna was going to refuse. "When I was in the deepest doldrums, so distraught about losing my son, I learned that mixing ingredients and making something delicious to share with neighbors and friends helped bring my spirits up just a notch. We pine for your spark." She gulped. "Sorry, ma dear, that was a bad choice of words."

"Maybe," said Rayna. "Though I'm not at all sure I have any spark left."

She looked so sad; it just about broke my heart.

Chapter Twenty-One

Pellegrino and Bros' are interested in making the kind of food that's equivalent to the third abstract painting, he said. This kind of food forces those who make it to "doubt everything including themselves."

—Jonathan Edwards, "A Travel Writer's Bad review of a Michelin-Starred Restaurant Went Viral. The Chef Responded With Images of Horses," *The Washington Post*, December 13, 2021

By the time I herded my group back to the car and drove across town to the parking lot outside Houseboat Row, I felt dog-tired. From the quiet in the car, I thought they were finally worn out as well. The lights in our houseboat gleamed, signaling that Nathan was home. Probably wrung out from the town hall brouhaha and possibly hungry.

I walked the ladies to Miss Gloria's houseboat and wished them good-night. "Let me know in the morning what time you're due in the kitchen. Hope you get a good night's rest; it's been a darn busy day."

"I'll say," said Violet. "We should have been working out to get ready for you folk." They disappeared into Miss Gloria's cabin, giggling over snack possibilities and wondering whether they were too tired for a cup of tea.

Nathan had moved out onto our deck in the dark, a beer in his hand. Ziggy woofed when he saw me. I kissed Nathan and stooped to pat the dog.

"Are you hungry? I can fix you something?" I asked.

"No thanks, I grabbed a sandwich on the way home."

I took a seat in the lounge chair next to my husband and reached for his hand. "What a day. What a night. How long were you at the meeting?"

"The police grilling ended soon after you left. You saw the worst of the crazies. But then we went back to the station to organize a plan. One thing those irate people were right about: this case needs to be solved. The department is starting to resemble a bad sitcom."

"Did you have any luck with that witness, Ellen?"

"She didn't have much more than what you and the rest of the county already heard." He grimaced and took a pull on his beer. "I did get the names of her husband and their friends. I'll follow up and see if someone has a clearer memory of the person running from the murder scene. What else did you and the old ladies get up to?"

"Best not to call them old ladies to their face. You might get hurt."

He laughed. "I know that much."

"We had dinner at Salute." I described our meals only briefly, as Nathan didn't have patience for food details unless they were related to police work. Then I explained our theory about how someone in a high perch might have seen something related to the murder.

"After dinner, we went to Hugh's View and heard Martina playing classical guitar. She's lovely—a bit shy, really." I described what she'd said about Rayna's one visit to the gym.

"Then we realized that our waitress at Salute has a studio on Dey Street right across from the bed-and-breakfast. We walked over—just to take a look. But the lights were on and we had her phone number on a napkin. Before I could stop this from happening, Miss Gloria texted her, and up we went." I summarized that conversation, talking fast and shading the order of events the tiniest amount before Nathan could focus on the fact that we shouldn't be contaminating witnesses.

"It occurs to me that there are two dark-haired men mixed up in this case. Harry, one of the baking contestants—we don't really know a thing about him. Plus Arvid."

Evinrude hopped onto my lap and butted my hand with his head, demanding attention. I was glad to have a minute to figure out how to break the news about the agent's double identity to Nathan. "Short story, Marlene the artist is convinced that Arvid is really a practitioner of Chinese medicine named Tim Trahant." I told him the rest.

"This was news to Violet and Bettina?" he asked, his expression worried.

"They were floored. Gobsmacked. Chagrined. All of the above," I said. I glanced over at Miss Gloria's houseboat to see her kitchen and living room lights flickering off. Nathan's gaze followed mine.

A Clue in the Crumbs

"I'll need to interview the sisters first thing in the morning. Can you set that up?"

I texted Miss Gloria and arranged an eight AM rendezvous on their deck.

Hope we're not in trouble, she texted back. I answered with a smiling emoji. I had no idea.

"I'm pooped," I said to Nathan, "and I haven't a clue what's going on with this case or why our Scottish guests are mixed up in it. Why in the world would their agent have a double identity, and why did he disappear? I will be happy for you to sort it all out." I held my hand out to lead him to bed.

"I'll be there in a bit," he said, but he looked a million miles away.

Chapter Twenty-Two

I want to swallow, but the food just sits there, moist and unwelcome, and I start to panic: Eggs. My mouth is full of eggs.

—Tom Perrotta, "The Squeamish American,"
The New York Times Magazine, October 7, 2007

The three women were lined up on one of the lounge chairs like guilty schoolchildren when we arrived the next morning. Nathan took his seat on a folding chair that Miss Gloria had set out for him. I was grateful that he hadn't chosen to tower over them by remaining standing. They were probably terrified enough without that. He tried to smile.

"I understand that there is some mystery surrounding your agent, some sense that he may not be who he said he was?"

Violet and Bettina nodded in melancholy unison.

"If you don't mind," Nathan said, "take me back to the first time you met him. Your first interaction. What was he like? What did he say?"

The sisters exchanged glances. "Out of all the possible agents, he was the only one who came to Peebles to meet us," Bettina said. "The others we met at the TV station in Edinburgh."

"He made a bigger effort than the others?" Nathan prompted.

Violet leaned forward, one hand on her sister's knee. "Truth, if you must know, he insisted on coming to us. Our producer suggested we meet everyone at the station, for the sake of our privacy and safety, of course, but also to judge everyone in the same setting. Arvid talked us into this arrangement."

"He wanted to see us in our natural habitat, our kitchen," Bettina added with a snicker.

I couldn't help laughing along with her—that was such a perfect description.

"He came to your house, and you brought him to your kitchen," Nathan prompted. "Was there anything about his request or his visit that made you nervous? Maybe set off a warning bell that you brushed off at the time?"

The sisters looked at each other, and for a moment I worried that one of them had noticed something off with Arvid, but they both shook their heads.

"We sat all together at the table and served him tea and our favorite strawberry loaf cake with a strawberry drizzle, plus cookies, in case he was allergic to strawberries. Some people really are," said Violet, as if Nathan might disagree with her. "He was darling. We both found him charming, and then he was so kind about my son. He knew all about Joseph's fall."

"Did it sound as though he'd read the accounts in the newspapers?" Nathan asked. His voice was gentle, but I got the sense he was getting very concerned and didn't want to show this and scare them.

"Now that's a good question, ma dear," said Bettina. "I suppose we assumed that to be true, and how else would he have known?" She glanced at Violet, looking more worried as the conversation went on. "His aunt had died recently, and I gather they were close, so he felt a connection with us that way."

Nathan said, "It seems he really wanted the job."

The ladies nodded.

"What are the benefits of acting as your agent? Do you pay him? Does he reap royalties from the television show? Does he make money in other ways that I'm not thinking of?"

Violet heaved a big sigh. "We never wanted to go down these paths, believe me. We didn't want to make money or to be concerned with other people making money from us. We enjoyed baking and tried out for that TV show on a lark. Those blasted cinnamon scones carried us along like surfers on a big wave."

Nathan chuckled, and I laughed out loud at the image of these two ladies on surfboards.

Bettina picked up the thread. "Ours is a complicated arrangement with Arvid, because we already had a contract with the television station. But as the idea has expanded to your country, it's obviously gotten more lucrative. He did those foreign-rights negotiations, and for that he takes fifteen percent. We were told that was standard."

"What about the bakeware?" Nathan asked.

Violet nodded briskly. "Again, fifteen percent of our income if he sells it into new markets."

"If I could sum it up," said Nathan, "if you do well, he does well."

"Seems only fair," said Bettina, narrowing her eyes a bit. "Are you saying there's something wrong with all this?"

"Not at all," said Nathan. "I am merely trying to establish the clear motives for him pressing to become your agent. Some

162

of them are financial. What about outside of the money? Why might he have been so persistent?"

"I suppose if he adored spending time with us, that would be an incentive." It was Violet's turn to snicker. "He seemed to like us buckets right from the beginning. He knew a lot about us, including our personal history and our baking history. Listen, he even brought a half dozen of our cinnamon scones to that first meeting. He'd made them himself using our recipe."

I was thinking that this took a lot of nerve—to bring baked goods to two of the masters, using their own instructions.

"Not to be cruel, but they were curling stones," said Bettina. "Remember how we felt we had to choke one down anyway?" she asked her sister. "It took an entire pot of tea to wash those heavy mouthfuls down." They tittered with laughter.

Nathan smiled, but he was all business, not about to get distracted. "What about fame in other ways? Endorsements or other food opportunities? I don't know the food world very well, so I would love any ideas about what might draw someone into it."

"It used to be that food rock stars were built on a foundation of cooking and baking skills, or nifty writing, or creating incredible restaurants," Bettina told him. "But now so many celebrities are jumping on board, plus tons of wannabe amateurs, it's very hard to tell who can really cook. A talented editor and food stylist can make something look and sound outrageously good when the cook can't bake his way out of a paper bag."

"TikTok," added Violet sadly. "Every single one of those people who came to the station wanted us to jump on TikTok. Have you looked at those videos?" She practically glared at Nathan.

He held his hands up. "Only if a witness says we will solve the crime that way. Other than that, no interest here."

"Most of the big stars are kids," said Bettina, planting her hands on her hips. "I mean young enough to be our great-great-grandchildren. Sure, we know what we're doing in the kitchen, and we are charming as old ladies go, but we are not TikTok material."

"Neither am I," said Nathan, his face serious though his lips twitched like he was hiding a smile.

All four of us burst out laughing.

"It isn't *that* funny," said my husband.

But it was, kind of.

"Unless I was going for a retro video of a cop imitating a log," he added with a wink.

That got us all laughing again, including Nathan.

"I don't want a bunch of teenyboppers in skimpy clothing sending instant messages or whatever to my handsome husband, anyway," I added, grinning at my guy.

After finishing the interview with the sisters, Nathan and I paused for a minute on the dock to powwow. Connie and Claire were just emerging from their houseboat.

"Morning!" my friend called.

"Morning, Aunt Hayley," said Claire in her little-girl lisp.

"How goes it this morning?" Connie asked.

"It's complicated," I said, dipping my head at my husband.

Connie winked and hurried her daughter by us. "We'll catch up with you later."

"I'm going to go talk to your artist friend Marlene," Nathan told me. "Just a follow-up. Do you think she'll cooperate?"

"I am sure she will, though nobody loves to see the police department show up at their work space."

"In your professional opinion, would someone really murder another person because they wanted fame in the food world?"

A Clue in the Crumbs

I laughed, because this would be so far from what Nathan could imagine. He was an eat-to-live kind of guy, though he tried hard to be complimentary when I spent a lot of time cooking. Food wasn't his thing.

"I think there's lots of money in this food world," I said. "Along with lots of failures of people who thought it would be easy money but don't have what it takes. You need a certain kind of magic, which Violet and Bettina have in spades. But who would've thought a couple of old Scottish ladies would become television stars? It's hard to predict."

"Are you going to the set this morning?" Nathan asked.

"Yes, it's easy-dessert day. I think Mom is making a chocolate loaf cake. She definitely wants me there."

"By now, would you say you know Martina a little bit?" he asked.

I nodded. I didn't know her like an old friend, but I had a sense of her as a person that I thought was true. "I don't get a feeling that she would be responsible for any of this. I think she knows in her heart that her talent is music, not baking. Any number of murders that might eliminate some of the competition won't change that. Nor did I get the sense that she knew Rayna's husband."

"Though you describe her as physically strong. Could it be that she felt protective of Rayna after she came to the gym?"

"Yes, that's possible. I'll keep an eye out and report anything I notice," I said.

"Also, if you get a chance to chat with the third musketeer, Harry, get to know him a little. Find out his food aspirations or sensibility, if either of those is the correct term. But don't scare him off." Nathan sounded stern and utterly serious. "At this point, I very much doubt the murder was food related, but we can't overlook any possibilities."

"Got it."

He leaned over to give me a quick kiss and hurried up the dock's finger toward the parking lot. He paused and looked back.

"I'm going to try to set up a time to chat with this Key West acupuncture dude, Michel. If you'd like to go with me?"

"Oh, definitely," I said. "Text me when you're headed over that way."

Chapter
Twenty-Three

The smell of good bread baking, like the sound of lightly
flowing water, is indescribable in its evocation of inno-
cence and delight.
—M. F. K. Fisher, *The Art of Eating*

By the time we arrived at Williams Hall, the big kitchen was
abuzz. To my surprise, Rayna had returned to the set, and
the staff was clustered around her, offering support. She looked
a bit pale, but her hair was pinned up in a pretty twist, and
she was wearing a cheerful yellow shirt under a flowered apron.
After greeting her warmly, Violet and Bettina moved behind the
counter to get their makeup touched up and then stepped in
front of the cameras and lights.

The producer clapped his hands. "Places, everyone! We are
very far behind on taping and need everyone to cooperate fully.
No drama today, people!" More hand clapping from the producer and some hoots from the audience. He pointed at the
camera people.

Violet smiled broadly as the cameras focused on her face.
"We are so happy to welcome all of you back to *The UK Bakes!*

Key West Edition. Today we are featuring quick desserts, with a focus on not-too-sweet but ever-so-delicious loaf cakes. This kind of cake is perfect for a supper dish when the chef does not have the energy or time to make a full layer cake."

"Or motivation," said Bettina with a laugh. "We are always, always motivated to eat pudding in our household, but baking a cake can seem daunting. All those layers, all that icing!" The sisters giggled like besotted teenagers. "We have asked our competitors to bring their favorite loaf cakes. Our special guest, Janet Snow, along with her trusted assistant, Sam, will be showcasing their chocolate loaf cake with vanilla glaze. Martina Bevis will be providing a quick Key lime pound cake, Harry Sweeting has chosen an old-fashioned poke cake, and Rayna Humboldt will be mixing up her sensational version of strawberry cake with strawberry drizzle."

I remembered the sisters mentioning last night that they'd baked their strawberry loaf when Arvid, now aka Tim, called on them in Peebles. My mother would wilt if she knew that recipe was one of their favorites. Did that mean Rayna already had a leg up? Who knew, maybe they hated chocolate or were allergic to it. Although who in her right mind hated chocolate? My mind was already in a death spiral, and my mother's would be spinning faster.

Behind me, I heard her whispering to Sam.

"You see, even the name she gave to her cake sounds more appealing than ours. Drizzle. Who wouldn't want a strawberry drizzle? No way we win this thing. They are already describing her as sensational."

"I thought you didn't want to win," Sam said in a hushed voice. He'd covered the mic on her collar with his hand.

"Remember, we're only here as placeholders, enjoying the ride."

"But weren't we holding Rayna's place? She's here now, right? We're fifth wheels . . ."

Sam hugged her shoulders and shushed her so she wouldn't distract from the sisters' explanations. He was also probably hoping her words wouldn't be picked up by her mic.

"All of our contestants will be baking at the same time, and we've given them exactly an hour and a half to produce their showstoppers. Although we shouldn't call them showstoppers, as that word may be intimidating."

"So true," said Violet. "These are meant to be homey cakes that an amateur could produce without undue angst. Our bakers may use their allotted time in any way they choose. Some recipes call for extra time in preparation, while other bakers with a dense cake may need the actual oven time."

"If you finish early," said Bettina, "feel free to check your Instagram feed—or better still, add to it with photos of the irresistible Scone Sisters!" She chuckled in delight at her own joke, and Violet chimed in.

The four contestants began to unload their ingredients from bags onto the counter. I signaled to my mother that I'd be working in the next room and gave a thumbs-up. It wouldn't help her nerves to have me hovering around watching. Besides, by this point in the week, I was far behind on my work for *Key Zest* and short on brilliant ideas. One of the things I'd learned over the past couple of years as an e-zine journalist was that grinding out words was the only solution when brilliant ideas and time seemed in short supply. As a writing mentor had once told me, the only thing that couldn't be edited was a blank page. My mother had tons of support, with Miss Gloria planted on a stool right in front of her station and Sam standing by to offer encouraging words and hand her whatever was needed.

I worked for almost an hour, managing to buff up the review of Salute, draft the beginning of an article on local homestyle lunches, and edit the opinion piece about rising restaurant prices in town. In the background, I registered the sounds of oven doors slamming and the cheery noise of the Scone Sisters chatting with the small audience. My nose twitched. Was something burning? I took a deep breath and decided with relief that it smelled more like cake batter hitting a hot oven element than flames licking wood. Hopefully, it wasn't my mother's cake.

Violet's reedy voice floated over all the noise of the kitchen. "Five minutes to showtime, ma dears!"

Then oven timers went off, one after the other, so I saved my work, slid the laptop back into my backpack, and hurried into the kitchen. All four cakes had been pulled from the ovens and removed to pretty blue oblong plates to cool. My mother and Rayna were in the process of painting sugary glazes on the top and sides of theirs. Mom looked half-crazed, glancing every few minutes over at Rayna's station, her face utterly glum.

The producer's assistant rang a bell. With the camera people trailing behind, the sisters prepared to make their way down the counter, stopping next to each of the bakers to hear their stories and taste the warm confections.

Martina went first. "Tell us about your cake, dear," said Bettina as she sliced the end off, revealing a bilious green color. I could tell that the sisters were fighting to suppress horror-stricken expressions.

"I can't remember exactly where this recipe came from," Martina said, "but I've made it my own over the years. It's fast and guests love it, and it comes together in no time. You just take one box of white cake mix, then add one box lime gelatin and a vial of green food coloring." She held up the empty boxes for the cameras to zoom in on while she listed the rest of the ingredients.

I was too stunned to absorb them all. This might have been the perfect quick recipe to wow hungry teenagers, but it wasn't what I'd choose for a TV bakeoff that would be judged by prize-winning bakers. But she seemed so pleased with her offering and so certain that the sisters would love it too. They each took a bite, nodding with faint smiles on their faces.

"Thank you, dear," said Violet, squeezing Martina's wrist. "You must certainly make a delightful and welcoming hostess." Not one word about the cake.

Harry was next. He stood stolid and unsmiling but announced proudly, "This is a poke cake that comes from my mother's side of the family. Because of the time limitations as a busy working mother, she came up with a recipe using strawberry Jell-O and Cool Whip." He sent an angry glance at Martina, as if she'd stolen his idea. "Once the cake is baked, holes are poked into the product with the handle of a wooden spoon, and then the liquid gelatin is poured into the holes. The crowning glory is a layer of Cool Whip. Believe me, this cake is unbelievable!"

From the looks on the Scone Sisters faces, I thought he was probably right. Once again, I found it incredible that someone would bring fast-food ingredients to a sophisticated baking show. Plus I was pretty sure the recipe came right off the back of a Jell-O box. The sisters nibbled politely, then asked a few more questions and moved on to Mom's chocolate loaf cake.

"So interesting that you chose a vanilla glaze, rather than chocolate with chocolate," said Bettina. "Tell us about that?"

The camera swung around and zoomed in on my mother's face. She had frozen solid.

Sam stepped in close to my mother, who had a deer-in-the-headlights-not-going-to-move-until-I'm-flattened look. He leaned over to speak into her lavaliere. "She loves a good chocolate cake, but my favorite is vanilla. In other words, we might call this a marital compromise cake," he said, flashing a wide grin.

"We can't wait to try it!" said Violet, as she sliced into the loaf. "My sister and I have the same argument over and over. I'm a vanilla kind of lassie, and she is strictly chocolate." They each tasted, this time exclaiming over the rich chocolate and perfect vanilla glaze contrast.

The last stop was Rayna's station, where Violet invited her to talk about the gorgeous pink-slathered cake in front of them.

"This cake is best when strawberries are in season, as they are now in South Florida," said Rayna. "You might think that the high water content in the berries would ruin the texture of the cake, but this isn't so. The glaze comes in at the last minute with a burst of berry." She explained how she'd soaked the berries in confectioner's sugar to draw moisture out, then used the flavored sugar flecked with berries as the base for the glaze.

"It is perfectly lovely," said Bettina. She cut a slice and offered a triangle to her sister, and they both nibbled. I watched both of their faces as they struggled to contain their reactions.

"Could we stop the cameras rolling, please? Something isn't quite right here," Violet said, signaling to the producer and cameraman. She put a comforting hand on Rayna's back and leaned in a bit closer. "We watched you make it, so we know the ingredients were added correctly. This combination sounded irresistible to both of us, and it looks beautiful too. I don't know quite how to say this, but I wonder if it could be that your sadness is leaching into your work?" She offered a bite to Rayna, who nibbled cautiously, like a suspicious cat. "Can you taste it? The glaze is perfect, but the cake is salty, like tears."

Rayna began to cry, first a trickle, then sobs. She bolted from behind the counter, pushing through the audience and hurrying down the length of the kitchen counter, past the long dining table, and into the adjoining room. We were left looking at each other, puzzled and concerned. I tapped a forefinger to my chest, signaling to Martha and the sisters that I would follow her and check up on how she was doing.

She was sitting at the desk that I had recently vacated, her forehead on the wooden surface, her hands covering the back of her head, still sobbing. I pulled a second chair up next to her and gently rubbed a circle on her back. "Could I make you a cup of tea?"

Rayna lifted her head to look at me, her face puffy and raw. "Actually, that would be lovely. Three sugars and a piece of your mother's lovely chocolate cake, if they're offering."

I returned to the kitchen and explained the situation to Martha, who helped me make the tea and slide a generous slice of my mother's cake onto a small, flowered plate. At the last minute she added another slice for me and put the food on a tray.

"Thank you. Wish me luck," I said.

While Rayna sipped the tea and we both ate cake, I tried to get her talking. "It seems as though in some ways it may have been too soon to return to a public performance like this one. Maybe we pushed you a little too hard last night?"

"Maybe," Rayna said in a soft voice, "but what else am I to spend my time doing? The bed-and-breakfast is closed to guests for the time being, so there's no work to be done there. No meals to prepare for my husband. His sister has arrived, and she's taking care of all the funeral arrangements."

That struck me as a little bit odd, because wasn't she the widow? Wouldn't she have known her husband best of anyone and wanted to have a say in how he was remembered? I couldn't think of a way to ask whether she wanted this to happen. "That's nice that you have support."

"Besides, it wasn't my tears that ruined the cake; it was Harry."

"Harry?" I asked. "Harry's sadness leached into your cake?"

She looked impatient. "I'm quite certain he switched up my ingredients. But I'll never be able to prove it unless they got it on film." Rayna sighed.

"Why would he want to ruin your cake?" I asked.

She shrugged gracefully. "He either wants to win—fat chance of that—or he doesn't want me winning. Your husband is a police detective, right?"

I nodded.

"What has he said about how close they are to solving my husband's murder?"

"He doesn't talk too much about his work. But he's interviewing a lot of suspects and following up on leads, which makes me think they haven't homed in on anyone in particular. Not quite yet. Maybe, if you wouldn't mind, you could talk to me about the night he was murdered? But even before that, about the fire? It would seem like such an odd coincidence if those two events weren't connected."

"It would." She put the fork she was holding down on the plate and blinked teary eyelashes over her clear blue eyes. I waited until she seemed collected enough and ready to talk.

"Do you mind telling me about the night of the fire?" Maybe talking about the fire would be less fraught than describing her husband's murder. "Let's start there."

"That night, I was busy in the kitchen, proofing the dough for cinnamon rolls, which we'd planned to serve to our guests the next morning. Once they were rolled and formed and set out to rise, I returned out back to our cottage to get dressed. We stay out there during the high season, but I prefer to bake in the big kitchen because of the space and the oven. Plus guests enjoy smelling the scent of the breakfast treats."

"I can imagine the scent of your cinnamon rolls right now." She smiled, and I sensed her shoulders relax. "You were going out that night?"

"I had tickets to *The Full Monty* at the Waterfront."

The Waterfront Playhouse was a local theater known for high-quality performances using a mixture of local and imported talent, mostly musicals that would sound familiar to potential theatergoers. It was located on Mallory Square, less than a half mile from Dey Street, and would have been convenient for Rayna to attend. It was easily walkable from her home—an advantage, because finding parking in Old Town was a nightmare, especially in our busy season.

"Did your husband go with you?" I asked.

She shook her head. "He plays in the Southernmost Bocce League on Monday nights and would not miss that ever." Her face paled as she seemed to realize she'd spoken about him in the present tense. She squared her shoulders and took a sip of tea. "He loved that team more than about anything or anyone else on this island. He'd known many of those guys since he was a kid."

"He grew up in Key West. Was he a Conch, then?" Locals born in Key West bore that nickname, and it was considered a badge of honor.

"Yes. Third generation." She blotted her eyes with the tissue I handed her, then crumpled it and dropped it into her teacup. I stayed quiet to give her the chance to figure out how to continue.

"Once the show was over, I heard sirens and could begin to smell smoke. At first, I didn't think much of it, because the town is so crazy and there are always ambulances responding to some crisis or another. Heart attacks, people falling down drunk, homeless people harassing tourists—it could have been anything. But the closer I got, the stronger the smell became. I was horrified to see that all the action was at my home."

"That must have been so scary," I said.

"Terrifying. Worst of all, once they finally put out the fire, they began to suspect arson. There was no reason why our home would spontaneously combust. Once the fire was out and the suspicion of arson was declared, our customers had to be resettled at other hotels and B and Bs. You can imagine how difficult that was at this time of year."

I nodded. Key West had gotten busier and busier over the past couple of years, but it positively burst at the seams during the winter high season. Hotel and bed-and-breakfast rooms were filled and commanded extraordinary prices for last-minute openings. "Were you and your husband allowed to stay?"

"As I mentioned, we have a cottage that we fashioned out of a shed at the back of the property, where we stay during the busiest times so we have some privacy. After the authorities put out the fire and cleared the area, we were allowed to return." Her shoulders shuddered. "But I was sick with disappointment that Violet and Bettina wouldn't be staying with us. At that point, I wasn't planning on entering the contest, because Vincent was dead set against it. At least this way, I would have gotten to meet them."

"The good news is that you're here and you do have a chance to work with them after all. They are lovely, aren't they? And so is your food." I paused, thinking about the salty cake. I could sort of believe the business about her sadness infusing the cake, but wouldn't a simpler, more straightforward explanation be sabotage? A rat in the kitchen, as she suspected? "Wonder why your husband didn't want you to compete?"

She shook her head, more tears flowing down her cheeks. "He was quite rivalrous when it came to my attention and my time. He loved me so desperately." She glanced at me, and I smiled with encouragement. "He had a suspicious side to his nature, always suspecting someone would try to take advantage. I don't know what made him that way, but no amount of persuading could change his mind once he'd decided that someone would cause him harm."

It wasn't at all clear to me why she'd decided to go against him and enter the contest anyway. "You got home first, it sounds like. Then at some time that evening Vincent must have arrived?" I prompted.

"I texted him right away," she said. "But he's very focused on the games on bocce night. He never looked at his phone until after they'd finished and had a few beers. Quite naturally, he was horrified and furious once he arrived."

"Of course," I said. I decided not to mention that we'd seen him in action, struggling with a police officer. "Do you mind if I ask where you were when they discovered Vincent's body the next night?"

"In bed," she said sadly. "In the cottage. I was so wrung out by the fire—we were up half the night. Plus the drama of the contest and all. The only thing I wanted was to not think about anything. I took a long bath and a sleeping pill, and I was dead to the world by eight PM."

"So awfully tragic," I said, reaching out to take her hand and giving it a little squeeze.

I had so many more questions, but her facial muscles had begun to tremble, and she seemed to be closing down emotionally. She'd abandoned her tea and left most of the cake, while I'd devoured every crumb of chocolate and scraped the droplets of icing left on my plate with the tines of my fork. All that to say, she probably wasn't going to answer anything else.

We heard Violet and Bettina call for everyone's attention in order to discuss the last day's baking challenge. As Rayna and I hurried to the kitchen, I had a text from Nathan. He'd been able to make a date with the acupuncturist in twenty minutes. Could I meet him there? *Yes*, I texted back.

I would have to make it work, because I didn't want to miss it.

The Scone Sisters were in front of the lights again, reviewing the results of the loaf cake competition. Rayna's strawberry cake with strawberry glaze had been edged out by my mother's chocolate, probably because of the salty taste. The others were not in the running this time. The sisters asked the bakers to stay for forty-five minutes so their backstories could be videotaped.

A Clue in the Crumbs

I pushed through the onlookers to tell Miss Gloria that I would be back in time to pick them up and ferry them to Houseboat Row.

"Keep your eyes open," I said. "Definitely let me know if anyone hears from Arvid." Another thought sprang to mind. "You know how Lorenzo mentioned that show *Rat in the Kitchen*? Sniff around a bit and see if there's any reason to think Rayna's cake might have been sabotaged. I know we all looked at the ingredients when the bakers laid them out, but maybe someone slipped a measure of salt into her sugar?"

Miss Gloria nodded seriously, making me hope I wasn't egging her on into danger.

Chapter Twenty-Four

"Outlaw Cook" was a revelation . . . This is the only cookbook I've ever read that understands how men really eat: over the sink, in the dark, greasy to the elbows.

—Alton Brown

Nathan pulled into the parking lot of the acupuncturist's office after me, and we both got out of our vehicles, pausing under the small roof shading the back entrance for a quick kiss.

"Everything okay?" he asked, studying my face. "You look a little drawn."

"Not terrible," I said. "Mom's freaking out, even though her chocolate cake was a winner. Rayna's cake may have been doctored with salt—she suspects Harry, unless it was flavored with her tears, as the sisters suspected."

He rolled his eyes. The police wouldn't consider sadness leaching into a cake to be a reasonable explanation of the facts.

We walked up the stairs to the second floor, and I noticed that the steps listed a bit to the left and creaked as we put weight on them. I wondered how a person with a bad back would even make it up here for treatment. I was a little nervous, not used to operating as Nathan's working sidekick. But I figured he would be less comfortable with nontraditional medicine than I was, and that was probably why he'd asked me along.

We sat in two chairs in the small waiting area until a thin man with curly hair, wearing shorts and sneakers, came out of the office.

"Please come in," he said, in a slight and utterly charming French accent. "I am Michel Gehin." He looked at me.

"Hayley Snow," I said, "and this is Lieutenant Nathan Bransford. Nathan, my husband, is investigating the murder case. You might have read about it—the man stabbed in the back on Dey Street?"

Michel nodded, looking perplexed about why we might be coming to him for information.

"It hasn't been shared widely yet," said Nathan, "and hopefully will not be until the case is solved"—he glowered at the acupuncturist—"but a particular baking pan belonging to two Scottish women who are here to film a cooking show was also found at the scene."

"Baking show," I corrected him with a smile.

"Anyway," said Nathan, "the two women had hired an agent to represent them in the marketing of their bakeware as well as field other opportunities that might come along as a result of the show. The man's name is Arvid Smith. Is he known to you?"

"I don't know him right off the top of my head," said Michel. He ran his fingers under his chin. "Of course, if he was a patient, this would not be something I could share."

"Of course," said Nathan.

He was squinting at the man's face, as if trying to assess what he was telegraphing outside his words. Was the agent one of Michel's patients? It seemed unlikely and bizarre, but what wasn't unlikely and bizarre in this case so far?

"The thing is, there is some suggestion that the man is not who he represented himself to be. He might possibly be a practitioner of Chinese medicine known as Tim Trahant," Nathan added.

Michel nodded thoughtfully. "I do know Tim. He visited Key West from Connecticut several months ago to give a lecture on recent research in acupuncture points."

"I have no idea what that means," said Nathan. "Could you enlighten me?"

"Acupuncture works by stimulating the central nervous system so that chemicals are released to improve healing. Each point"—he held up his right palm and tapped his thumb—"is related to a different part of the body."

Nathan looked skeptical. "What do you know about Mr. Trahant?"

"I'll help if I can, but I don't know him well. He started out with a career in physical therapy and athletic training but became more interested in Chinese medicine and acupuncture. He's uniquely qualified to understand how the body works with the mind."

If Nathan was thinking along the same lines as I was, he would be wondering what in the heck this could have to do with the work of being the Scone Sisters' agent.

This morning Nathan had asked Bettina to AirDrop him the photo of Arvid Smith with his arms around the sisters. Now he held it up to show Michel. "Is this man Tim Trahant?"

Michel peered at the phone and then nodded. "Yes, that is him. Certainly it is."

"As far as you know, does he have regular business in Key West?" Nathan asked.

"As far as I'm aware, he was only here for that brief weekend conference. But I had a very busy week, so I wasn't able to spend time with him outside of the lecture. He's very interested in new research about suicide and homicide points."

Nathan frowned. "Suicide and homicide points? Does that mean something he might do would make the patient he's treating feel homicidal?"

Michel held up both hands. "No, no, quite the opposite. Releasing the chi at a certain point would reduce those feelings."

I wasn't sure how helpful this was. Vincent Humboldt had clearly been killed by the stabbing or bludgeoning, not with a thin acupuncture needle. Did he even know Tim Trahant? Chances were slim, but this was a question we needed to pursue. Maybe Nathan knew more about Rayna's husband than he had told me. Like maybe he'd been one of Michel's patients and had therefore been invited to the lecture?

Nathan thanked Michel, and we left the office.

As we made our way down the narrow stairs and outside into the heat of the afternoon, Nathan said, "You might be asking yourself why we're spending all this time on the silly agent. It's because he's disappeared and he lied about who he is, and that makes him look darn guilty. It's never a good idea to disappear when there is a suspicion of murder." He said that last bit sternly, as if I might consider going into hiding. Or rather, as if he were rehearsing for what he'd tell his colleagues at the police department. Because this case was turning out to be a big hornets' nest, and he would know that I could see that for myself.

"I'm not really wondering, because his fate is so closely tied up with our Scottish friends. They are such darling women, and I hate to imagine that he's taken advantage of them in any way or that any troubles he's having will drag them down. I can't think why this would happen, but do you suppose it's possible that either he's been killed or kidnapped?"

"He was a strapping young man who looked like he worked out a lot. I don't suppose you noticed the muscles?" asked Nathan, grinning.

I batted my eyelashes at him. "You know I don't look at any other man's muscles. But I agree, it would have been hard to take him down without a gun. Assuming he was kidnapped, where would it have happened? Why? Where is he being held, or alternatively and far worse, where is his body?"

Nathan said, "It wouldn't be the first time a criminal executed a second crime to try to cover the first. But it's more logical that he's gone into hiding. I need to get back to the station. Do we have any plans for tonight?" His face looked hopeful, and I knew the hope was that I would say no. He went along with pretty much any social engagements I set up, but he was definitely more of an introvert than me and needed time off from my usual hustle-bustle to recharge.

"Unfortunately, we haven't discussed it. When I go pick up the ladies, I'll try to steer things in that direction. I suspect they're exhausted too. But you can be excused if it turns out we have something on the docket."

He gave me another quick and grateful kiss and got into his SUV, and I checked my phone. According to Miss Gloria's latest text, they were running late at Williams Hall and I still had a little time left.

A Clue in the Crumbs

I sat in the parking lot, thinking about all the possibilities. We'd spent time getting to know Martina, and lots of time thinking about the question marks in Arvid aka Tim's background and identity.

But nobody seemed to know much about Harry, except that he was from Big Pine and was a terrible baker. Although that was an unkind way to put it, even if true. Surely he had some idea of his limitations in the kitchen? Or did he have some compelling reason to want to get close to the Scone Sisters unrelated to food and baking?

I Googled his name, looking for signs of previous trouble. Not much came up, except that he'd had an accounting business and had been a volunteer tax accountant for seniors and lower-income residents at the Big Pine library. I remembered that our new librarian in Key West, Kim Rinaldi, had worked at the Big Pine branch of the county library in her previous job. She might have an inside scoop on this guy, as it was a very small town where pretty much everyone knew everyone else. And everyone else's business.

Chapter
Twenty-Five

The pastry was way too much, and the filling was way too little. As someone said to me when I mentioned it, "Of course the recipe in the book doesn't work. He didn't want to give it out."

"Tarte Sablée au Chocolat," *David Lebovitz Newsletter*, May 17, 2022

Because of the high-season traffic, it took me longer than usual to get from White Street to the library on Fleming. As I alternately drove and waited in a crush of vehicles, I considered my approach with the librarian. Since Kim was still considered new to her position and would be eager to get to know the community, she'd probably agree to talk with me. Once I got my foot in the door, I'd figure out how to coax her to answer questions about a former volunteer.

Two Conch Tour Trains and a trolley delay later, I edged Miss Gloria's Buick into a narrow parking slot behind the library and went in the back door of the pink stucco building.

Inside the main space, Kim was just leaving the circulation desk. I recognized her as the friendly redhead from a spotlight article in the *Keys Weekly*. I introduced myself as a new editor at *Key Zest* and asked if she had a quick minute to chat. After we were seated in her office, I took a little time to ask how she was settling into the new job and told her how I'd found an old Woman's Club cookbook in the Friends of the Library's donation pile that had helped solve a murder. Then I came to the point.

"I have a favor," I said. "I'm hoping you can help. I am spending a lot of time at the bakeoff at Williams Hall this week. The two hosts are staying with my next-door neighbor. I'm sure you've heard about the fire and the murder?"

"Yes, it's awful," she said. "Do the police think the murder is related to the baking contest?"

"They aren't sure yet, but the dead man is the husband of one of the contestants. She's the best baker of the bunch. I suppose it's possible, even if not likely, that someone wanted her out of the running. So we're covering all the bases." I didn't describe what I meant by *we*, but I would if she asked.

She nodded thoughtfully, probably puzzled about what this could possibly have to do with her.

"I wondered if you're familiar with a man named Harry Sweeting?"

A funny look crossed her face, the kind that portended someone telling me they were so sorry, but they were unable to help for reasons of confidentiality, et cetera. Then came a knock on the door, and former library administrator Michael Nelson poked his head into the office.

"I thought I saw you come in. Hayley and I go way back," he said to Kim. He repeated the story about me solving a crime with a cookbook. "Not only is she whip-smart, but you can trust this woman with anything," he added as he left the office.

"Surely Harry isn't baking?" Kim said, then paused. "Anything I say would be privileged information . . ."

"Of course," I said. "Absolutely."

Kim fingered her necklace, a charm of an open book dangling on a silver chain. "I've never eaten something that he prepared, but he didn't strike me as a baking sort. He was perennially sour. He attended every county meeting that was open to citizens and complained to the commissioners."

"About anything in particular?" I asked.

"Spending too much, spending too little. You name the issue, Harry complained. That's all public record," she added, narrowing her eyes.

Which I took to mean she wasn't gossiping, only sharing easily accessible information. I nodded in encouragement. "How was he as a volunteer?"

"He wasn't much different—unfortunately, we fielded a lot of complaints. He criticized his clients for inadequate record keeping, poor fiscal choices, lousy documentation, and so on. We had to start screening potential assignments to include people we knew to be thick skinned, because he was surly and rude. If I had to say, he seemed like a man who had been thwarted in his personal life, and he spread that unhappiness everywhere." She sighed and plucked at the charm again. "I believe his wife left him last year for the electrician who'd been doing repairs on their home. He put on a tough front, but I suspect it was a terrible blow. Honestly, I felt sorry for him. He was kind to volunteer with the taxes, because not everyone has those skills. But I was also relieved when I no longer had to serve as his cheerleader."

"Was he always grumpy like that with people, or can you pinpoint a change?"

"I'd say it got worse after his wife left." She paused, as if wondering whether to say more. "Maybe he had some trouble with his financial planning and accounting business too. That was hearsay, so I can't say for sure."

"Was he ever violent, to your knowledge? Either toward his wife or anyone else?"

"Not to my knowledge," she said firmly. "If you don't mind . . ." She tipped her head at her computer.

"Of course; you must be so busy. It was a pleasure to meet you."

As I drove back to Williams Hall, I tried to summarize what I knew about Harry. Reading between the lines, should we worry that if he flunked out of this contest, he would sink into a slough of despair? In other words, how much did winning mean to a man who might already be feeling fragile? Was it possible that he would lash out? It didn't really make sense that he would have killed Rayna's husband before the contest had even begun. Unless, of course, they had a connection unrelated to baking. I still wondered why he was there in the first place. Face facts: His flavor combinations were discordant, and the sense of lightness so important to baking was entirely absent from his creations. In other words, he might have the personality to murder someone, but I hadn't found a motive.

Martina had missed the mark in her baking in a different way. Her heart was pure gold; she hugged the dishes from her grandmother's kitchen close in order to remember the woman. Entering this contest seemed to be a way of thanking this precious relative and telling the world about her. But did she honestly have no idea that her baked goods were flops? How would she feel if she was dismissed from the contest? Shocked and hurt, at the very least.

Rayna was a cipher too, half wanting to kowtow to her husband and the other half wanting to break away from his restrictions. How did she really feel now that he was gone? I had no idea, other than fragile. My psychologist friend Eric always reminded me of this: what people presented on the outside might have virtually nothing to do with what was inside. People were good at protecting their tender inner selves with outer shells, like mollusks. To find out what it was really like in another person's mind, you had to sit quietly and patiently so that that soft inner being didn't feel threatened as it emerged. Move too abruptly, they'd retreat, and you'd lose your vantage point.

As I trudged up the stairs to Martha's kitchen, I puzzled more over the murder. It occurred to me that I still knew little about Vincent and Rayna's marriage. I remembered that Rayna had mentioned her sister's encouragement to enter the contest. Was this sister in town because of Vincent's death? She would be likely to have more insight into their relationship than most people. For some reason the sentence that Palamina had used to criticize my work came to mind. *Go deeper, Hayley.* I knew that was what I needed to do to understand Rayna right now. She wasn't going to tell me who she really was. Her husband was dead, murdered, and she didn't appear to have close friends. But she had a sister. And I needed to find her.

It would also be good to interview Vincent's sister if we could. She might not have killed her own brother, but from the way Rayna had described her, she was bossy and controlling. Also, one or the other of them, the sister or the sister-in-law, might be able to shed some light on Rayna's black eye that my friends had mentioned earlier this week. But right now I needed to figure out a plan for dinner. Who was counting on me to arrange something, and what could that something be? I sighed. Sometimes being the resident food critic felt like a full-time job.

By the time I reached the kitchen, most of the onlookers had cleared out, as well as Harry, Martina, and my mom and Sam. The crew for the show was packing up equipment for the day and moving the boxes against the far wall. Miss Gloria was slumped with her head on the big dining table and appeared to be dozing. Violet was studying a booklet of notes at the far end of the counter. Rayna was still there, chatting with Bettina at the nearest end of the island. The bits I could hear sounded like a pep talk.

"You are a natural baker," I heard Bettina say. "It would be practically criminal if you're not part of this. No one blames you for today's cake. Anyone can make one mistake measuring, and you've been under enormous stress."

Rayna gazed at her. "Do you think it's possible that someone sabotaged my ingredients, like Harry? I mean before the taping started. That's the only logical conclusion, because I remember distinctly measuring and remeasuring. I was afraid my mind wasn't all there."

Bettina patted her on the back and said in a kind voice, "We will look into that, I promise. I will alert the producer and other staff to keep a very close eye on Harry and Martina. There's no way that it could've been Janet or Sam. Winning this contest wasn't something they sought out. They only filled in as a favor."

The producer approached the two women and waved Violet over to join them. "We're set with the individual contestant interviews, thank you. But I believe your agent wanted some trial video for the bakeware advertisement. We can't reach him"—he scowled at Bettina as if she were responsible—"but since you're here now . . ."

Violet wilted visibly at his words, and I noticed how truly exhausted she looked.

After glancing at her sister, Bettina turned to the producer. "We still haven't received the boxes of bakeware that were shipped. We'll come early tomorrow to finish the taping using the few pieces we wisely packed in our own bags. We're feeling peckish and wabbit, ma dear, as you can see. That's hungry and exhausted to you." She patted her sister's back.

"Sounds good to me. Nine AM on the dot?" he asked.

"Sure." Bettina turned back to her sister. "I'll do the last bits of the cleanup and organize for tomorrow. You should go home, ma dear, and take a nap. Remember, we still have dinner with our sponsors tonight. I've got a second wind, and I'm perfectly capable of calling an Uber when I'm finished."

"I would be happy to help," Rayna offered. "I've got nothing to go home to."

"Sure?" Violet asked, studying her sister's face and then glancing at Rayna.

"Sure," said Bettina back.

"I could stay," I started, but she cut me off.

"If Rayna is able to help a bit and you can take the ladies home, we will be tip-top in no time."

Chapter
Twenty-Six

One of the secrets of cooking is to learn to correct something if you can, and bear with it if you cannot.

—Julia Child

I gathered up Violet and Miss Gloria and their belongings and we headed downstairs to the car, which I had luckily parked nearby. "This has turned into a bit of a rat race," said Miss Gloria. "I thought I was a pretty peppy old gal, but this schedule has worn me thin."

"You and me both, dearie," said Violet, her head wobbling against the upholstery of the back seat. "I don't know what we'd do without you, Hayley."

My phone rang, and Miss Gloria snatched it up from the cupholder in the console between us. "It's Nathan," she said as she accepted the call. "What's happening, dude?"

I heard Nathan laugh, then ask her a question. "He wants to know about dinner obligations. Some of his pals are going to the gym and then out for burgers on Stock Island." She covered the receiver with her palm. "I think he's yearning for a night off."

I had Miss Gloria put him on speaker. "Honey, you should go. Violet and Bettina have plans. Miss Gloria and I can forage and make this an early night. We're all a little wrung out from the goings-on this week."

"Are you sure?" he asked.

"I'm positive. See you when you get home; just don't drive tipsy. The Key West cops are tough on that, I hear."

Once we'd parked at Houseboat Row, the two ladies hurried up the dock for naps and I took Ziggy for a walk. "Sorry, buddies," I said as I snapped on his leash and then rubbed Evinrude's head. "You guys are getting the short end of the stick this week."

We trotted at a fast clip over the Palm Avenue bridge and then the same distance back the other way to get my heart rate up and burn off a few halfhearted calories. Finally, I fed the two furries and settled onto a lounge chair under a big umbrella with my computer and my phone. I sent what I had to Palamina at *Key Zest*, promising her an insider scoop into the Scone Sisters' bake-off. I hoped that would make up for a lackluster performance in my lead article aka opinion piece. In the end, it felt hard to trash anything about the restaurants of Key West. Wasn't everyone doing the best they could with what they had? Plus I had to live here, and I couldn't bear the idea of being despised by the restaurant community, even if my criticism was well deserved.

Then I answered a few emails and skimmed through the Key West locals Facebook page. I remembered that Rayna had mentioned her husband was a regular at the Southernmost Bocce League, so out of curiosity, I navigated to their page.

Before league play begins tonight, at 5:30, we'll have a brief time to share memories and stories about Vincent Humboldt, God rest his soul, and tip a can in his honor.

Someone had posted a meme featuring a man holding a can of Budweiser and a bocce ball, whom I assumed to be Vincent. I had seen him for a few moments the night of the fire, and then again in Martha's kitchen—the resemblance was clear. I looked at the time on my phone, then glanced over at Miss Gloria's place. She and Violet were emerging from the cabin, looking a little fresher than when I'd left them. I hopped over to Miss Gloria's deck, the animals trailing me, and explained my idea.

"If you don't mind another night out," I said to Gloria, "how about popping over to the bocce courts to see if we hear anything interesting about Vincent? Then we could grab a bite somewhere."

"Ready when you are," Miss Gloria said. "I had no plans other than calling the boys and listening to them fret and fuss about whether I'm fading away living alone. I can do that later. Let me run a comb through my tresses, and I'll be good to go." She rubbed a hand over her tousled white curls until they stood up in peaks like the meringue on my recent banana cream pie. Then the screen door slammed shut behind her. Violet and I exchanged looks and grinned.

"She's amazing. I hope to have half her zip at that age," said Violet.

"You will, I'm certain. Will you be okay here by yourself?"

"I've learned that one is never alone on Houseboat Row," said Violet, smiling as she stroked the cats stretched out on either side of her. "Besides, Bettina should be here shortly, and we're to be picked up for dinner at six."

Chapter Twenty-Seven

Neighbors bring food with death and flowers with sickness and little things in between.
—Harper Lee, *To Kill a Mockingbird*

The bocce courts were located at the corner of White Street and Atlantic Boulevard, kitty-corner across the street from the ocean, the AIDS Memorial, and the dog park. The courts were busy pretty much anytime I drove by, particularly in the evenings. The surface was a beautiful rust color, like a red clay tennis court, with cement walkways between the playing areas and chairs at the ends for the players and onlookers. Tonight there were white and blue balls scattered across the red courts, but no one was playing. The small crowd gathered under a white tent marked the place where Vincent's memorial was being held. As we walked closer, I could see they were dressed casually in shorts and T-shirts, some in bare feet, others in flip-flops.

Miss Gloria grabbed my hand to slow me down. "This time, let me do the talking," she said. "My dearest hubby Frank spent a lot of hours in this neck of the woods, so I probably know half the people here, and I know the lay of the land. In fact, I'm sure

I met Vincent a time or two back in the day. So leave it to me, okay?"

I snickered but nodded my assent. In the past, before visits that we'd made together to investigate other cases, I'd been the one telling her to keep her random thoughts to herself. She absolutely meant well, but sometimes her enthusiasm wasn't thought out. Tonight, though, it totally made sense to let her take the lead.

As she'd promised, she was greeted warmly by several of the onlookers. "Gloria! We've missed you," one man called. "Come over here for a big hug."

"We are sorry for your loss," she said to the group at large. "This is my former roommate, Hayley. We're friends of Rayna's, and we wanted to come and pay our respects to all of you, too, who've lost a friend. Some of you will remember that my husband, Frank Peterson, spent many happy hours here, and that made for a happy marriage. Nothing like a little alone time to make the time together feel sweeter."

A chorus of guffaws followed.

"Frank was a lovely man," said a burly man with a white crew cut. A gray shirt stretching tightly over his chest and stomach read *Key West: Close to perfect, far from normal.* "We named him the closer, because every time his team looked like they were finished, they called on him and he pulled them through to victory."

Miss Gloria moved nearer to him, smiling broadly as he told a story about a memorable game her husband had played a role in winning. After he'd finished, he squinted, his gaze shifting from my friend's face to mine. "You said you're friends with Rayna?"

"She's part of the baking event at Williams Hall that we're assisting with," I said. Not exactly accurate, but I hoped the description was close enough to be believable.

"Vincent and Rayna didn't have the same kind of marriage you and Frank did, more's the pity," he said to Miss Gloria. Then he added, "You were always welcome here, even if your technique was weak." She laughed and sputtered in protest.

"How did the marriages differ?" I asked.

"Theirs was much shorter, for one thing. For another, being lighthearted is a great attribute in a spouse. I couldn't have described either of them that way." He looked at Gloria for confirmation. "Your husband was always happy to see you stop by, and so were we."

"Rayna didn't come to watch often?" I asked.

He shook his head. "I don't know if he preferred she wasn't here or if she didn't like the scene. The few times she did show up, he got tense."

This made me wonder if he didn't like to share her with the public. Or had she come to nag or drag him home? "Did they fight publicly when she came?"

"Only the once." He stared at me hard. "The lady over there is Vincent's sister. I'm sure she'd like to hear from you." The man tipped his chin at a dark-haired woman wearing a white sweater and a black skirt, but before we could start toward her, another man called the gathering to order.

For about twenty minutes, we listened to the players tell stories about the dead man. I'd attended this kind of event more often than I liked to think about over the past few years. Usually at a funeral, or especially a less formal memorial service, I listened for the subtext. People were unlikely to come right out and say the man had beaten his wife or cheated his business partner, but you could tell a lot about a person's character from what wasn't said. Tonight, I concluded that while Vincent Humboldt wasn't universally adored, he wasn't hated either. He was admired for his competitiveness, and several of his friends mentioned how he had mellowed and improved over the years. When the more formal sharing of memories ended, I still had no idea why he would've been a target for murder. Not among this crowd, anyway.

Miss Gloria approached a small knot of players, but I lingered in the background. As an older lady with connections through her husband, she might get more from them without me hovering. "This must have been such a shock," she said. "Have you heard anything about who murdered him, and why?"

I couldn't catch their answers from my distance, so I let my attention wander to the rest of the people on the courts. I wondered whether Rayna had not been invited to this gathering or whether she'd simply chosen not to come. When I noticed Vincent's sister standing by herself, I went over to chat.

I introduced myself and expressed my sympathy. "What a terrible time for your family," I said. "Do you also live in Key West?"

"Definitely not," she said. "We were both born here, but I couldn't wait to get out. This town is entirely too small for my liking. In fact, it has the worst of everything: small-minded local people and a bunch of yahoo tourists who think it's Nirvana. To me it felt suffocating."

A harsh assessment, to my mind, but I certainly wasn't going to argue. "I bet Rayna is grateful that you're here." A fact that I wasn't at all sure of, based on what Rayna had said.

"Probably not, to be frank," she said. "But someone needed to take charge. She was hapless when it comes to financial affairs, so he kept her out of theirs. She was the kind of person who panicked when she made a mistake—even something as simple as balancing the checkbook. Vincent was such a whiz at that stuff—he managed a lot of other people's money, so he had to be. Plus they signed prenuptial agreements, as neither was a young person when they married. I'll do my duty and get out as quickly as I can."

From the grim set of her lips and eyes, I doubted she would say much more. "Did Rayna's sister come?" I asked. "At a time like this, having family to lean on means the world."

She squinted suspiciously. "She doesn't have a sister." Then she stalked away, leaving me surprised and perplexed. I could swear that Rayna had told us it was her sister who persuaded her to enter the bakeoff. Either I remembered wrong, or someone was lying.

As I turned to find Miss Gloria, I was astonished to see Rayna herself approach from the parking lot. She was wearing the same clothes she'd had on earlier today and looked more disheveled. I could hardly believe that Vincent's friends would have chosen to exclude her, even if the marriage hadn't been perfect. Sometimes the work of grief was harder with a complicated loss. The group of players and onlookers fell silent as she got closer.

"I saw the note on Facebook that you'd be talking about Vincent," said Rayna. "I hoped you wouldn't mind that I came."

After some awkward moments of silence, the man with the gray shirt and crew cut approached her and drew her into a stiff hug. I wondered whether we should stay longer to see how Rayna was received. On the other hand, regardless of whether their marriage was flawed, this was a private, emotional time, and it felt like we were intruders.

"Ready?" whispered Miss Gloria, who'd come up behind me. "I doubt we'll squeeze much more out of this crowd right now. They've got a lot on their plates."

Chapter
Twenty-Eight

I know that food can't heal our fractures, and that sometimes a salad is just a salad. But I heard this one gives
you a glow.

—Eric Kim, "This Chicken Salad Has It All,"
The New York Times Magazine, June 22, 2022

After a little back-and-forth, we settled on trying for a table in the café above Louie's Backyard. This restaurant on the top floor did not take reservations and served a menu of inter-esting small plates. To our astonishment and delight, a couple had just finished up at one of the two-tops looking out over the fancy restaurant below and then to the water. We each ordered a glass of rosé, then settled on sharing tempura fried green beans, a beet, walnut, and goat cheese salad, stuffed shrimp, and shak-ing beef.

"We can always add more later if we're still hungry," I said. I lifted my glass to clink hers. "Cheers."

My friend clinked back and took a big swallow. "That was awkward there at the end when Rayna showed up, didn't you think?"

I nodded. "They should have invited her, even if it was his thing and his friends and not hers. Even if there was something strange going on between them." I unrolled my napkin and spread it over my lap. "What kind of husband do you think he was?"

"Not the kind that I would marry," said Miss Gloria, adding a wry laugh. "What did you make of Rayna's sister-in-law?"

"Not the kind of relative I'd hope for," I said, thinking of Nathan's sister. We weren't much alike, but even over a short visit to Scotland, I'd grown to appreciate her and like her. I knew we'd grow closer over the years, given the chance to spend more time together. I hadn't gotten that feeling about Rayna's sister-in-law. "I'm puzzled about what she said about Rayna's sister. Rayna said she was the one who convinced her to enter the contest, but this woman said she doesn't have a sister."

"Weird. Maybe that was a fluke and they've never been close, and Rayna thought it better to pretend she didn't exist. Maybe something awful happened between them a long time ago—a fight over money or a guy or who knows what. Families fall out for the strangest reasons. That reminds me—shoot! I never called Frank Jr. I think he actually believes I'm an old lady quivering in my dark living room straightening the doilies on the end tables." She rolled her eyes. "As if the only thing I've got going on is waiting to talk to them!"

As we enjoyed the first plates of crispy, salty green beans and tender beets dotted with creamy goat cheese, I told her what I'd learned about Harry from the librarian. "He clearly isn't a beloved curmudgeon, if her opinion is a reasonable sampling. However, I haven't so far heard anything that would make me believe he had it in for Vincent. On the other hand, I probably should do some internet searching myself. Maybe he's been involved in violent incidents that she didn't feel comfortable sharing."

Miss Gloria was distracted by the buzz of her cell. She glanced down and looked at me, her faced a little worried. "It's Violet, wondering if we've heard from Bettina, by any chance. Their ride is at the pier to pick them up, but her sister didn't come home. I don't like this. I don't like it at all. She's one of the most punctual and reliable people I know."

I reached for her free hand and gave it a squeeze. Hopefully, they were overreacting. How well did my friend really know Bettina anyway? Maybe she'd gone on a walk or started to read something or even lain down for a catnap at Williams Hall. "Let's not panic. I assume she tried texting and calling?"

Miss Gloria tapped that into her phone and then nodded. "Of course, she called her right away. Bettina's not answering."

This did feel worrisome. "Did she mention where they're going to dinner?"

More texting. "They have a reservation here, downstairs."

"Maybe Bettina was running late and decided to come straight to the restaurant? Tell her I'll pop downstairs to take a look and then"—I was thinking on my feet—"why doesn't she come right over? If Bettina's not here, we can help her figure things out. If she is here, no harm done. Just don't eat my half of the shaking beef." I said that last to lighten what had started to feel like a heavy, gray cloud of worry. It didn't really make sense that Bettina would shoot off on her own when they had a definite plan with important sponsors. This dinner sounded like a big deal, and besides, from everything I'd seen so far, the sisters worked as a team.

I dashed downstairs and took a quick spin through the restaurant, both the inside and outdoor sections, and then down a few more steps to the bar overlooking the water that shimmered in the glow of the dock's lights. I could hear the rush of the waves, the clink of silverware, and the hum of conversations—a glorious night to be outside enjoying a cocktail or a special dinner. But Bettina wasn't there. I texted Violet and told her that news and that we'd meet her downstairs on the porch.

We had just about enough time to gobble the rest of our meal and pay for it before the text came that Violet and her dinner companions had arrived. We clattered downstairs to meet her.

Violet introduced us to the sponsors for the Key West segment of the contest. Cory Held I already knew, as *Key Zest* rented space from her realty, Preferred Properties. Kitty Clements was a longtime Key West resident, both a local theatre performer and a philanthropist. I hugged them both and then turned to Violet.

"I've still had no word from Bettina, and now I'm really getting troubled." Her lower lip quivered like a toddler about to lose it. Miss Gloria enveloped her in a big bear hug, and I patted her back. She glanced at Kitty and Cory. "I'm so sorry, but I'm afraid we're going to have to reschedule dinner."

"Would it be helpful if we stayed?" Cory asked.

"Oh no, dear, thank you," Violet said. "We'll be in touch as soon as we know something."

I invited Violet and Miss Gloria to take seats in the rockers on the porch as the other ladies left. "Let's think this through systematically. The last time we all saw her was when she offered to stay behind and get cleaned up and organized for tomorrow," I said. "Isn't that right? Rayna stayed with her as well. Have you tried texting her? We know for sure that she showed up at the bocce courts, as we saw her there. She may know whether Bettina mentioned a change of plans."

Violet smacked her forehead with her palm. "Why didn't I think of that? But I'm too nervous to text and wait for an answer. I think I'll just call."

Rayna's phone rang three times. Finally, she picked up, and Violet explained that Bettina had not shown up for dinner and she was starting to get very concerned. "Did she say anything about going to meet someone before she headed home? An errand, maybe? Hayley and Gloria are here too." Violet put her on speakerphone so we all could listen in.

"Oh dear," said Rayna, "she was fine when I left her. We stayed about another forty-five minutes to get things organized for tomorrow, and then I planned to walk home to get the car and drive to the bocce courts. I invited her to come with me, suggesting I would drop her off at Houseboat Row. She said she was perfectly capable of taking an Uber and happy to wait. She was very excited about the upcoming dinner. That's it. I'm so sorry."

"When you left Williams Hall, did you notice anyone else lurking there? Or maybe pass someone on the street near the building?" I asked.

"Someone nefarious or suspicious," Miss Gloria added. I almost laughed at the way she wrinkled up her forehead and nose, but now was not the moment to tease her.

There was a pause on the line. "There was a dark-haired man, maybe medium build and a little less than average height. I held the door for him on my way out." Her breath caught. "Oh my gosh, I hope she didn't come to any harm."

"To be clear, the man wasn't Harry, right?" I asked.

"Oh no, not Harry. I would have recognized him. I think so, anyway. I've been in such a fog since Vincent . . ." Her voice choked up.

"Understandable," I said. "But if you think of anything else you might have noticed, call right away, okay?"

"Of course," she said. "Now I feel like this could be my fault. Is there something I can do to help? I'd be happy to come over, if that would be of any use?"

Violet said, "No, ma dear, I don't think so. But thank you and get some rest if you can. We'll see you tomorrow as planned. I'm sure she's fine and just got distracted by one of the sights of Key West."

But when Violet hung up, she looked distraught. She rocked back in her chair, pressed her hand to her eyes. "I have a very bad feeling about this. I keep thinking about Arvid . . ."

"Oh my," said Miss Gloria. "Would Arvid harm her?"

Violet began to snuffle.

I really hated to bother Nathan during his much needed and deserved night out with his pals. But this could become an emergency. My fear that something terrible had happened to Bettina was almost as strong as Violet's. I dialed him up and explained the situation. "Maybe you could do a quick check to see if there've been any calls about an older woman in an accident or something? I hate to bother you—"

He cut me off. "Don't be silly. I've been in meetings all afternoon, so I'm not up to speed, but let me check."

In the background I could hear the clanking of weights and a few grunts that told me he was at the gym.

He came back on the phone. "There was an incident outside Williams Hall. An older woman with a head injury was taken to the emergency room. No identification on her, but the description might match Bettina. Was she wearing a white blouse and blue plaid skirt?"

I looked over at Violet, who nodded.

"Oh, good gravy," said Miss Gloria, gripping Violet's hand as she dissolved into tears. "We'd better head out to the hospital right now, because it has to be her."

"I'll meet you there," said Nathan in his gruff don't-even-think-about-arguing-with-me voice. "Fifteen minutes tops."

Chapter
Twenty-Nine

That love has certainly shaped Stanley Tucci's life and
career, in which cooking and eating seem to be the glues
for every relationship, the sidebars to every adventure,
the grace notes of every achievement.
—Frank Bruni, "Hollywood Ending, With Meatballs,"
The New York Times, October 2, 2012

Violet, Miss Gloria, and I piled into the old Buick, and I
drove as quickly as traffic would allow. I figured I could do
some fast talking if we were stopped for speeding. We crossed
over Cow Key aka Cheryl Cates Memorial Bridge to Stock
Island and took a quick left by the golf course. I lurched into
the parking lot adjoining the emergency room, and we flung
ourselves out of the vehicle and hurried toward the entrance.
I stopped at the information desk and explained that Violet's
sister had been brought in with a head injury.

"We need to see her right away," I ended. Which was not at
all how emergency rooms worked—acting at the whim of fran-
tic relatives—but we must have looked desperate enough for the
clerk to check with a higher-up.

"One of you can go in, preferably the blood relative," she said when she'd hung up the phone.

Violet stepped forward, and I whispered to her that we would be in as soon as we could evade the authorities. At least that got a chuckle. Miss Gloria and I paced around the waiting room until I saw my husband rush in. He was wearing gym clothes, and the gray jersey fabric below his armpits was damp with sweat. He looked adorable but also fierce. We trotted over to greet him at the front desk, where he was talking with the same clerk who had repelled us.

"Come on," he said, waving us to follow him. "We can all go back for a moment."

A police officer was stationed outside one of the cubicles, and Nathan spoke with him briefly. Then he motioned again for us to come along.

Bettina was ensconced in a hospital gown on a gurney located between two curtains that separated her from other patients. Her usual neat bob was disheveled, and she looked pale, with a bandage over her forehead, and her hair around the temple was matted with what appeared to be blood.

Her eyes brightened immediately. "Oh ma dears, you are a sight for sore eyes and faces. I didn't mean to ruin all of your evenings by dragging you down here."

Her sister squeezed her hand and gently shushed her. "Where else would we be, ma dear?" Violet turned to the rest of us. "The doctor should be in shortly. There seems to be a little disagreement about whether to keep my firecracker sister overnight."

"I'm really quite fine," said Bettina.

Given her hospital gown and bandaged head, I wasn't sure this could be accurate.

A Clue in the Crumbs

A nurse bustled into the room. "We're going to keep her overnight for observation, although I predict she'll be more trouble than she's worth."

Violet laughed, but I could see how scared and worried she was.

"The rest of you need to wait outside," the nurse said firmly.

But before she could shoo us away, Nathan said, "Unless this patient is headed to surgery or the morgue, I will be questioning her about the attack on behalf of the Key West Police. Her friends will remain in the room."

The nurse glared at him but then retreated through the curtains with a warning. "We'll see what the doctor has to say about this."

"Do you feel well enough to tell me what happened?" Nathan asked Bettina in a gentle voice.

"Yes, I feel fine," she said, touching her forehead gingerly with her fingers. "Just a bit of a sore head. As you know, I was cleaning up and organizing our goods for tomorrow's morning shoot, with Rayna's help." She glanced at her sister, a smile lighting up her face. "You'll never guess—an officer showed up with our wooden knife box. They found it behind the dumpster. I opened it up to see—it still smelled of home, thank goodness. The only thing missing was the big carver. They won't release that until they finish the forensics."

The smile fell off her face at the mention of the probable murder weapon.

"That's a wee bit of good news," said Violet, patting her sister's hand. "But do go on and tell us what happened next."

"When we were almost finished, Rayna wanted to walk me out, and that's where my memory stops." Bettina paused, looking puzzled. "No, that's not entirely it. She agreed to leave, but only after she arranged to call me an Uber, and I said I would be fine waiting, that I'd finish up in a wee while, and she should go ahead home. I'd been asking her more about her husband and whether she knew of anyone who wished him ill. I probably shouldn't have pressed her. What with her husband being murdered and all the drama around that, she looked exhausted. She was torn about leaving me, but she was going to some kind of memorial gathering. I assured her I would be fine—I'm not a helpless old lady."

I started to ask whether she'd noticed anyone around her on the way out of the building or once she was out on the street, but Nathan got there first. "No one approached you or talked with you, as you remember? Either inside Williams Hall or out on the street?"

She shook her head and then winced. "Next thing I know, I'm waking up in the hospital and police and doctors are around me. The annoying thing, aside from the fact that I'll now be marred with black-and-blue, is that my purse is gone."

Nathan said, "Unfortunately, we've had a little problem with purse snatching in town lately. Do you remember seeing anyone around you who might have been watching and waiting for a victim? Did you feel threatened or concerned by any passersby?"

I knew he didn't want to put ideas in her head by suggesting that her assailant could've been someone who'd come down from Miami looking for drugs and drug money, but there had been a run on that sort of crime lately. Sometimes the perpetrators masqueraded as Uber or Lyft drivers but grabbed the belongings of unsuspecting tourists who thought they were getting a ride. My next thought was to wonder whether this incident could be connected to Vincent Humboldt's murder, however unlikely that was.

"Sorry, ma dear," said Bettina. "I remember nothing like that."

"I wonder if Rayna noticed anyone lurking," Nathan mused.

"She didn't," said Violet. "I already talked to her when I was beginning to worry about my sister's no-show."

"Although she did mention seeing a man with dark hair and medium build," I said. "Remember? She thought he was entering the building as she left." Unfortunately, that description could include half the residents and visitors in town, including both Arvid and Harry.

"Did you carry anything of particular value in your bag?" Nathan asked. "What did it look like?"

"Standard-issue scuffed-up blue leather old-lady purse," said Bettina, drawing a laugh from all of us. "It's a whopper, so I can fit in anything I'll ever need. Fortunately, Miss Gloria insisted that we leave our passports in her little safe at the houseboat. I had some dollars and some British pounds sterling, but probably not more than forty between those two." She rubbed a hand over her forehead, fingering the edges of the white gauze. "A vial of blood pressure medicine, my date book, driver's license. Things that will be a nuisance to replace, but I can't imagine who else would want them."

Her face fell. "Plus our knife box. I didn't feel comfortable leaving that in a strange kitchen when we'd already lost it once."

"We'll get it all back safe and sound," I said, patting her hand.

A doctor in a white coat, her hair tied back in a ponytail, bustled into the room. "The nurse said this room is oversubscribed with visitors," she said sternly, but I swore she winked at Nathan. "I'd like to get this patient discharged if someone can promise to stay with her tonight."

"Definitely," said Miss Gloria, pressing into Bettina's side and grasping one hand. Violet was doing the same on the other side of the bed. "We won't let her out of our sights."

Chapter Thirty

People are lonely. They want to be part of something, even when they can't identify that longing as a need. They show up. Feed them. It isn't much more complicated than that.

—Sam Sifton, *See You on Sunday*

Nathan insisted on walking our three women friends down the finger of the dock to Miss Gloria's home, keeping a tight grip on Bettina's arm all the way and giving instructions to make sure she was tucked right into bed. "No alcoholic nightcaps, no midnight walks, no sleuthing escapades, okay?" I heard him ask in his fierce cop voice.

I could picture the meek expressions on their faces as they answered. "Yes, Officer."

I waited for him on our deck with the animals, as Miss Gloria's houseboat would be crowded enough without me hovering. I remembered that neither of the sisters had been able to eat dinner because of the emergency room rhubarb.

If anyone's hungry, I texted Miss Gloria. *Happy to bring something over. I have lots of delicious goodies stashed in the freezer.*

I watched the string of fairy lights sparkle to life on the deck and then a warm yellow glow light up each room. I knew exactly how cozy the houseboat would feel inside, especially with Nathan checking the locks and inspecting every nook and closet. The ladies would feel as safe as they possibly could, given what had happened today.

Since no one seemed to need me urgently and I was super behind in my work, I began to copyedit an article for *Key Zest* that Palamina had sent me, summarizing entertainment on the island for the coming week. Monday, the writer mentioned, was a relatively slow day. Most theaters didn't have productions on Monday, and some restaurants were closed. On the plus side, the bars in Key West were always open.

If I owned a restaurant—and I had no plans for that, ever—I would definitely keep it open on Mondays and give my staff a different day off. Imagine the traffic I might inherit from all the other kitchens that were closed! One of my favorite seafood restaurants, Seven Fish, did this, and it seemed to work well for them.

I heard Nathan call good-night to the ladies, then felt the slight bobble on our houseboat deck as he came aboard.

"Are they all settled in?" I asked. "How is Bettina feeling? Do you think we made the right move, lobbying the staff to release her?"

He kissed the top of my head as he walked by the chair where I was working, headed to bed. "I think they'll be fine. Violet's sleeping right next to her—on the outside of the bed, so if there's a problem, she'll know about it. Believe me, this incident scared them, and if anything goes wrong, they'll call us right away."

I closed my laptop and followed him into the bedroom. "What did you think about the acupuncture guy?" I asked. "We never got a chance to talk about that."

"I don't like the fact that this agent dude not only has a second identity but now has vanished without telling the sisters anything." Nathan's face looked grim and worried.

I nodded as he disappeared into the bathroom to wash up for the night. "For all we know, he could have been the one who clocked Bettina and put her in the emergency room. The question is, why? Why pretend to be their agent, the person who has their best interests at heart, always, but then knock her out? There's something about the rewards of this contest that we don't understand."

Nathan returned to the bedroom, a towel draped over his shoulder. "Of course there is. But we won't solve it tonight." He tossed the towel and the gray T-shirt he'd been wearing into the laundry basket stashed in the closet and rubbed his eyes. "I'm beat." He got into bed. "Come give me a kiss, and let's go to sleep."

After a kiss, I spooned in next to him. He drifted off quickly into light snores, but my mind continued to race. Knowing from experience that I could lie there a long time without sleeping, I got up and carried my laptop out to the deck.

I typed Tim Trahant's name into the search bar and came up with a list of links related to his work. As Michel the acupuncturist had told us, Tim had been trained first as a physical therapist, then grown interested in Chinese medicine. For a few minutes I watched a YouTube video from a talk he'd given several years ago at a retreat focused on mind and body. This was definitely the guy also known as Arvid Smith, though neither this nor the other links about Tim showed any mention of his work as an agent. On the second page, I found a link listing his mother's phone and address in Northern California. (Was nothing left private in this modern world? Apparently not.) I glanced at the oven clock. Ten thirty here meant seven thirty there. Not too late to call. I punched in the number and, after a woman answered, quickly introduced myself. "We're trying to track down Tim Trahant."

"Oh dear, is he all right? He's not been in touch the past few days, and that always makes me worry." Her voice tightened with each word. "I hope he's not mixed up . . ." She stopped speaking before clarifying what he might be mixed up in.

"He's fine," I assured her, though I wasn't sure of that. I explained that I was phoning from Key West for two dear friends who were working with Tim—I hoped this would satisfy her while still being vague—and asked when he'd last called.

"Who did you say you were?" she asked, sounding suspicious now.

I actually felt better that she was asking—I wasn't trying to scam her, but some other caller might be. "I'm working with the Scone Sisters from Scotland. Maybe you've seen their TV show, *The UK Bakes!*?"

"I love them!" she said. "You said Tim is there too?"

"Yes," I said. "They adore him."

"How in the world did he meet television celebrities?"

I laughed, because I honestly didn't have the answer. "It's something, isn't it? When's the last time you spoke?"

The date she gave me corresponded to the day we'd seen him on Miss Gloria's deck, when he'd gotten a phone call, excused himself, and never come back. "Did you by any chance have an emergency that evening? He left our home rather abruptly after a call."

"No, I can't think of a thing," she said. "We had a normal chat."

"Do you have any reason to think he might be in trouble?" I asked. "You mentioned him being mixed up with someone?"

After several minutes of silence, she said, "He was troubled as a teenager. A risk taker. He challenged any authority that he was presented with, including that of my husband and me. Oh dear, I did think he'd grown out of that nicely."

As her voice was sounding increasingly trembly, I hurried to reassure her as well as I could. Then I added, "Do you know anything about his work as an agent for the Scottish ladies?"

"Agent?" she said, sounding confused and more worried. "He's not an agent; he does acupuncture. Which I never could quite understand—releasing the body's energy with needles and all that. But he was the most unusual of my two boys, always flitting toward new subjects. He's very empathetic too; we knew that from when he was a child."

She was on a roll now, and I didn't have the heart to cut her off, even though exhaustion from the week's excitement had suddenly hit me hard.

"When my sister realized she'd been cheated by that awful financial adviser, he flew right in to talk with her." I could tell she had begun to cry. "Wasn't a thing he could do, because the money was already gone, but he was a comfort anyway. That was the beginning of her downhill slide. A month later she had the first stroke. Oh, I miss her so terribly. We spoke every day, and I don't know what to do with myself at one o'clock when we'd each make a cup of tea and chat. She lived in Miami, so teatime was four PM for her and one for me. The time feels so empty now. Tim helps with that, he does."

"He sounds like a wonderful man," I said. I wished it didn't look like he was behind Vincent's death, because I would hate to have to break the news to her that her lovely son was also a murderer. No mother wanted to hear something like that. "I promise to be in touch the instant we hear from him. Oh wait, one more question. Does he have any special interest or expertise in baking?"

A peal of laughter rolled out through my speaker. "Oh lordy no. That man can't hard-boil an egg. My sister always says that's not a fair way to judge culinary skills, because everyone likes their eggs cooked differently. She's right, as usual. But even though Tim can't cook, he was always kind enough to watch *The UK Bakes!* show with my sister and me, because he knows we love it. He helped set us up to view those Scottish ladies bake on Zoom so we could all watch together. They were so sweet, and he seemed to really enjoy their programs almost as much as we did. He felt so badly hearing about Miss Violet's son." She barely took a breath. "I can't think why in the world he'd be pretending to be an agent for those lovely ladies. I don't even know that he's been to Scotland. Between us, my other worry about that boy is money. He's so kind to give it away, and to spend it, so he always seems a little short."

I thanked her for her time and hung up. Poor lady had her tenses all mixed up about who in her life was alive and who was dead. I hoped that her son wasn't gone permanently. Even more than that, I hoped he wasn't a killer. Or—this thought rushed into my head next—a charlatan taking advantage of seniors. He'd clearly known about Violet and Bettina as they baked and chatted toward their own brand of stardom. Had he masqueraded as an agent in order to fleece the sisters, the way someone had cheated his aunt? I guessed they stood to make a lot of money, between the TV shows and the special baking equipment. If I would pay more than market value for a polka-dotted dish with the Scone Sisters' logo on it (and I would), I suspected there would be a lot of other foodies who'd do the same.

I quickly called Mrs. Trahant back. "I thought of one more question. Do you by chance have the name of the financial adviser who took advantage of your sister?"

"Dear me, no," she said. "Once we settled her affairs, I shredded every bit of that."

"What name did your sister go by?" I asked. She had no reason to trust me, but maybe she'd spill.

"Lorraine Avemor," she said.

I thanked her again and hung up. The more I knew, the more confused I felt. Unfortunately, this connection with the sisters on television made Tim look guilty. Like he'd identified them as targets and bored in right where they were most vulnerable.

There was another loose end we hadn't tied up—the fire. Who was really behind setting up the ladies to stay at that bed-and-breakfast? If Tim the agent had organized this, would he have set the fire? Maybe try to ruin Vincent's business? This didn't make sense, and the sisters had even said he'd lobbied against that arrangement. Besides, he would stand to lose a lot if the Scone Sisters were injured or their event was impacted. That made me think it was unlikely that he'd hurt Bettina either. If she'd been badly hurt, she wouldn't be able to perform. When they lost money, he lost money, right?

Was it Rayna who'd encouraged them to come? She didn't seem to have enough chutzpah to do such a thing when her husband wanted her to have nothing to do with the contest. Speaking of her husband, why had he been so dead set against her competing? The question remained: Who had invited them to come? Maybe I could ask Rayna about this. I certainly couldn't ask Vincent, because he was dead. I'd like to ask Tim aka Arvid, but he was missing in action.

I jotted down the questions in a note: *Who set the fire? Who killed Vincent, and why choose the Booth sisters' knife and porcelain? Who knocked Bettina out and stole her purse? Why? Why did this Arvid Smith aka Tim Trahant change his identity and his career? Why did Rayna's strawberry tea cake turn out so salty? Did someone sabotage her ingredients?*

Also, I remembered I'd completely forgotten to fill Nathan in on our trip to the bocce courts. Not that we'd come away with any big news, but he needed to have all the pieces of the puzzle in order to figure out what was really going on. I shut down my computer and returned to bed.

Questions that I hadn't covered in those notes kept popping into my head as I tried again to sleep. What were Rayna's relationships with both Vincent's sister and her own—if she had one? In addition, it occurred to me that I knew next to nothing about how Cory Held and Kitty Clements had ended up sponsoring the Scone Sisters here in Key West. We'd said hello briefly earlier this evening, but then we'd been swept into the emergency room crisis and abandoned them abruptly. Certainly we could learn more about them while chatting with the sisters tomorrow. I focused on my three-part breathing, as a yoga instructor had once taught me, and finally drifted off to sleep.

Chapter
Thirty-One

To retrieve the memories and sensations of the past, Proust relied mainly on the taste of crumbly cakes moistened with lime-blossom tea. The rest of humanity relies on songs.
—David Remnick, "Paul McCartney Doesn't Really Want to Stop the Show," *The New Yorker*, October 28, 2021

Nathan and I went over to Miss Gloria's boat once we saw that the ladies were up and about. I'd woken up super early and taken the extra time to whip up a batch of strawberry scones; the strawberries I'd purchased a few days ago wouldn't have held much longer. Besides, all those ladies deserved a treat baked by someone else.

"How are you feeling?" I asked Bettina. I set the plate of hot scones on the table and nodded a yes to Miss Gloria's offer of coffee.

"A bit like something the cat dragged in," she admitted. She looked like that, too, with a bruise blooming on her forehead and a few streaks of blood in her hair. "Though I'm certain I would have slept much worse in that hospital bedlam. Or perhaps not."

She flashed a wry smile at Violet. "My sister woke me up every hour to make sure I was still alive, as the nurse instructed. I am alive," she added, "just a wee bit grumpy."

We all laughed.

"I certainly wasn't going to let you drift off to meet your maker and leave me to do this tour alone," Violet said, pretending to huff. But the sweet love on her face told me she would have done about anything for her sister.

Bettina turned to Nathan, who was dressed for work, and antsy to get there from the looks of him. "Anything new on the case of the old-lady-purse snatcher?"

"Nothing yet, but I won't let it drop, I promise you," he answered. "Hayley and I came up with a few more questions." I'd confessed to calling Tim's mother once he was up and on his second cup of coffee. He was not happy, even though he was interested in what I'd learned. "Does the name Lorraine Avemor sound familiar?"

The sisters looked at each other, but both shook their heads.

"I know we've discussed this before, but who booked you at Vincent and Rayna's bed-and-breakfast?" Nathan asked.

"Arvid wasn't keen on that arrangement." Bettina smoothed the gray curls away from the bruise on her forehead. "Right, Violet?"

She nodded. "It all happened in such a rush once Martha Hubbard and the people at Williams Hall agreed to host our contest. There were sponsors who'd been persuaded to foot the bill. In exchange, we would be obligated to charm them at a private dinner. I suspect they suggested it.

"By the way," added Violet. "I suspect they are deeply disappointed about our no-shows last night. We may have to grovel."

"Who are these sponsors?" Nathan asked.

"Their names are Kitty Clements and Cory Held. From what Arvid told us, they are rabid foodies and particular fans of ours." Her face fell from delight to disappointment. "Of course, now we don't know what to believe among the things he told us, do we?"

I exchanged a glance with my husband. We both knew those sponsors. They were longtime Key West residents who were very generous with a variety of charitable organizations and active in the local arts scene. Unlikely to be killers.

"I can stop into Preferred Properties while I'm at work and have a chat with Cory," I said, glancing at Nathan. "If that's all right with you?" Her real estate company was on the first floor and rented space upstairs to Palamina for *Key Zest*.

Nathan nodded his okay. "Stick to the facts, and let me know as soon as you've connected. Either I or one of the detectives will talk with Mrs. Clements." He turned back to the three women. "Please, no brave stunts today from any of you. Call me if at any moment you feel endangered. I think we'll learn in the end that last night was a random and unfortunate purse snatching. We're very likely to find your bag in a trash bin once they've stripped out the money."

They thanked him, but I couldn't help thinking he'd added that last bit so they wouldn't worry about Bettina as a target. Most of the crime we heard about in this town happened at night and involved too much alcohol. Sometimes drugs.

Once Nathan was off to work, I returned to our houseboat and tried to focus on the articles that were due to my boss shortly. But I found it hard to concentrate. My mind kept drifting off to Tim aka Arvid's mother and aunt. I Googled his aunt, Lorraine Avemor, and came up with her obituary and an article about a group of senior citizens in her assisted-living facility who'd suffered financial losses related to unscrupulous but unnamed advisers. This made me think of Arvid the agent, though I couldn't imagine he'd bamboozle his own aunt.

Once the sisters and Miss Gloria were dressed, I ferried them to Williams Hall for the final leg of the contest. On the ride over, they seemed deflated, a bit joyless, as if the sense of fun that lighted them up from within had drained out. Whether it was the fire, the murder, the attack on Bettina, or all the above, they seemed more anxious than excited. I knew they weren't themselves when they chose to take the elevator rather than the stairs. The news had traveled quickly through the kitchen staff, the camera crew, and the other contestants, and everyone crowded around Bettina to check on how she was feeling and ask questions about what had happened.

Rayna reached them first. "This is awful. I feel so terrible that I left you in that position. I should have insisted on driving you home myself."

Bettina patted her arm. "You had no way of knowing, ma dear, that a crazy person would come after an old lady. You have so much on your plate, you mustn't worry one instant about me."

Next, my mother and Sam came up to wish her a speedy recovery and offer any assistance needed.

Finally, Martina approached her to give her a gentle hug. "Be careful with a blow to the head," she said. "We've seen this with a few of our customers at the gym who've taken falls. There can be effects for days afterwards, so you should take it slowly. Don't worry if you find you've forgotten things; often the memories get clearer with time."

"Thank you, ma dear," said Bettina. "It's true that my poor mind is a sieve right now. Trust me when I say that my sister and my friends are not going to allow me to get into any more trouble." She glanced at the workers and audience, who were all waiting for the filming to begin. "Seems like we should get this party started today."

"Thank goodness," said the producer. "We have desserts to make. Let's get the sisters in makeup and see what can be done with that shiner."

I thought I noticed a quick flinch from Rayna, as if she might have some experience with covering up bruises. I also realized that Harry was the only one of the contestants who'd had nothing to say to Bettina. The only thing bright about him was the lime-green shirt he was wearing. He stood behind the counter glowering while everyone else greeted her, then stomped off to sit at the big table near the piano.

This might be my one chance to talk with him alone, so I trailed behind him and took a seat across the table. "It's so brave of you to make an appearance competing on a cooking show when you don't have a lot of experience," I said, adding a big grin. "I don't think I'd have the nerve. I'm curious about why you decided to take this on."

He stared at me like I was asking him to get undressed.

"Everything I do in my work is in my head," Harry finally said, tapping his skull with one knuckle. "I wanted to try something using my hands, and I know my grandmother loved to bake. So why not?"

"I guess," I said. "It's sweet that you're using her recipes." I paused, hoping that would get him chatting. It did not. "It's awful what happened to Bettina. Do you remember seeing anyone suspicious lurking around the building yesterday as you left?"

"No," he said flatly. "I'm as mystified about all of this as the rest of you. I left before most of the others and didn't notice anything out of the ordinary. At this point, I want to get on with this stupid contest and see it in the rearview mirror." He frowned, the lines on his forehead creasing. "If I wasn't afraid it would make me look guilty, I'd quit."

I suspected he was lying, but I didn't know about what exactly or for what reason. I reminded myself that it was not my job to solve the crime or even identify the suspect. Nathan only wanted to hear observations and thoughts from my quirky point of view, hoping a different perspective could shine a light on this problem.

Harry looked restless, but I had one more important question. "Did you know Vincent Humboldt?"

The expression on his face snapped shut. "We'd run into each other at Chamber of Commerce meetings and so on. We live in a fishbowl. Sooner or later you meet everyone. I neither liked nor trusted him. Period." He wheeled his chair back, stood up, and left without another word.

On my way out to work, I paused to talk with my mother and Sam for a moment. I kept my voice low. "Keep an eye on things today and call me or Nathan if anything seems off-kilter, okay?" I summarized more details of what had happened to Bettina last night, to their expressions of horror and worry.

"Nothing can go wrong as long as everyone's here together," I said, hoping this was true. "I think Violet and Bettina were scared enough about last night that they won't allow themselves to be cut out from the pack. Keep your ears open, too, in case you hear anyone talking about the murder or the attack. Or anything, really. It's so confusing. Don't turn your backs on Harry. I'll be back in a couple of hours to see the end of the taping."

I gave my mom a quick hug and whirled around to head toward the stairs. Rayna was waiting near the door for me, and I nearly slammed into her.

"So sorry," I said, patting her shoulder. "How are you doing this morning?"

She blew out a big breath of air. "It's going to be a long haul, this dealing with grief and anger. Vincent wasn't perfect, but I loved him. And he didn't deserve to be murdered in an alley."

I squeezed her arm again. "I can't imagine how painful this must be for you. I know the police are working hard to solve your husband's murder. One question that we can't seem to get clear on is how the Scone Sisters ended up being booked in your bed and breakfast?"

She broke into a giant grin, the first real smile I'd seen in several days. "That's easy: Vincent invited them. He knew I wanted them there because I'm such a huge fan. So he reached out to the producer. I was thrilled, because Vincent and I had been arguing over whether he would let me enter the contest. At least this way, I'd get to know the sisters. Their silly agent tried to talk them out of staying with us, but he sure didn't seem to mind getting booked gratis into his own room."

Interesting that she remembered the agent as unhappy with the lodging choice. "Who was paying for their rooms?" I asked.

Now she looked puzzled, as if I were asking strange or ridiculous questions. "They have sponsors, people who were recruited by the higher-ups in the television program. You probably know them—Kitty Clements and Cory Held."

So now we were coming full circle, except the answers were not clarifying who'd been responsible for the mayhem this week.

"Was there anything going on between Vincent and Harry?" I asked. "He acted strangely when I asked him if they were acquainted." I tipped my head toward the counter where Harry was talking with the producer.

"Vincent was pretty sure he was a cheat. He thought he was skimming off the top of his clients' accounts, but he didn't have enough evidence just yet to call him on it."

The producer yelled for all the contestants to gather around the sisters to discuss the day's work.

"Have a good day, and good luck with your creation!" I told Rayna.

I drove across town on Williams Street and south on Southard and parked in the lot behind Preferred Properties. With any luck, Cory would be in and willing to talk with me. I stuck my head into her office.

"Do you have time for a quick question?" I asked.

She looked up from her computer and smiled. "Are you selling that adorable houseboat? I'd have several potential buyers in no time."

"Never," I said, smiling back. "It's heaven on earth. I know that you're one of the sponsors for Violet and Bettina Booth's events this week, and you've heard about the murder in the alley near the B and B where they were to be staying. Last night, Bettina was attacked outside Williams Hall. That's why she didn't show up for dinner."

"Oh no," she said. "We knew they had to cancel urgently, but I never imagined that. They are the sweetest women. I feel terrible about them having problems in our town."

"Do you remember who arranged for their lodging? Was it their agent, Arvid Smith?"

She shook her head. "I don't think Arvid wanted them staying there. But Vincent Humboldt was insistent, so we agreed. Besides that, you know how busy town is during this time of year—I knew it would be almost impossible to move them." At least that was consistent with what Rayna had said.

"Did Vincent know them?" I asked. "Do you know why Arvid was against it?"

"I'm sorry," she said. "It seemed like typical island politics, so I stayed out of it until it was settled, and they asked for a check to cover the cost of the rooms."

"One more question," I said. "Do you know a man named Harry Sweeting? He's one of the contestants in the bakeoff this week."

Her friendly face morphed into a scowl. "You know I can't tell you the details, but he's not a nice man. He's ruthless and will run over whoever's in his way to cut a deal. He knows enough about real estate to be dangerous. That's all I can say."

Upstairs in the office, I hollered out a quick hello to Danielle and Palamina and retreated to my nook at the end of the hall. I loved this cozy space with its slanted ceiling, to which I'd tacked my favorite articles and photos, and its bird's-eye view over bustling Southard Street. The street was busier than usual as the town geared up for tomorrow's Saint Patrick's Day celebration. Already green tutus and beads and *Kiss me, I'm Irish* T-shirts were in full display. Very rarely did Key West celebrate a holiday on one day only—Halloween and Christmas decorations and parties, for example, went on for weeks. Saint Patrick's day was a close runner-up. I sent a quick text to Nathan about my conversation with Cory. *I'll go over to pick the ladies up midafternoon, and we'll figure out a plan for dinner. Probably soup on the deck, as I suspect Bettina will be dragging.*

Just about the time I hit send on that message, two alerts came into my in-box. One was from my mother: *You better get over here, as things are going downhill fast.* The other, from Martha Hubbard, said essentially the same thing but without the emojis and hysterical tone. I packed up my computer and paperwork and headed down the hall to the stairs. This time I knew I needed to stop for a second at Palamina's office and assure her that all was on schedule.

I pasted a big grin on my face. "We're having a little meltdown at the Williams Hall baking contest. I need to run over and put out fires. But not to worry, all my assignments are in the works! I know you'll be pleased."

I bolted out before she could argue.

Chapter
Thirty-Two

Turned out eggs, much like memories, were unforgiving.
—Sonali Dev, *Recipe for Persuasion*

I drove as quickly as I could back across town and found a parking space a few blocks away on Fleming Street. As I dashed up the stairs to the kitchen, I could hear yelling even through the closed door. It sounded like a man and a woman fighting.

"I know you've sabotaged my ingredients, and now I have proof!" The voice was Rayna's, and I suspected it was aimed at Harry.

As I opened the door, I heard Sam's soothing voice. "Let's all calm down for a few minutes and see if we can get this sorted out."

But his bid for calm was overrun, as the other two continued to shout. Then I heard a splat and watched a bowl of whipped cream drip down Harry's face and onto the front of his shirt. I'd seen a similar scene at a key lime pie contest Christmas before last. My first impulse was to laugh, but it hadn't been funny then—it had led to a vicious murder. It wasn't funny now either, because the rage on both of their faces was real. The producer, the cameraman, and Martha had rushed forward to pull them apart, but that only changed the target of Rayna's hysteria.

"I'm telling you—go taste what I have set out, and you'll see for yourself. He's replaced my sugar for the key lime pie with salt. He wants me to fail. As if his disgusting leaden baked goods would ever win any contest anywhere. I've seen your faces when you taste them. Tell him, tell him!" She broke down in hysterical weeping, and Martha took her by the elbow and steered her to the back pantry.

Across the room, Miss Gloria, Violet, and Bettina were seated at the big table in the open dining area. They looked both shocked and exhausted, and Bettina's face was white as meringue.

I headed over to their table. "Are you all okay? What in the world happened?"

"Those two have been sniping at each other all morning," said Miss Gloria. "Finally, it was like someone threw a can of gasoline on a little fire. Whoosh! You saw what happened next."

"Is it true that he replaced her sugar with salt?" I asked.

Violet shrugged, looking far from her usual perky self. "My sister wasn't feeling well, so we backed away from the chaos when they began to fight in earnest."

"You know what," I said, "I think this day needs to be ended here and now. Stay right here, and I'll be back for you in a minute. We'll go home to the houseboat and get a good nap and a good meal and early to bed."

I strode off toward the pantry and knocked on the closed door. Inside, Rayna was hunched on a stool by the window, with Martha hovering nearby. "I think we need to call it quits for today," I told Martha. "Bettina isn't feeling well"—I held my hands out—"and everything appears to be chaos in this kitchen. She needs some TLC and a break from the pressure."

"Agreed," said Martha. She patted Rayna on the back. "Rayna's having a bad day too."

Rayna said, "He really shouldn't be allowed back into this contest. He's mean and he's awful, and he's tried twice to sabotage me and his food is the worst. I wouldn't be the least bit surprised if he was the one who killed my Vincent."

"Why would you think such a thing?" I asked.

"They did some business together. Vincent suspected Harry was cheating people, and he told me he was going to call him on that. Next thing I know, my husband's been stabbed to death."

I met Martha's eyes above Rayna's bowed head. "I think we all need a break. We can start over tomorrow." I heard a fresh wave of hubbub out in the kitchen. I hurried out to see three Key West police officers surrounding Harry.

"You are under arrest for the murder of Vincent Humboldt. You have the right to remain silent. Anything you say may be used in court against you," said a uniformed officer I didn't know.

Harry protested, but the officers pulled his hands behind his back and cuffed him. They marched him out of the room and down the stairs, the onlookers watching in shock. I was dumbfounded about how quickly this had happened. The police must have learned something new and very incriminating to make a sudden arrest. From what I'd been hearing, no one seemed to like Harry much, but only Rayna had accused him of murder.

Within minutes, I was able to collect the three ladies and whisk them out the door. "Come on, the car's only a few blocks away, and then I'll deliver you home to Houseboat Row. I suspect everybody needs a good rest. I'll make some vegetable soup. I can pick up a loaf of nice olive bread at Old Town Bakery, and we'll relax this evening. We've had a little bit too much excitement the last couple of days. We'll save our strength for the final taping and then Saint Patrick's Day dinner tomorrow."

"Ditto on too much excitement," said Bettina, her eyebrows peaking. "We certainly had no idea what to expect, and this beats all. I hope we all survive the denouement. Do you suppose the cameras were rolling during that altercation? It could make for high drama and higher ratings."

She nattered all the way home and down the dock onto Miss Gloria's boat, with Violet gripping her elbow. She sounded a bit unhinged, and I worried again that we'd pushed too hard to spring her from the hospital and return her to hosting the contest. I couldn't wait to call Nathan and find out what they'd learned that had led to Harry's arrest.

Chapter
Thirty-Three

May you escape the gallows, avoid distress, and be as
healthy as a trout.

—Irish blessing

The next morning, I woke later than usual, my body and
mind exhausted from the week's insanity. We'd managed
to get our friends to bed early after a comforting supper of soup
and bread, followed by a coconut cream pie from Fausto's grocery store. Everyone had seemed relieved about Harry's arrest,
if saddened by the information Nathan had been able to share:
Right before he was murdered, it appeared that Vincent had
filed a whistle-blower complaint against Harry, blaming him for
siphoning off money from his clients. It remained to be seen
whether the murder had been an impulsive act after an argument, or whether Harry had gone over to the bed-and-breakfast
planning to kill him. Harry was denying everything.

That news aside, we'd also learned that Rayna's ingredients
had definitely been tampered with, though no fingerprints were
found on her equipment other than a few of her own. They had
yet to tie Harry directly to the attack on Bettina, but Nathan

expected he'd fold under further questioning. As my psychologist friend Eric had mentioned more than once, the best predictor for how someone would behave in the future was how they'd behaved in the past.

"Remember that today is Saint Patrick's Day?" I asked my husband once we'd plowed through bowls of my homemade granola with berries and were both caffeinated enough to speak coherently about the obligations of the day.

Nathan sighed. "I couldn't very well forget. Aside from New Year's Eve and Fantasy Fest, this is my least favorite Key West holiday."

I couldn't blame him for feeling that way. Saint Paddy's Day fell in the middle of a long string of spring break weeks, meaning that college kids and older people behaving like unmoored teenagers crowded the island. There was more trouble on the streets than usual, with overconsumption of alcohol and fighting. On the day itself, ersatz Irish people from up and down the keys and all the way from Miami traveled south for the day to participate in bar hops and booze cruises. Green beer was de rigueur and lime-green tulle the costume of the hour. The police and fire departments would be busy from dawn to the wee hours of the following morning tamping down arguments and transporting drunks to jail. If they were lucky, the town wouldn't suffer a real tragedy, only nuisance calls.

"I promised Violet and Bettina that we'd do a tiki hut sunset cruise. I figured that's a good way to keep them off Duval Street. Not to mention safe from any other bad guy who has it in for them." I laughed, as though this would never happen because Harry was behind bars. "The boat only seats six guests, and counting you, we'll be five. So there won't be a crowd. At

Gloria's insistence, I ordered costumes for everyone. Even Ziggy has a green tutu if you can persuade him to wear it. Can you meet us at Schooner Wharf by five thirty?"

I hadn't told him about this plan ahead of time, guessing he might hate it. The longer he had to think about it, the more excuses he'd find to weasel out of coming.

"Not a chance in H-E-double-L," he said, softening his quick response with a grin that highlighted the dimple in his chin. "In other words, I'm a hard no. I don't think Ziggy's interested either. I do appreciate the invitation, and I think it's a good plan for the ladies. But if you're going for a promotion to captain in the police department, you can hardly parade up and down the main drag or sail the seas of the harbor in a green tutu."

"Maybe you could tell the boss you were acting undercover?" I suggested.

"Under investigation would be more like it," he said. He got up from the table to stash his dishes in the sink and give me a quick kiss.

"We'll see you back here around seven thirty, then," I said. He wasn't going to change his mind, and I couldn't really blame him. "I'm going to start the corned beef in the Crock-Pot this morning so I can work in the office. With all the excitement of the company and the baking show, I've fallen way behind. Mom and Sam should be here around seven to give me a hand."

He looked a little befuddled.

"You remember we're serving dinner tonight on our deck?"

"Sort of," he said, then winked. "I'll be here."

Once he'd left for work, I dragged the huge and rarely used slow cooker we'd received for a wedding gift out of the open storage space above our bedroom closet that passed for an attic.

While my hunk of corned beef browned in the pot, I sliced a big red onion and cleaned and chopped three leeks. Pushing the beef to the side, I added those vegetables to the bowl of the cooker with a dollop of olive oil. I poured a bottle of Guinness beer over all of it, along with the seasoning packet that came with the beef. I'd add potatoes, carrots, celery, and cabbage when I came home for lunch. With the heat set to low, the dog walked, and both animals fed, I headed to the office for the morning.

* * *

I was already deep into my lunch roundup when Palamina clip-clopped upstairs on her trademark heels. She called Danielle and me into her office for a flyover of this week's issue of the e-zine. She looked even more wound up than usual.

"Hayley," she said, pursing her lips and tapping tapered fingers on a printout of the work I'd sent her. "I appreciate that you're attempting to keep your relationships with the city's restauranteurs intact, but I think you need to call them out for this article. There's no point in trying to make a big splash about price gouging without naming names."

We argued back and forth on this until Danielle suggested the compromise of mentioning the most outrageously priced dish at several places. "This way you're calling out the dishes without blasting the restaurants. Maine lobster for seventy dollars, for example. Or truffled pork chops for almost fifty." She wrinkled her nose. "On a side note, the smell of truffles is disgusting. I don't even like walking by a table where someone's eating truffles. I can't wait for the current *truffle this and truffle that* trend to be over." She winked, seeming to notice that she was losing Palamina. "But I'm running off the rails, aren't I? All I'm suggesting is stick to a few outrageous dishes. That way you'll be critiquing the trend without harming the establishments."

Palamina looked at her with a whisker of admiration. "We'll need a rewrite then, Hayley," she said, still assessing Danielle. "On my desk no later than seven, okay?" She returned to her computer, and I retreated to my nook.

If I could keep up a blistering pace, and if I skipped running home for lunch, the pie making at Williams Hall, and the cruise itself, I'd be able to turn everything in before seven. Then I could pick up the ladies at the harbor and get us all home for supper. I texted my mother to see if she or Sam could run by the houseboat to add the prepared vegetables to the Crock-Pot midday and let the dog out. Then I called Miss Gloria and explained the revised plan. Work, work, and work.

"We've already paid for the whole boat, so you won't be obligated to party with strangers."

"It's okay," she said. "Since when have I minded meeting new people? You've neglected your job all week to squire us around. We'll take an Uber over to the harbor and we'll be fine. Honestly, could you picture your big handsome hulk of a husband on a tiki boat?" she asked.

"Not really," I said, grinning although she couldn't see me. "But I would have enjoyed a happy hour on the water, with or without him. How about if I pick you up when it's over and bring you back home?"

"Perfect," she said. "Please don't worry about a thing. We'll have a ball, and we can't possibly find trouble unless we get mowed down, and you know that won't happen."

A text came in from the waitress/artist woman whose studio was on Dey Street. *You told me to let you know if I saw or remembered anything new. This may be nothing, but call me?*

I dialed her back immediately.

"I've noticed lights going on in the bed-and-breakfast at night. On the third floor, which must be the attic." She sounded tentative. Worried. "I don't know if this means anything, but it's odd, because the B and B isn't yet open for business after the fire, as far as I know."

"I'll pass that on right away," I said. "Tell me, did you ever see or hear any fighting or arguments between Rayna and Vincent, the owners?"

She took some time before she answered. "You know living here yourself that Key West is a loud place, and often people behave in ways when they're visiting that they never would at home. Almost like the lid has been taken off a pressure cooker. I've learned to tune those noises out. It sounds odd, but the louder it gets outside, the quieter it gets in my head and the more clearly I can work. I don't know if that makes sense, but it's how my brain works. I can only say I've been working very well the last few weeks."

"Meaning maybe they've been fighting more lately?" I asked.

"I'd say that's true. But I couldn't say exactly over what."

I thanked Marlene and hung up my phone as Danielle came down the hall, holding up her phone. "Oh dear," she said. "My sweetie just texted me. They've released Harry Sweeting because the judge determined there wasn't sufficient evidence to hold him." She grimaced. "It's like catch-and-release day at the jail," Danielle told me. "They let all last night's drunks go too. Some of them are probably back on their barstools already."

She continued with a story about a guy who'd called an Uber from jail to take him straight to Sloppy Joe's. But my mind had snapped back to Harry Sweeting. This news felt disturbing, because it meant the real murderer was still at large. Unless Harry was the murderer and his release had been in error. At least the police would probably be watching him. I worried that the sisters were in the killer's cross hairs, even though I didn't understand why. A tiki boat was probably the safest place on the island. Still, I felt nervous.

I called Miss Gloria again and told her I was going to pick them up at Houseboat Row and take them to the harbor. I'd also retrieve them at the end of the cruise. You never knew who was driving an Uber, who might take an opportunity to steal a group of chatty old women and whisk them off the island. To what end, I couldn't imagine. But my number-one priority was keeping them safe.

Chapter
Thirty-Four

It is more fun to talk with someone who doesn't use long, difficult words but rather short, easy words like, "What about lunch?"

—A. A. Milne, *Winnie the Pooh*

Just after four o'clock, I returned to Houseboat Row to pick up the three ladies. They seemed to have shrugged off the pall thrown over all of us by the murder and, most of all, Bettina's attack. They were dressed in their Saint Paddy's Day best and excited about the cruise.

I found a place to park near the harbor and walked my friends out to the correct dock. All the excitement of the week, along with the fact that a killer was still on the loose, left me feeling a little anxious about being separated from the women—I felt like a mom who'd dropped her kid off to kindergarten, I imagined. Except that these were older ladies, way more fragile than the young tourists, despite being dressed in similar green tutus and headbands with leprechauns bouncing above them on metal springs.

The tiki boat looked exactly like a tropical bar, with a thatched roof, six stools placed around the circular bar top, and the captain and her helm positioned inside the circle. The captain was a well-tanned woman named Chris who looked to be in her late twenties. It didn't help my confidence level that she'd dyed her blonde hair green for the day and wore a tutu herself.

"I won't be able to take the cruise today," I told her. "Please keep in mind that your passengers are senior citizens—all of them—and I'm worried about their safety." Probably scaring her half out of her mind, I began to quiz her about the safety record of the company, the route they'd take, and whether her equipment was up to code and up to date.

After noticing my obvious anxiety, Chris invited me to watch her safety demonstrations—life jackets for everyone were available, plus two easily accessible ring life preservers that would be thrown out if someone fell overboard. "I've captained this very boat for over seven years and never had a single complaint," she said. "Besides, the craft wasn't designed to go over six knots an hour, and I'm an expert at avoiding the wake of other boats so it won't even feel tippy."

Nodding reluctantly, I snapped a photo of the ladies and the captain grinning in front of the boat. I wished them a fun trip and watched them board and launch. Hopefully, they'd have a grand time and wouldn't come back too tipsy. I noticed that a voice mail from Marlene had come in while I was busy.

"I was looking at our drafts from the night of the murder again, and there were so many broken pieces in my drawings. Shards of things. I'm puzzled, because this is not my style, so I began to think maybe I was influenced by something I'd seen or heard. I'm not sure what that would be." She paused. "And maybe one other thing: some papers blew over to our yard the other night that I thought might be important. It looked like bits and snatches of financial records, but the edges of the paper were brown, as though they'd been burnt in a fire. I could only make out part of one name: *Lor Av.*"

Good gravy. Was that Tim aka Arvid's aunt? I sent Marlene a text asking her to call the police about the papers. Since I was almost there anyway, I swung by Dey Street. A UPS truck was parked in front of the bed-and-breakfast. I parked my car behind his and hurried over to the driver, who was returning to his truck from the direction of the artists' compound.

"Happy Saint Patrick's Day," I warbled, thinking this was no time to be subtle. "My husband has been working on the murder case." I gestured at the B and B. "I'm sure you've heard about it. I wonder, do you remember delivering any heavy boxes to the B and B, maybe the day of the fire or the one after? They would have been marked fragile," I told him.

He nodded. "I do remember, because they were shipped from England. I think there were four big boxes. No one was home to take delivery, but the owner has always insisted that I leave any and all packages regardless. He said he didn't have time to be tracking them down. So I tucked them under the porch behind the house, which is what we agreed in the past. Then I left a notice at the cottage." He offered a quick *mind your own business* salute, shifted into drive, and pulled away.

I crept around the side of the B and B, past the blackened sections of the porch to the back, even getting down on hands and knees to peer underneath. There was no sign of any abandoned boxes. I texted that tip to Nathan too, then drove back to the office to put the final polish on my piece.

Miss Gloria texted halfway through the ride to tell me they were having the time of their lives. *Captain Chris wants me to remind you that she has a lot of experience. She's "never lost a passenger yet."* That last bit was accompanied by a laughing emoji and followed by a short video of the three ladies holding up steins of green beer and whooping with laughter that set their leprechauns dancing. The blue-green water of the Gulf sparkled behind them, and it looked like they were having a ball. I was so glad we'd arranged the trip.

* * *

An hour later, I waited on the dock in front of the Schooner Wharf bar, feeling a low-level but lingering sense of dread. I studied the bustling harbor as the various craft that had ferried tourists out for their sunset cruises began to appear on the horizon. There were large sailboats and Hobie Cats with their decks crowded with live bands and drunk tourists dancing, and a smattering of smaller craft like Jet Skis, which all seemed to be driving too fast. I was grateful again that Danielle had suggested the tiki hut for the ladies—they wouldn't have blended in well on bigger boats with a younger audience, a lot of alcohol, and live, loud music. Saint Patrick's Day ratcheted the energy of the party scene even higher than usual. Around me, cups of green beer were being consumed by people dressed in green— green T-shirts, green beads, green tutus, green top hats and ball caps and wigs and more. The music pounding from the bars was more "Danny Boy" and "Molly Malone" than "Wasting Away in Margaritaville" today.

Groups of green-clad tourists who'd taken faster boats began disembarking from their cruises. The tables inside the open-air bars that lined the waterfront were also crowded with visitors, probably enjoying a respite from their own cold-weather lives.

Off in the distance, I spotted the tiki hut lurching slowly into the harbor. It looked like the best of kitschy fun. Miss Gloria and I always included this activity on a list of possibilities for visitors, but prior to the Scone Sisters, none had jumped on it.

I squinted into the reddish gleam reflected in the cirrus clouds left behind after the sun dropped below the horizon. Something didn't look quite right. Their boat was going faster than I'd ever seen a tiki hut move, not the maximum speed of four to six miles per hour, according to both the website and the captain. They appeared to be chasing someone on a Jet Ski. A man, I thought, with dark hair and a green shirt the color of Harry's. I tried to reassure myself by reminding my busy brain that three-quarters of the people on the water were wearing green today. The Jet Ski changed directions abruptly and headed toward my friends.

As I watched in horror, a second small watercraft emerged from behind their tiki hut and crashed into their boat from the other side. Harry's Jet Ski slammed into the tiki hut too and toppled everything over, including the youthful captain and my sweet old lady friends. The passengers' and the Jet Ski drivers' heads emerged from the murky water, and they dog-paddled furiously. They were too far out for me to do anything helpful, so I dialed 911 and explained the problem.

Then I watched as Miss Gloria managed to grab one of the ring life preservers and the captain scissor-kicked toward the other women. Then I saw the Scone Sisters swimming with strong strokes toward the green-shirted Jet Ski's driver, who had also been dumped by the force of the collision. They appeared to be dragging oars behind them. Once they reached him, they used their oars to herd him toward the tiki.

I bolted down the wooden decking that led to the *Yankee Freedom*, a larger boat that ferried visitors to the Dry Tortugas, shouting, "Help! Man overboard!" as I ran. Not that all the passengers were men, but that was the phrase came to mind.

Good lord, where were the police? No nearby sirens predicted a quick rescue, and none of the other boats in the harbor had changed course to head toward the tiki. I hopped over the NO ENTRANCE sign hanging from a chain, dropped my backpack on the dock, kicked off my shoes, and dove in, determined to save their lives.

I swam as quickly as I could toward the splashing shapes in the water, reaching Gloria first. "Are you okay?" I sputtered, grabbing the other side of the ring that she clung to.

"Fine," she said. "Don't let Rayna get away!"

Rayna?

I kicked hard to the far side of the boat, which bobbed lopsidedly in the current. Chris the captain had a blonde-headed woman by the hair and was shouting at her in a stentorian voice. "Given the power vested in me by the United States Coast Guard, you are under arrest."

If I hadn't been so scared and worried, I might have laughed. She sounded a bit like she was conducting a wedding. "You heard her," I shouted back. "Do not try any funny business; the police are on the way." But why was Rayna here?

Another figure bobbed up next to her; this time it was Arvid aka Tim. He had a stubble of whiskers on his face and dark moons under his eyes, and he wore a lime-green shirt.

What the hell? I muttered to myself. Was he in cahoots with Rayna? Where was Harry? I considered swimming over to try to pretend to arrest him, but I was pretty sure he would outmatch me. At that moment, the Scone Sisters swam over, surrounding Arvid and treading water on either side of him while still brandishing their oars.

"Stay right where you are, you impudent rascal," yelled Bettina in a fierce voice.

I dog-paddled in place, ready to cut him off if he tried to escape. Finally, in the distance, I heard the welcome whoop of sirens. A Coast Guard boat swooped in, scooped the women out of the water, and then dragged Rayna and Arvid onto the deck.

"I don't know exactly what's going on here," said the captain of the Coast Guard boat, "but I want everyone's hands on their head until the police get it sorted out. Do you need assistance?" he asked me, as I clung to one of the tiki's pontoons. "We're full up here right now, but I can come back."

"Thank you, I'm fine."

I swam back to the dock where I'd left my belongings and pulled myself hand over hand up the rusty ladder that extended into the water. Both Rayna and Arvid stood at the end of the dock, hands on their heads as instructed. My three women friends were explaining to the police officers who'd arrived on the scene how they were pretty sure one of these people was the correct murderer of Vincent Humboldt. They tripped over each other's words, excited to tell the story.

"This man," said Bettina, pointing to Arvid, "was supposedly our agent. Supposedly the man who was looking out for us in every way, from finances to lodging to whatever. Instead, he knocked me out and stole my handbag."

Arvid began to protest, babbling something about Rayna's attic and how he'd come to save the sisters from her evil. Rayna began to yell over him, flailing and thrashing at the officer who came over to attempt to take control. He finally snapped her into handcuffs, and Rayna drooped to the ground like a pin-pricked balloon. She gazed up at the sisters.

"I didn't mean to hurt anyone, especially you," she said to Bettina. "I only wanted to get my ring out of the knife box." She began to weep hysterically.

The officer in charge shook his head, looking hopelessly confused, and pointed to Rayna and Arvid. "You two are headed for the department, where we can get to the bottom of this. And you three"—he gestured first at the ladies and then to the fire department EMTs who'd arrived on the dock with gurneys— "are headed to the hospital to be checked out. How about you, Captain?" he asked Chris, who was still clinging to the tiki boat, kicking hard to push it closer to the dock.

"I'm fine," she insisted. "No harm done. I must stay with my craft."

"I'm fine too," I added, though no one had asked. "If any of this isn't covered by insurance, please let me know," I called to Chris. "We don't want you to lose your job." I had been furious with her at first for not taking care of my dear friend and the Scottish ladies, but as the events were explained in high, excited voices, I realized that she had done the right thing. She'd tried her best to dodge the incoming Jet Skis, and when that failed, she'd distributed lifesaving equipment and stuck with her passengers.

"I'll be right behind you," I called to Gloria, Bettina, and Violet as they were ensconced on gurneys and rolled off, looking ridiculously excited by the events.

Once the ambulance had pulled away with the ladies carefully belted in, I ran to the car to meet them at the hospital. I dug in my backpack for the phone and saw three missed calls and three voice mails, all from Miss Gloria's sons. I listened to them as I drove, the intensity of their concern increasing with each message: they were waiting at Houseboat Row but no one appeared to be home. Did they understand the plans incorrectly? Was their mother all right?

Oh brother, we were all in trouble now.

Reluctantly, I texted them to take an Uber or a cab to the hospital. All was well, their mother was fine, but I'd rather tell them the whole story in person.

Chapter
Thirty-Five

"The kitchen is tough," Mr. Ottolenghi said. "It's one
of the last bastions in civilized culture that sets out to
crush the spirit."
—Ligaya Mishan, "A Chef Who Is Vegetarian in Fame
If Not in Fact," *The New York Times*, April 26, 2011

I followed the ambulances in Miss Gloria's Buick, wrapped in
a beach towel I'd found stashed in the trunk. The traffic was
brutal; I was held up for fifteen minutes by first a Conch Train
and then a fender bender that blocked the road leading to Palm
Avenue.

By the time I reached the hospital and parked in the lot,
there was no sign of my friends. I checked in at the front desk of
the emergency room and was directed to take a seat in the waiting area. After fifteen minutes of my anxious pacing, the ladies
emerged down the hall that led from the treatment rooms to the
lobby. They were dressed in hospital scrubs and carried plastic
bags that I figured held their wet clothing. In fact, a green tulle
tutu stuck out the top of Violet's bag. Miss Gloria had managed to preserve her leprechaun headband in spite of the harbor

shenanigans, and she still wore it, though it was a little worse for the wear.

"They've released you already?"

"We're right as rain," said Violet. "They couldn't find a single reason to detain us."

"Your sons are on the way," I told Miss Gloria. "I don't think they're happy about all of this. They said they hadn't heard from you in ages and got worried." I wanted to add, *I'm not happy either. You could all have been killed, and maybe you should lose the headgear to show you understand the seriousness of the moment.*

Instead, I asked, "How are you feeling?" Every other question I could think to ask would sound like Nathan. I never appreciated it when his first words after a semidangerous stunt were "What were you thinking?"—even though, as I'd gotten to know him better, I'd grown to realize that he was scared for my safety, relieved more than angry. That's how I felt about Miss Gloria now. This whole mess wasn't exactly her fault—after all, I was the one who'd booked the cruise. But they should have called for help rather than tracking scary people down themselves.

That conclusion sounded a bit too familiar.

"You've had quite an introduction to Key West," I added, smiling at the Scottish ladies.

"Tonight was a wonderful adventure, wasn't it, Violet?" Bettina asked, glancing at her sister.

"Capturing that woman made me feel as though I was really alive, as if I was doing something completely meaningful." Violet looked at me, her brown eyes soft with tears. "You can imagine that hasn't been so easy since my Joseph was killed."

I took her fingers in my hand and squeezed gently. "I can only imagine how hard that's been." I cleared my throat. "But I'm so confused. You think Rayna is the murderer, not Arvid?"

"Oh, definitely," said Bettina, sitting up straight and bristling with excitement. "I don't know where Arvid has been the last few days, but he showed up at exactly the right moment. Once your smart po-lice figure that out, I told him he's invited for dinner at your houseboat. Hope that's okay, ma dear. I always welcome an unexpected guest, but I know not everyone feels that way."

"Of course," I said, laughing at the fact that she could even think I'd be worried by one more at the table at a time like this. "I can't wait to hear his story. That reminds me, I was going to invite Lorenzo too." I pulled out my phone and sent off a quick text.

From the window of the emergency room, I spotted two stocky, middle-aged men in winter coats pile out of an unfamiliar gray sedan with their luggage. They hustled across the hospital parking lot and headed toward the entrance. The sons, Frank and James, had arrived. Their body language was, in a word, tense. For a second word, I'd choose angry. I rushed over to greet them, hoping to head off an unpleasant conflagration.

"Welcome," I said as they swept in through the automatic door. "Everyone's fine; no harm done. Your mom will be so glad to see you anyway."

"Hello, Hayley," said the older of the two, Frank. He was the one I most often talked with when they were checking in on their mother. He pecked me on the cheek. The younger son, James, only nodded, his expression stony.

I waved them over to the corner of the waiting area, where the three ladies sat together, wearing surgical masks around their chins and hospital bracelets on their wrists. Honestly, they didn't look much the worse for wear, though they did appear a bit damp still, with their perfect gray and white bobs drying in funny strands, like mops used several days earlier and left out on a porch to dry. Certainly, their cheerful demeanor had not been subdued. They appeared to be laughing over a private joke.

Miss Gloria sprang up to hug her sons, her bedraggled leprechauns dancing, and introduced them to her Scottish friends.

"Your mother is a bonnie lass, pure dead brilliant, not one bit afraid to fankle with that ill-hertit rascal." This was from Bettina, who had lapsed into Scottish slang with the excitement of the last few hours.

"You should've seen us in the water," added Violet. "Once the tiki hut tipped over, we all had to dog-paddle for a good fifteen minutes," she explained to Miss Gloria's sons. "My sister and I are quite hardy, accustomed to the cold and damp and windy winters and cold swims where we come from in Peebles, Scotland. So you see, we don't chill easily."

"But I've gotten used to the tropical weather, and my teeth were chattering like castanets by the time the rescue crew fished us out," Miss Gloria said. "All we needed were a couple of flamenco dancers," she added, laughing so hard she could hardly finish the sentence.

"They wrapped all three of us in foil packets, as if we were a row of baked jacket potatoes," added Violet. "Getting ready to be served for lunch slathered with coronation chicken."

Now we were all laughing at the image she had painted. Except for Frank and James, who were not smiling, certainly not laughing, and had not contributed a word to the conversation.

A Clue in the Crumbs

"The wee trip itself was amazing as well," said Bettina to the men. "We got to see where the liveaboards are moored off Wisteria Island. A bonfire had been set on the island itself, and we were so curious about who might have been sitting around the fire. Were they cooking dinner? What would they be talking about? Wouldn't it be fun to hire a craft to ferry us out there so we could meet some of those squatters and have a proper chat?"

"Splendid idea," said Violet. "There was wildlife all around the tiki hut too," she added.

"I was the only one to spot a giant stingray burst out of the sea and slap his belly on the water," said Miss Gloria. "According to Chris—she was our captain—there is some kind of parasite that attaches to their stomachs, and they have no way to scrape them off. So they leap out of the ocean, and smack!" She clapped her hands together to mimic the motion. "Knock those suckers loose."

"But we all saw the dolphins. Or are they called porpoises? Anyway, it was magical to watch them arc out of the water," Violet added.

Frank opened his mouth to speak, his face radiating barely contained anger. He took a breath and planted his hands on his hips. "We are not finding any of this all that entertaining, and certainly not funny. Our mother is an old lady, and this is her third near-death experience since she got involved with you. Or have I miscounted?" He glared at me. "We can't afford any more stunts. Because the next one could kill her." He turned to look head on at Miss Gloria. "Maybe you can understand that we are terrified for your safety, and right now we don't particularly care about the sea life you cataloged."

I had no rebuttal, because those things were true. If you counted the time she was thrown into the water off the island of Iona in Scotland, she had had four close calls. Bad idea to remind her sons of that. I thought about explaining how she hadn't really approached death except for the once, which had been before I really knew her, and that she had popped back brilliantly from each episode. But I was afraid my protests would only make them angrier.

"We've put a deposit down on a lovely apartment at an assisted-living facility two miles from my home," Frank continued. "My wife will be able to stop by most days to check on our mother. James and I will see her on weekends. We will be able to bring her to one of our homes for the holidays. We will feel a great weight lifted off our shoulders to have her nearby. I know you've tried your very best to look after her, Hayley, but it isn't enough. Look what's happened here." He held his hand up to stop me from speaking or protesting. "Besides, we are family, and you are not. End of story."

I felt completely sick to my stomach, my whole body heavy, like someone had punched me in the solar plexus and knocked the wind right out of me. I hadn't done a good job looking after her—in fact, I'd egged her on in adventures that were too much for an old lady. Now her dear friends and Key West family of choice would all pay, with her absence. Not to mention my friend herself, who would be devastated about moving.

Meanwhile, Miss Gloria appeared to fold in on herself as her son spoke, shrinking small and pale and looking, well, old. She removed her leprechaun headband and stuffed it into the plastic bag that she clutched on her lap. This was not my lively, spunky, wise friend. This was a shell of an old woman, and she was headed toward living alone in a sterile apartment surrounded by other old people. Regardless of how much I loved her, I was only a neighbor. My voice didn't amount to much. Apparently, Miss Gloria's didn't either.

Violet put a finger up and looked hard at James and Frank. "If I might put a word in? You don't know me or my sister, but we know Gloria. We also know what it's like to be old and to be thrown on the senior dung heap. Everyone thought we'd lead small, meaningless lives after my son died. But we haven't done, not at all. For some elderly citizens, this type of living arrangement that you describe might be just the ticket. For Gloria, it would be a death knell."

Bettina was nodding in agreement, and she took up the conversation as soon as her sister stopped for breath. "Yes, she did raise you boys, and you do share blood. But that was a long time ago, and Hayley is her emotional family now. The family lodged deep in her heart." She leaned across her sister to clasp my wrist. "And Nathan. And Janet and Sam. And Mrs. Dubisson. And all the people on this dock that is her home, even the Renharts next door, who are beloved even if a pain in the bahookie. What about her animals? Does this place you've selected allow two cats? Sparky is her glorious, glossy black moggy and T-Bone the most adorable orange bairn. You can't possibly ask her to choose."

Frank interrupted. "One pet and only on the first floor, which we were not able to reserve at this time." He cleared his throat. "But residents do transition frequently, and then new apartments open up. I'm sure she can find a home for these animals with one of her friends. If not, I'm certain the SPCA would take them."

By now Miss Gloria had tears in her eyes, and so did I. This mess was my fault. I never should have let the women go alone.

Someone needed to talk them out of taking such a terrible risk. And I should have insisted Miss Gloria call her sons every week, no matter how busy she was.

"Aha," said Violet, pointing a finger at Frank. "Transition? You mean to say die. These places always want to sugarcoat it. Although they say people with pets in their lives do tend to live longer. Then you said your wife would be stopping by every day. Has she agreed to that? What kind of relationship has she had with your mother over the years? You need not embarrass yourself publicly in front of us, but in quiet, you might be thinking of this."

I'd heard enough about Henrietta aka the angry gremlin to know the answer to this. There was not a lot of love lost between my friend and her daughter-in-law. Miss Gloria was looking progressively more cheerful as the Scottish ladies talked, almost like a flat tire getting pumped with air.

Finally, she turned to face her sons. "This isn't *Miracle on 34th Street*. You can't just commit me for choosing to be happy and optimistic. I may be old, but I plan to get much older. And I hope to do so gracefully and with joy. Perhaps you hadn't heard that the eighties are the new sixties?" Her face softened as she looked from one to the other son. "Your father and I had planned to live out our lives here. It's where we both felt the most at home. Hayley is certainly my family—and the others are too, exactly as Violet and Bettina described. If I should get to the point where I'm unable to care for myself, we can revisit this conversation. But I have friends to call on and professionals to hire, should I need them. I have a spare room where a caregiver could live, and believe me, there are plenty of kind people looking for work on this island."

As my friend talked, I watched her sons, wondering if they looked a little relieved that their mother had taken a stand. Had the grim frowns on their faces relaxed a bit? Or was that wishful thinking?

Suddenly, I noticed that agent Arvid had come down the hall from the examining rooms and had been listening in on our little group. He seemed to be waiting for an opening. He took a step closer. "You don't know me, but I would have given anything to see my mother and her sister knocking around, so full of life, the way these women are. For what it's worth, I'd advise letting them go until they can't. In my professional opinion, that time is a ways off for this marvelous young lady." He put his hand on Miss Gloria's shoulder and squeezed tenderly.

Frank stared at him as though he was deciding whether to blast him—and all of us—for interfering with his mother. He finally spoke, focusing on Miss Gloria. "You are the most exasperating woman." He glanced at his brother, who gave a curt nod. "Okay, but we'll be checking on you."

"Okay? You mean I can stay here in my own home?"

Her sons nodded.

Miss Gloria clapped her hands. "I'd be thrilled if you can arrange more visits so you can see for yourselves how things are going. When's the last time you came to Key West? I know it's inconvenient and that my houseboat might seem cramped, but I will gladly make you a hotel reservation and pay for it myself. We are family, after all." She popped up and crossed the room to embrace them each in turn.

"Anyway," she said, turning back to the rest of us. "I'm famished. And I'm sure my friends are too. Adrenaline and dog-paddling will do that to a gal. Did you tell the boys what's for dinner, Hayley? What can we bring, besides two extra guests?"

"Could you make it three extras?" Arvid asked, looking sheepish. "I'd love to come too."

"Speaking of mothers, you should call yours sooner rather than later, as she's probably worried sick about you," I said to Arvid aka Tim. "I'm afraid I got her all wound up with my phone call the other night."

"And I for one would like to hear where you've been, young man," said Bettina, her voice a little stern, as though she were his mother.

"Me for two," said Violet, crossing her arms over her chest. "Who the heck are you really, anyway?"

Chapter
Thirty-Six

Food may not be the answer to world peace, but it's a start.
—Anthony Bourdain

Eleven people at a dinner table on our deck was definitely setting a record for our houseboat. Before our guests arrived, we turned on the fairy lights around the deck and lit a dozen tea lights on the table. Once I'd shooed Evinrude off the tablecloth, the place looked magical. My mother and Sam came first, helping me with putting the last touches on our Irish dinner.

James and Frank, who had followed us home from the hospital in an Uber, shed their winter coats and brought over Miss Gloria's two extra folding chairs. Arvid aka Tim arrived shortly after. Lorenzo came last, trotting down the finger of the dock bearing two bouquets of tropical flowers.

"For the Scottish ladies," he said, offering them to the sisters with a shy smile on his face.

"We are so thrilled to meet you," said Violet, flinging her arms around him and squeezing. "If only we'd had a card reading earlier this week, you might have saved us a lot of trouble."

Nathan poured everyone flutes of prosecco, and I passed a plate of French cheese puffs that I kept in the freezer to heat up for just such occasions.

"What can you tell us about what happened this week?" I asked Nathan. "Did Rayna really kill her husband?"

He nodded solemnly. "We think so. They'd been arguing about the sisters and the contest all week, and he finally told her she couldn't be in the contest, period. She says she was so upset and angry that she dragged his financial records and baseball card collection outside, sprayed them with gasoline, and set them on fire. She had no intention of burning the building, but these things tend to spread . . ."

"No predicting what might happen with an accelerant," Bettina added.

A lightbulb went off for me. "Her alibi was the show at the Waterfront theater, but there is no show on Monday nights!"

"They fought again the next morning, and she said he was so angry. He noticed the boxes of dishware that had been delivered. When she got home, he was in the process of smashing up the porcelain and throwing it into the dumpster across the street. Thanks to Marlene's tip and Hayley's persistence, that's exactly where we found it."

"What about the knives? And the attack on Bettina?"

Nathan said, "Rayna was so angry when she saw what her husband was doing that she grabbed a baking dish and hit him. Then she picked up the knife that had fallen out of the box and stabbed him. Afterward, she had the presence of mind to wipe the handle clean, deposit her clothing in the public trash can, take a bath and a sleeping pill, and go to bed."

"Yikes," said Miss Gloria. "Don't mess with Rayna."

Nathan nodded. "We've interviewed Vincent's bocce friends and his sister at some length today. They hadn't been married that long, a matter of years rather than decades. After the first few months of their honeymoon period, things between them got progressively worse." He glanced at me. "Your friend Paul the baker finally admitted that he wouldn't have been shocked to hear about either one of them hurting the other. They fought all the time in private. In some online reviews about their bed-and-breakfast, people were beginning to notice and comment on the tension."

With our dinner guests all buzzing around Nathan for more details, I felt I could turn my full attention to the kitchen.

The corned beef and cabbage dinner that had been simmering all day in the Crock-Pot was ample enough that if we'd had to tackle it alone, Nathan and I would have been eating leftovers for a month. My mother and Sam had brought over the killer Irish lemon pie that she'd planned to bake for the contest, along with salad and their freshly baked Irish soda bread. Nathan had stopped at Key West Cakes to pick up two dozen cookies cut in the shapes of shamrocks and leprechauns and sprinkled with bilious green sugar. No one would go hungry. It was so wonderful to have relatives whom I loved spending time with and who loved to cook and entertain. With the amount of work I had to do this week, it would have felt impossible to throw a dinner party alone. Not to mention the zaniness of the bakeoff and trying my best to protect the older women. But with lots of help from my mother and Sam, I was thrilled to welcome all the out-of-town guests to our table.

"Five minutes to dinner," I said, returning to the deck. "I don't have a seating plan, because I hadn't planned for quite such a party!"

"It looks and smells fabulous," said Lorenzo, with a huge smile. He took a seat in the middle of the table, and the sisters fluttered to either side of him. Miss Gloria's sons sat on either side of her, across from Lorenzo, with Arvid/Tim and the rest of us settling into the remaining places.

"I didn't realize that Scottish people celebrated Saint Patrick's Day," said Frank, looking at Bettina and Violet.

"Scots enjoy a party, almost any party," said Bettina with a hearty laugh. "Besides, our countries are close enough that we do share ancestors." She held up her glass. "To the Irish Scottish peoples, and most of all, to our dear friend Miss Gloria, who brings us on the most astonishing adventures. Slainte!"

"Slainte! To Gloria!" we all shouted out. I watched her eyes fill with tears again—happy this time.

"The queen of Houseboat Row," added Violet.

"Perhaps the dowager mother describes it more aptly," my friend said, grinning hard with delight.

Once we'd filled our plates with corned beef, cabbage, potatoes, and carrots as well as salad and bread, Nathan said, "Now, it's nothing to do with St Patrick's Day, but I sure would like to hear how you recognized Rayna, and how you managed to convince your tiki boat captain to get involved in these shenanigans." He didn't look entirely happy, though he was trying to put a friendly face on the question so our friends wouldn't hold back.

"At first, it was a matter of self-defense more than anything else," Miss Gloria said. "As for our captain, on the voyage out to sea, we filled her in about the contest and the fire and the murder. She'd already heard about a lot of that on Facebook, of course. Then we started talking about how discouraged the police department sounded about catching the bad guy. How we knew we had the puzzle pieces of the story, but no one could quite put it together."

Nathan broke in, using his sternest voice. "We would have shortly reached the same place without putting you ladies at risk. In fact, we were closing in on the woman."

Miss Gloria reached across her son to pat Nathan's arm, looking up at him and batting innocent eyes. "I bet you were, as you have very smart people in your department, starting at the top. However, the longer we talked about the case with our tiki captain, the more obvious it became that Rayna, rather than Harry, had to be the murderer." She began to tick the evidence off on her fingers. "Harry looked guilty at first. Hayley learned that he had become mean since his wife died last year. It showed up in his work at the Big Pine library, where he volunteered to help people with taxes, and all those county commission meetings, where he became the resident grinch. He worked as a financial adviser, but he didn't appear to be well loved by his customers. In other words, he didn't seem to be the kind of man who could talk someone out of their soft drink, never mind their life savings. Plus he came across as desperate about winning the competition, even though his food was basically atrocious to the point of inedible."

Violet interrupted her to add her own opinion. "You see, while we couldn't identify a specific motive, the whole picture fit the profile of a man who would murder to get what he wanted. Since both Vincent and Harry worked in financial services, we concluded they'd had a falling-out, and maybe a fight that led to the attack."

Bettina rested her carefully buttered piece of Irish soda bread on the side of her plate. "Honestly, there were some bits that didn't fit. Then we saw that dark-haired man driving so crazy on his Jet Ski, and that confirmed our theory. You know those optical illusions where some people see one picture and others another? In this case, our unconscious minds were primed to think it would be Harry coming after us. We assumed that he was trying to escape from being captured by the police, and we roared after him."

Tim had been quiet up until now, focused on consuming the huge plate of food in front of him. His eyes twinkled with affection as he looked at the sisters. "Instead, it was me, going after Rayna," said Tim.

"We never expected that," said Bettina. "Because you'd disappeared like a hot steam in the morning sunlight."

"Rayna fooled us all around," added Violet, frowning. "We felt so sorry for her, losing her home and husband. And she baked like a dream. We always give great cooks and bakers the benefit of the doubt."

Bettina leaned in to look down the table at Nathan. "We overlooked the fact that she had all the motive in the world because of the way that man treated her, bullying her and trying to suppress her baking talents. But we didn't believe she had the heart of a killer. Someone who bakes like an angel can't be hiding evil inside at the same time. It would have shown up in her food. Or so we thought."

"What does that mean?" Nathan asked.

"A person with only good in her heart cooks with love," said Violet. "This shows in the finished products. All of Rayna's baked goods were magical, up until the moment they weren't."

Frank reached for the last piece of bread in the basket. "Anybody else want to fight me for this? It's incredible. I thought I didn't like soda bread," he said. "What is that unusual flavor?"

"Thank you," said my mother. "Probably the caraway seeds, which are quite controversial as ingredients go. That last slice is all yours." He nodded his head in thanks.

"What do you mean by 'showing up in her food'?" Frank asked Bettina.

"Bad feelings turn milk and cream and butter sour and make dishes taste bitter," she said. "If you're paying attention, it's easy to tell. Except we didn't put two and two together after the session with the sour cake. We thought she was so sad that the tears made her cake taste salty. She insisted that someone else—and she suspected Harry—had switched up her ingredients."

"I was guessing that part of the problem was too much lemon zest," Violet said. "I know you don't think there is any such thing as too much zest, but there is a difference between us. One of the few." She laughed gaily and squeezed her sister's hand.

"I didn't have a chance to taste it. Did you get the sense she'd forgotten the sugar?" I asked.

The sisters looked at each other, brows creasing with intensity. "Almost like she substituted one of those fake sugars. Baked goods never quite taste right that way. Or maybe a combination of fake sugar and salt. Then we got all focused on the question of supposing someone did sabotage her recipe, how would it have been done? Was there space in the pantry? Did a lot of people go in and out so it might not have been noticed?"

Bettina sighed, and Miss Gloria nodded along with her.

"The cake was a glaring clue that we overlooked. I suspect she'll eventually confess that she switched the ingredients, intending to blame Harry and get him kicked out of the contest. She recognized that he might know something was off with Vincent's work and their marriage. Something lethal."

Violet added, "We assumed that poor woman didn't have a bitter bone in her body. Sad, yes, but bitter, never. As for other suspects, certainly, our agent had not proven himself to be reliable, dependable, or believable. *Hello, my name is Tim, but call me Arvid.*" She lifted her eyebrows in Tim's direction, and he looked instantly chagrined.

"We were glad and grateful that he found us the beautiful bakeware with the most amazing logo, and we fully intended to use it and sell it on our tour," said Bettina, talking about him as if he weren't right there at the table. "Though we weren't keen on some of his terms. But we couldn't figure out why in the world he'd want to kill Rayna's husband. Unless the two of them were fighting over the chance to profit from a couple of old ladies." She held up a forefinger when she could see that several of us had questions. "Hold on to those thoughts."

"We also considered Martina," said Miss Gloria. "She's strong enough to belt him over his head with heavy porcelain and knock him cold, and then stab him. But again, we all agreed her music never sounded a sour note. Even if she can't cook, she plays guitar like an angel. Unless she was supremely good at compartmentalizing and not showing her true self, how could she possibly have the heart of a killer? Although we may want to rethink that theory, since it wasn't true of Rayna."

She turned to glare at Tim aka Arvid. "We are most grateful for your assistance at the harbor. However, you, sir, have some 'splaining to do. Why were you even there? Where have you been the last few days? How did you know Rayna was dangerous?"

He ducked his head in agreement. "First, I need to apologize. No matter what my reasons were or how good, I lied to you ladies and talked you into believing I was someone that I'm not. That was wrong, and I'm sorry."

"After I talked with your mother," I said to Tim, "I began to think that you'd figured out a way to take financial advantage of our friends. That's why you flew to Scotland to charm them into accepting your offer of representation."

He looked horrified. "I hope you didn't tell that to my mother! That wasn't it at all," he said. "I wanted to protect them, as no one had with my aunt." He sighed. "It's a long story."

"We have all night," said Nathan in a gruff voice, and the others around the table nodded in agreement.

"Okay." Tim swallowed hard. "Mom and her sister were best friends, always. Even though they lived on opposite coasts, they talked almost every day. They had tea together on FaceTime. It was so sweet. Sometimes I'd sit in with them via Zoom and listen to the stories. They became very interested in you two." He looked at Violet and Bettina and smiled. "They admired your friendship so much, as I think it reminded them of themselves. They began watching your TV shows and became a little obsessed. The same things that drew other people to you appealed to them. You share a genuine love that people crave for themselves in their own relationships. Besides that, you are so funny and so obviously adore the job you're doing. They loved how much you wanted to share all of this with viewers. Honestly, it was irresistible."

Violet leaned across the table and patted the back of his hand. "Oh, ma dear, how you do go on. You are making us blush."

"But it can't have all been a love fest," said Miss Gloria. "We do want to hear about the reason you changed your name and lied to our friends."

He swiped at the sweat that had beaded on his forehead. "True. Almost two years ago, my aunt hired a new financial adviser. I wasn't paying much attention, and neither was my mother. Before we knew it, he'd weaseled into her confidence and drained her bank accounts. But slickly, in such a way that it wasn't obvious nor was it quite illegal, so he couldn't be prosecuted. We tried, but there was no way to recover her funds. I do believe that was what propelled her into that first stroke and then a downhill slide. We lost her five months later. Mom hasn't been the same since."

The sisters made noises of sympathy and patted his hands.

He fell quiet for a moment. "I grieved her too, of course, and I grieved the great loss of their friendship." He looked intently at Violet, then Bettina. "Mom and I watched your program all the time because it made us both feel closer to her. Then you started talking about needing a logo and wondering whether you should hire an agent and so on. I knew you were in a vulnerable position, Violet, because you'd lost a son. Honestly, grief addles a person's thinking."

"Surely we talk too much," said Bettina, clucking her tongue. "If only we hadn't blathered on about our private business on public television."

"It's hard to say," said Tim. "Because viewers love your openness, and they could relate to your loss. Like my mother and me, people admire the way you found a path to begin to recover. I think you have probably helped a lot of your fans navigate their own losses. Having lost someone dear in my family, I began to think I might be of some use, especially to Violet. But I didn't think you would take to it if I told you straight out that I practiced Chinese medicine and had no experience with representing celebrities." He gave a mirthless chuckle. "So I lied." He turned to face the rest of us. "Lest you think I'm a charlatan like Vincent Humboldt, I've always been good at negotiating. And I did have a brilliant idea for their logo and a friend who could execute it."

"You saw the result, Hayley," said Bettina. "Aren't those baking pans to die for?"

"They are," I said. "I plan to order a whole set as soon as they're available to the public."

Nathan looked horrified, but to his credit, he didn't immediately pounce to ask where in the world I would possibly store any new kitchen gear.

"That's my story," said Arvid/Tim.

"Back up a minute here," Nathan said. "You seemed to have skipped over some important questions. For example, what were you doing giving a seminar on acupuncture in Key West? How did you manage to weasel your way into the confidence of these ladies? What about Vincent—did you know him? Was he the one who swindled your aunt? Where have you been over the last few days?"

From the looks on the faces around me, I suspected they were thinking the same thing I was: these questions explained why Nathan was the professional detective and the rest of us were amateurs at best. Poor Tim was squirming under the light of Nathan's fierce glare.

I stood up. "Before our guest answers all those questions, can I get anybody anything? Another glass of wine? We'll have dessert once we have a chance to digest dinner." Sam helped me refill the empty glasses, both water and wine, and clear some plates away from the table. That would give Tim time to regroup and decide how to explain himself, I thought.

Once Sam and I settled back into our places, Tim began to speak. "I'll take your questions one by one. You guessed it," he said, looking directly at Nathan. "Vincent Humboldt was my beloved aunt's financial adviser. He never paid for what he did to her, along with the other people in his stable of suckers. He was so careful about his swindle that no one could pin it on him or prove that what he'd done was illegal. I'd already been in conversation with Bettina and Violet about the porcelain and the logo and representing them on tour when I heard they were planning to start out in Key West. That, as you can imagine, rang a warning bell big time. I was able to persuade the local acupuncturist to help me set up a seminar, thinking I could check out Humboldt while I was in town. The more I knew of him, the more urgent it felt to get into a position where I could protect Violet and Bettina. So I traveled to Peebles to see them and was able to talk them into allowing me to represent them."

"He was very kind and gentle, and very persuasive," said Violet.

"And so very handsome," added Bettina, who winked at Tim. He was blushing all the way from his cheeks to the roots of his hair.

"When I heard they'd been booked in the Humboldt bed-and-breakfast," Tim said, "I was horrified. I tried every which way to undo that. I did not believe they'd be safe staying there. The best I could do was book a room for myself so I could keep an eye on things."

"Are you certain you didn't set the fire that first night?" I asked. I was appalled at the prospect, and my voice came out sharper than I'd intended. But setting a fire in Old Town was not a small misdemeanor. A lot of people could have been hurt, not to mention the property that could have been destroyed.

Tim held both hands up. "I swear I had nothing to do with the fire—even if I wasn't unhappy with the results, meaning you ladies wouldn't be staying there and possibly falling under Vincent's spell. At least this way I knew you'd be snug and secure among friends." He smiled fondly at Miss Gloria.

Violet crossed her arms over her chest, looking determined. "Tim or Arvid or whatever your real name is, where the heck have you been for the last few days? Why did you leave so suddenly and not come back?"

"I think I owe you the whole story, embarrassing or not," he said with a grimace. "Rayna called that night we were all on Gloria's deck. She said she had an urgent favor related to her husband's death. She didn't dare tell me over the phone. Could I please come right away?" He sighed. "She'd asked me earlier, but I told her I had an appointment to meet with you ladies. This time she sounded brittle, at a breaking point, and I believed she needed me."

"I knew something was wrong!" Miss Gloria exclaimed. "I didn't know exactly what that thing was, but I was worried. So I called Nathan and Hayley home from their dinner."

Tim nodded thoughtfully. "You were wise to realize that—you were well ahead of me. I couldn't think what Rayna's emergency was or how exactly I could help. Maybe she found Violet and Bettina's missing belongings in a guest room? Or the attic? Had someone stolen them? Or she was moving Vincent's stuff to the attic and needed my help and was in danger of breaking down completely? Once I arrived, she asked me to carry a box upstairs, where she clocked me and tied my hands behind my back and my feet to a chair and slapped a piece of tape over my mouth. She told me she'd be up with meals."

"Those were the lights that Marlene saw in the attic over the past few days," I said.

"But why in world would she lock you up?" Violet asked.

He shrugged. "Earlier in the day, I went over there to see if I could pick up any remaining luggage. I chatted with her about the murder, asking if she knew Harry and whether he'd ever been in trouble with his customers. Had he ever worked with Vincent and did her husband mistrust him and so on. I suppose she thought I was getting too close to understanding the truth, even though I wasn't really."

"Meanwhile, for the rest of us who were in the dark, that left one serious suspect, as far as we knew," said Violet. She winked at my husband. "Detective Nathan wasn't sharing a word if there were other people in the running. But we were pretty sure the killer had to be Harry. Or Arvid."

Bettina picked up the thread. "At first, we thought it was Harry, for financial reasons, and then Arvid aka Tim because he'd disappeared in such a fishy way; we never considered Rayna seriously. She was so sweet that evening in the Williams Hall kitchen when she was helping me clean up and organize for the next day. One mistake I made was to ask her a couple of times about her sister." She looked at me. "We all wondered why her sister wasn't in town to help her with her with the funeral, remember?"

I nodded. "Her sister-in-law told me she didn't have a sister. Rayna flat out lied about that."

"Mistake number two came after I found her grandmother's antique class ring wedged into the corner of our knife box after your officer returned it to me," said Bettina. "Rayna must have suspected that she'd dropped the ring when she grabbed the knife from our box to stab her husband. That night in the Williams Hall kitchen, I found it where it had rolled into a corner of the box. I was so puzzled and wondered aloud with her if it might turn out to be important in the murder. So I stashed it in my bag along with our knives, for safekeeping, intending to give it to Nathan later. But then I got knocked on the head and forgot all about it."

"Did Rayna know you'd found it?" my mother asked.

"I'm sure I blathered on about *Goodness, what is this doing in my box?* and so on. She called me an Uber and pretended to toddle off to her home but circled back and hid in the shrubbery. When I walked by, she snatched the purse. But I fought a bit and lost my balance and hit my head. I only remembered what happened when I saw her roaring toward us on that Jet Ski. An image of the ring flashed to mind, and then I knew."

I turned to Tim. "We'd love to hear about how you got away from Rayna." I wasn't going to ask him for details about how she'd managed to tie him up and keep him sequestered in the attic, because he'd only feel embarrassed that a small woman had gotten the best of him. His face flooded pink, but to his credit, he told us anyway.

"She used plastic ties. I kept working on them every time she left the attic, sawing away on a little metal edge I found underneath the chair. Finally, they snapped." He held out his wrists, which looked reddened and chafed. "I followed her to the harbor and saw her get on a Jet Ski. I had a bad feeling she intended to make trouble for you women. My wallet was missing, but I managed to persuade the kid at the rental kiosk that I'd come back later and pay him double."

"This is why we agreed to have this man represent us," said Bettina. "He could talk a dog off a meat wagon." The rest of us howled with laughter while Tim made a face.

"Long story short, I followed her out into the harbor and saw her making an insane beeline for your tiki."

"I can't figure what she planned to do with the four of you after she tipped the boat over. Drown you one by one?" I asked.

"She said she never intended to hurt us, only tell us the truth before she fled town," Bettina said.

Nathan made a face. "We'll find out the true facts," he said. "She did confirm that she murdered her husband—they'd fought about the contest and things got ugly. The important thing is, she's in custody and every one of you is safe."

"We owe you a vote of thanks for saving our mother's life," Frank said to all of us around the table.

"Not to worry; we weren't going to go down easy," said Miss Gloria to her son. "You didn't see my pals managing Tim here with a pair of oars. Everyone underestimates the power of us senior gals."

When we'd served the lemon pie and sugar cookies and everyone was almost finished eating, Sam asked, "We never heard; what's happening with the contest?"

"You don't have to pretend that I was a winner," said my mother to the sisters, smiling. "Rayna was magical when she wasn't evil, ruining her own baked goods and trying to blame poor Harry. Anyway, I am so happy here on this island that I have no urge to travel. And besides, Sam would hate for me to be away. So even though I had a blast baking with you two, I will be happy to cede my position."

"Thank you for that," said Violet with a grimace. "The producer has determined that it will be best for us to move on to the next stop and delete the footage they collected this week. You were the one person who both acted normal and baked fabulous breads and desserts. It's a shame we can't showcase Williams Hall and Key West, but there were too many issues with our other contestants—one murderer and two with limited talent, and one of those with no charm either. The producer feels it could scare off potential sponsors and participants. He suggests we consider this as practice. The good Lord knows we needed it. We can be perfect next time."

She held her hand up for her sister to slap. Frank and James got to their feet, and Lorenzo followed. "Thanks so much for the hospitality tonight. We'll see you all tomorrow before we fly out in the evening."

Miss Gloria turned to look up at her sons. "I was thinking before you leave, you might want to visit the cemetery with me to say hello to your father." She'd had her husband buried in a small plot with space for herself next to him when the time came. She talked with him every time she did one of her cemetery tours—I'd been with her on several of these; it helped her feel close to him. It had saddened her over the years that her sons refused to visit. At this moment, in public, both of their faces held expressions of dismay, looking as though they were trapped, maybe deeply afraid of death and the dead, as I had been before meeting Miss Gloria.

"You know," Lorenzo said, leaning toward them and touching his chest, "that you carry your father in your heart and will always. But it's a comfort to Gloria to have his memory close by and imagine that one day—"

"Not anytime soon!" exclaimed my friend and neighbor.

Lorenzo grinned. "Of course. One day far in the future, she'll join him, and that makes her feel so content." By this point, we all had tears in our eyes.

The brothers looked at each other. "We have a flight out tomorrow afternoon, but we'd love to see the cemetery in the morning. Would you ladies like to meet Dad, too?" asked Frank. "He was quite a pip, a perfect match for our mother."

"We'd love to," said Bettina. "But now, perhaps you'll walk us home?"

Within minutes the deck of the houseboat was empty except for the detritus of the party, Nathan, Sam, and my mother. "Some party you Snow women throw," said Sam with a grin. "I'll help Nathan clear the dishes while you two relax."

"Do you think Miss Gloria and her sons are okay?" I asked my mother, once the men had gone into the kitchen.

"I think they will be," she said. "It's a hard transition, watching your parents age and the roles between you shift. I hope I'll have half the grace and the energy those three do when my time comes."

I felt my eyes get shiny with tears and got up to give her a big hug. I noticed Bettina and Violet approaching our houseboat with a large gift bag.

"One thing we forgot," Violet said.

"We wanted to give you this, with our thanks," Bettina added.

They came aboard, and I opened the bag. Inside was the square baking pan I'd coveted, with the pale-blue dots and the Scone Sisters logo.

"Because you're like a daughter to us," they said together, quickly flashing a guilty look at my mother.

"I'm happy to share. She's got a big enough heart to go around," said my mother, with the widest grin.

Recipes

Roasted Shrimp in Butter Sauce

Hayley Snow and Miss Gloria considered a lot of recipes to serve their Scottish guests, and in the end they agreed on garlicky, buttery, Worcestershire-laced baked shrimp with lots of good bread from Old Town Bakery to sop up the sauce. The shrimp can be served with the shells on for a more rustic, hands-on experience, but for their special and jet-lagged guests, Hayley decided to peel them in advance.

Ingredients

1 teaspoon paprika
8 tablespoons unsalted butter
1–3 large cloves garlic, minced
2 tablespoons Worcestershire sauce
Hot sauce or a sprinkle of dried hot peppers, to taste
1 bay leaf

Fresh rosemary, leaves snipped off stems
2 pounds extra-large or jumbo shrimp, peeled and deveined,
    thawed if frozen
1 lemon, sliced
Good bread for serving

Directions

Mix all ingredients except shrimp, lemon, and bread in a 9 × 13 pan. Heat in 400-degree oven until melted.

Remove from the oven, stir, and add the shrimp and lemon in a single layer. Roast for about 15–20 minutes or until butter is bubbly and shrimp are pink.

Serve with good bread for soaking up the sauce. You'll probably want a nice green salad to balance the richness of the shrimp.

Violet and Bettina's Cinnamon Scones

This recipe is our closest approximation to the cinnamon scones baked by the sisters in *A Scone of Contention* and now this book. Violet and Bettina reveal several secrets to making light scones. First, freeze and grate the butter and keep it cold between steps, working the dough as little as possible. Second, use the highest-quality cinnamon available.

Ingredients

2 cups all-purpose flour
2½ teaspoons baking powder
1 teaspoon ground cinnamon (don't skimp on quality here)
¼ teaspoon salt
½ cup (1 stick; 115g) unsalted butter, frozen
½ cup heavy cream (plus 2 tablespoons for brushing)
1 teaspoon pure vanilla extract
1 large egg
½ cup packed light or dark brown sugar

For the icing:

1 cup confectioner's sugar
3 tablespoons freshly brewed coffee
¼ teaspoon vanilla extract

Directions

Mix together the flour, baking powder, cinnamon, and salt. Grate the frozen butter onto a plate. Rub the butter into the dry ingredients using your fingers or a pastry cutter, until the butter is the size of peas.

In another bowl, whisk together the heavy cream, vanilla, egg, and brown sugar. Mix this lightly into the flour butter mixture.

On a piece of parchment paper, shape the dough into a disk, and with a floured knife, cut the disk into eight triangles. Put the scone dough back into the refrigerator while the oven heats to 400 degrees. Move the parchment with the scones onto a baking sheet. Paint the scone tops with the remaining cream and sprinkle them with sugar.

Bake the scones for 20–22 minutes or until they begin to brown. You could serve them as is, but why leave off the icing?

For the icing, whisk the confectioner's sugar with coffee and vanilla until smooth. If you don't like the idea of coffee, you could substitute milk. When the scones have cooled, drizzle them with icing.

Irish Soda Bread

Hayley's mother, Janet, makes this bread for her first entry in the Scone Sisters' contest. It's a quick bread (no yeast or rising) that is often served as part of a Saint Patrick's Day feast. Even those who think they don't like Irish soda bread love this recipe.

Ingredients

4¼ cups all-purpose flour, plus more for your hands and the counter

3 tablespoons granulated sugar

1 teaspoon baking soda

1 teaspoon salt

1 teaspoon caraway seeds

1 cup raisins

5 tablespoons very cold unsalted butter

1¾ cups buttermilk (or milk with 1 tablespoon lemon juice added)

1 large egg

Cook's note: If you want to use buttermilk, please do. If you have none on hand and would like a substitute, squeeze half a lemon into a two-cup measuring cup and fill to the 1¾-cup mark with whole milk. Set that aside to come to room temperature.

Directions

Mix the dry ingredients—the flour, sugar, baking soda, salt, and caraway seeds—together in a big bowl, Stir in the raisins.

Cut butter into the dry ingredients. The colder the butter, the lighter the batter. When the butter is pea sized, whisk the buttermilk or milk together with one egg.

Fold the egg-and-milk mixture into the dry ingredients.

Move the batter to a floured surface. (Parchment paper with a little flour sprinkled on it works well.) Dust your hands with flour and knead the dough briefly into a round. Again, the shorter the time, even as little as 30 seconds, the better.

Move the batter to a prepared greased pan. (This can be a pie plate, cake pan, or cast-iron skillet.) Those round pans help the bread keep its shape. Make a cross in the batter with a sharp knife.

Bake in a 400-degree oven for about 25 minutes. You can check the bread halfway through to see if the top is getting too brown. If so, cover with foil for the second half of baking.

Let the loaf cool for ten minutes or more before you slice it. Serve warm with more butter and possibly raspberry jam, or for breakfast, maybe with peanut butter?

Chocolate Loaf Cake
With Vanilla Drizzle

This cake was baked by Hayley's mother, Janet, in the quick dessert competition. It's easier than a layer cake and quite sweet enough for dessert, especially with ice cream. But it also could be served as a tea cake or even eaten for breakfast. An electric mixer is not required, as a whisk does the job perfectly well.

Ingredients

1 cup all-purpose flour
1 teaspoon espresso powder, optional
½ cup unsweetened cocoa powder
2 teaspoons baking powder
⅛ teaspoon salt
½ cup unsalted butter
2 large eggs, room temperature
1 cup granulated sugar
½ cup milk, room temperature
2 teaspoons pure vanilla extract
¼ cup boiling water

For the vanilla glaze:

¾ cup sifted confectioner's sugar
2 to 3 tablespoons milk
2 teaspoons vanilla extract

Directions

Preheat the oven to 350 degrees.

In one bowl, place the flour, espresso powder, cocoa powder, baking powder, and salt. (I sifted them together, as some of my ingredients came out of the freezer and were a little lumpy.)

In a small pan, melt the stick of butter and set it inside cool.

In a second bowl, whisk together the eggs and sugar. Whisk in the cooled butter, the milk, and the vanilla extract.

Whisk the two sets of ingredients together, and then add the hot water and stir that in.

Grease an 8 × 4 loaf pan, then fit a piece of parchment paper inside so a couple inches stick up along the longer edges. This forms a sling that will make it easy to remove the cake.

Add the chocolate batter to the pan and bake 40–45 minutes, checking with a cake tester to be sure it's done but not dry. Let the cake cool on a rack for half an hour, then remove it to a pretty plate.

In a small bowl, mix the sifted confectioner's sugar with a tablespoon or two of milk and 2 teaspoons vanilla. Once the cake is completely cooled, paint on the glaze. Serve exactly as it is or with ice cream.

Slow Cooker Corned Beef and Cabbage for Saint Patrick's Day

Hayley made this dinner in the slow cooker so she wouldn't be fussing with it all day. The whole dish took about eight hours cooking on low.

Ingredients

1 large red onion
3 leeks, cleaned well
7 (or so) carrots
3 to 4 stalks celery with leaves
10 to 12 small potatoes
1 head green cabbage
1 3.5- to 4-pound corned beef with seasoning packet (usually coriander, mustard seeds, peppercorns, bay leaves, allspice)
1 bottle Guinness beer

Directions

Slice the red onion; dice the leeks. Peel the carrots and celery and cut into 2-inch chunks. Wash and quarter the potatoes. Remove the outer leaves of the cabbage and cut it into quarters or eighths, leaving the core attached.

If you have a browning feature in your cooker, use it to brown both sides of the beef. Remove it from the pot.

Layer the sliced red onion and the chopped leeks on the bottom, then return the beef to the pot.

Turn the setting to low and add the beer and spices. Cook for four hours.

Add the carrots, potatoes, and celery. Cook for four more hours on low. When there are two hours remaining, add the cabbage if you can fit it; otherwise, roast it in the oven at 400 for 40 minutes. Trim the fat off the beef and slice it thinly.

Serve with lots of spicy mustard, plus Irish soda bread and a green salad.

Acknowledgments

T hanks so much for reading! I hope you enjoyed this install-
ment of the Key West food critic mystery series as much as
I loved writing about the Scone Sisters, Violet and Bettina. I am
very grateful to have my sister, Susan Cerulean, as my dearest
friend since birth, exactly like those Scottish sisters. Having her
in my corner makes all the bumpy parts of life more tolerable
and all the shining moments happier.

As always, I have many people to thank: Dorothy Breck-
enridge took the time to read through the entire manuscript to
fix my errors related to Scotland and Scottish ways of speaking. Julia Spencer-Fleming had the splendid idea that the sisters
should be showcasing special baking equipment, and she also
identified the knife. Thanks to Elizabeth from JRW for the idea
of scones as curling stones. Thanks to Leigh Pujado for many
chats about food, and Alison Roman. Gillian Butler offered me
advice on the fire scene. Ann Mason cleverly suggested the pastry shop name Au Citron Vert, and Ellen T. White came up
with the slogan *Key Lime Pie et plus*. Thanks to Judy Copek,
who may have saved me from a lawsuit with her suggestion of
naming the baking show *The UK Bakes!* Thanks to absolutely
everyone on Facebook for brainstorming clever ideas. Thanks to
acupuncturist Tim Trahant for loaning me his character.

Acknowledgments

Ang Pompano and Christine Falcone read every word I write and make insightful comments—we've been working together for over twenty years, and I'd hate to do this without them! Thank you also to the amazing writer bloggers at Jungle Red Writers for encouragement, inspiration, and a lot of laughs. I'm also grateful for the writing cooks at Mystery Lovers Kitchen, and my pals on the Friends of the Key West Library board.

I am sorry for any confusion about the names Marlene, Martina, and Martha. These wonderful characters are based on three real and talented Key West people, so the names had to remain the same. Marlene is really an artist, Martina a musician, and Martha a chef and photographer. Thanks to Marlene this time for sharing details about the work she and her husband do together. Thanks to Martha for showing me around her kitchen at Williams Hall, the model for the kitchen in the book and on the cover.

Thanks to my dogged and resourceful agent, Paige Wheeler. We've been working together since she miraculously sold my first book, *Six Strokes Under*. I appreciate all the grand folks at Crooked Lane, who produce such gorgeous books and get them out into the world. My team includes Matt Martz, Rebecca Nelson, Melissa Rechter, Madeline Rathle, Dulce Botello, Rachel Keith—I apologize to anyone I missed and thank every one of you! I also adore my independent editor, Sandy Harding, and the talented cover artists Griesbach and Martucci.

There is nothing more wonderful than an independent bookstore—if you have one near you, or one you'd like to support with online orders, please do! To booksellers and librarians who've bought the Key West series and spread the word—I am so grateful! I need to give a special shout-out to Suzanne

Acknowledgments

Orchard of Key West Island Books, plus the wonderful staff at Books and Books Key West, and my hometown Connecticut bookstore, RJ Julia. I feel so fortunate to have their support and am happy to buy way too many books at all those magical places for my greedy reading self.

As always, sincere thanks to my husband, John, for his love, enthusiasm, and sense of humor. I'm lucky to have him with me on this journey.

Lucy Burdette
Key West, Florida
December 2022